THE EDGE OF EXTINCTION

THE EDGE OF EXTINCTION

*Who will survive the
alien plague?*

ROBERT LIDDYCOAT

CONTENTS

Liddycoat is also the author of:

A WANDERING MAN

"An entertaining and thought-provoking examination of Western vigilante justice." Kirkus Review

"...rough-and-tumble, high-stakes Western provides a riveting read." Bookmonger Review

HIT AND RUN

"...action-packed, entertaining, and suspenseful...well crafted." Scribendi Review

FOR THOSE WHO SURVIVE AGAINST THE ODDS

The Edge of Extinction

Survivors

Vacationers Joe and Jan Jones
State Trooper Terry Streck
Hunter Bob Adams
Motel owners Stan and Joan Lake
Army Ranger Dennis Lake
Vacationers John and Mary Midder and daughters Vanessa and Teressa
Honeymooners Bill and Sally Morris
Salesman Devon Martinez
Dispatcher Wanda Patronis
Cruise ship server Alima Hosni

Glossary

Shayatan - Islamic Demon/demons
Iblis - Islamic Satan
Mahdi - Islamic Redeemer of Islam
Malak - Islamic Angel
Houri - IslamicVirgin companion in paradise
Daeva - Iranian Demons
Ahriman - Iranian Satan
Hajib - Islamic Head covering
Niqab - Islamic Face covering

Foreword

Survival is, of course, a work of fiction. Although actual buildings and landmarks are noted, they are described and used fictitiously. The people, events, and places are from the author's imagination.

However, the Cascadian earthquake and tsunami are real threats. A knowledgeable source, *Memo to City Council from Seaside Tsunami Advisory Group March 6, 2018*, was used to describe it. The description is as accurate as I could make it but is simply an educated guess.

Most authors list the help they received with the book and then say any errors are the author's. What about all those people? Didn't they see the blooper on page 208? Although I had some valuable help (and I need all the help I can get), any bloopers are mine.

Extinction is the rule; survival is the exception.
Carl Sagan

Prologue

The world of the Community was doomed. The singularity at the center of the galaxy would soon consume it. With all their ability and knowledge, the Community could not stop that from happening. Even the gravity drives they invented could not.

The obvious answer was to find another world—one farther out in the galaxy. A younger world. To that end, they sent out thousands of scout drones. These sailed in the gravitational sea at speeds beyond time.

For hundreds of years, the Community heard nothing. They knew the probabilities for a similar world approached nil. Yet there were many possibilities and finding such a world was their only chance. The alternative was to advance to the next level. Most of the Community, even those who evolved for a thousand years, wanted to live for many more before advancing.

As time moved on, the event horizon approached. Many more of the Community advanced. Perhaps they all would have to.

Though the drones could only travel using gravitational drives, they could communicate instantly. Obeying a gravitational law of instantaneous effect, the Community had the ability to communicate with the drones through the gravitational threads they left. Yet many were lost. The gravitational sea was in constant flux. Many threads were broken by random shifts.

Then one drone sent positive information. There is such a world! Eight hundred parsecs farther out in the galaxy, and similar enough to theirs to be inhabited. Billions of years of life in it yet.

The world was, unfortunately, inhabited by a lower-level biped, one evolved less than 50,000 years from true sentience. As information from the drone was processed, it became apparent that these bipeds were savage—and numerous. Over eight billion of the creatures prowled the land. The Community could not live with them. There was one obvious remedy: they would be exterminated.

A plan was devised. The world would be cleansed of the savages. As a precaution, the other search drones were not recalled. Some better world might still exist. Plans were laid for the current find. Even if they found another world, this world would be better off without the savages.

There were certain requirements. The ecosystem must not be affected. The indigenous animals must not be affected. These requirements ruled out the use of diseases that could mutate or cross genetic boundaries. The Community needed an exterminator that targeted the savages only. It must be humane. The kills must be painless and the exterminator must be relatively non-threatening.

Engineering and producing such an exterminator would take several years. Several more to deploy it, and another few to ensure success. This small amount of time was a minor inconvenience to them. But the event horizon was near. They went to work.

The area of land was calculated. The number of spores required to ensure coverage was determined. The specifications were agreed upon. The capsid must not interact with any life forms. It must be smooth. It must release the exterminatory factor at a precise time.

They studied population distribution. Accurately counting the number of savages was impossible; their population was in constant flux. Births and deaths happened with depressing speed. Wars, diseases, and famines plagued the savages.

Engineering the spores was difficult, even for them. The hardest and most important part was the timing. The exterminators must all be operational at the same time some years after deployment. The growth would necessarily have to be exponential during the last few hours. The spores would be dispersed proportionally throughout the world's inhabited landmasses. No area was to be missed. They would lie dormant and be allowed to wash down to acceptable production levels.

Inhabited deserts received very little precipitation, and water was necessary for exterminator production. It would be years before some could go into production. This was a minor factor. While developing the exterminators, the Community would build and set sail for the world in an Ark. In the relative years of travel time, the world would be without savages. Their existence would be erased.

The factories were built, and raw materials were provided. Working with numbers they had not before, the Community produced the payload. The spores were loaded on available drones. The flights were programmed. They were launched. Their movement was monitored. The savages of the planet might notice them, but they could do nothing to stop them.

The remaining Community would be saved.

After manufacturing the drones and deploying their exterminators, they built an Ark and attendant vessels.

CHAPTER 1

Year One

Bugs

People once thought the end of humanity would be Biblical, like Revelation: Armageddon, the Apocalypse. They envisioned the Four Horsemen riding through the gates of eternity to destroy the wayward people with colorful plagues, fires, and infestations.

Some thought humanity would end with an alien invasion. With massive ships and superior weapons mindlessly and mercilessly blasting humans from existence, apparently just for the fun of it, or maybe to steal some precious resource. The aliens were depicted as sadistic and malicious, kind of like despots on earth. Except they were almost always ugly. Or maybe they would be benign and humanoid, like *The Day the Earth Stood Still*. Punishing humans for their sins.

Some thought a cosmic disaster would end humanity, like a meteorite or comet or rogue asteroid. Smashing into the earth, darkening the skies, causing fire and brimstone. Or maybe a forever winter. Maybe a monster solar flare or nova burst would incinerate the hapless earth.

Some thought the end would come through a manmade disaster—plagues, viruses, or mutant pathogens triggering a zombie plague. Eating their way to the end.

Some thought it would come from a natural disaster. Supervolcanoes. Super earthquakes. Covering the earth with lava, ash, and/or tsunamis. Global warming flooding humanity. Ozone depletion frying the planet. Polarity reversal wreaking havoc on the infrastructure, driving mankind back to the Stone Age.

Some thought it would be a nuclear war. Blast and radiation poisoning, nuclear winter destroying all life. Except for cockroaches and one last soldier.

Some just did not even think about it.

These pathetic scenarios were depicted endlessly in movies, books, TV shows, video games, and whatever media was at hand. Most predicted that humans would eventually win, or at least survive.

None predicted the actuality.

However, one was pretty darn close.

As it turned out, the earth wouldn't be harmed at all. But humanity would.

Late September—this was the time it would happen, the start of fall in the northern hemisphere. Spring in the southern. The autumnal equinox. The vernal equinox. Death coming in both hemispheres. The die was cast. It was time to die—or live.

There was no warning. There was no mercy. To survive would require both luck and skill, and maybe something more. But it was the last day, the last chance for humanity.

CHAPTER 2

Joe and Jan

Joe and Jan Jones had a good vacation, and the last day started out well.

It was one of those rare, pleasant Sundays in late September in the city of Seaside on the north Oregon coast. A high-pressure system sat over eastern Oregon and Idaho, and a low-pressure system stalled over the Pacific Ocean. The soft wind rolling over the Cascades and Coastal ranges was warm. The week had been mild, without clouds. Soon the seasonal mist, clouds, wind, and rainstorms would roll in, but today felt like summer. The soft surf was three feet every ten seconds out of the west. The long, wide Seaside beach, stretching from Gearhart to the Tillamook Head, boasted lots of warm sand for kids to dig in.

However, the upwelling seawater along the Pacific coast was always cold, sitting at fifty plus or minus a few degrees, summer and winter. The lifeguard tower and warning posts had been taken down after Labor Day, and the sandy expanse look abandoned. Yet, in the afternoon, a few remaining brave vacationers screamed and laughed when the low rollers splashed against their legs, numbing their feet. Some braver ones waded out into the breakers under the watchful eyes of their family.

Vendors and restaurants on Broadway and the Promenade did a good business. Over the years, Seaside had become a year-round resort. And good weather was always a boon.

For the Jones, the week of summer vacation was over. They were headed back to their home in Portland, feeling the glow from a pleasant stay at the Sand and Sea. The had enjoyed late breakfasts at Pig n' Pancake or the Osprey Cafe and late dinners at Maggie's on the Prom or at Pier 12's Baked Alaska in Astoria. They spent sunny days walking the Seaside beach and Promenade, climbing the Astoria Column, or enjoying the Astoria Riverwalk. Visiting the local Lewis and Clark historical sites. Hiking the Tillamook Head.

They watched brilliant sunsets from their balcony, and sometimes the sun would give a soft green flash as it disappeared. They spent cool nights warmed by the fire.

It had been a good time.

That was soon to be in the past. Forever gone.

If it hadn't been for the deer, they would have had no future. They would have been dead, along with most of the rest of humanity.

Late they afternoon, they packed up, left the condominium, and drove down Beach Drive and up Avenue U to the gravel lot at the Trade Winds hotel. They parked and watched as the golden sun slowly turned to molten copper and sank into the calm, azure Pacific. Sitting comfortably, they took one last wistful look at the brilliant red, orange, and green colors lighting the sky and then at the darkening sea. They were endlessly amazed that they could actually watch the seemingly slow movement of the Earth turning on its axis.

The night was cooling. They walked down the avenue, went into the U Street Pub, and ate a leisurely dinner. They ordered coffee and sat for a while, quietly reminiscing, waiting for the evening traffic to ebb.

The night closed in. Well-fed and rested, Joe and Jan walked back to the truck, pulled down Avenue U, and turned onto Highway 101 south. They cruised leisurely along the recently repaved two-lane highway to the Highway 26 exit and headed east toward Portland. As it darkened,

Joe clicked on the high beams. Very few cars headed toward Seaside, and only a few headed to Portland. It was relaxing. Passing through a long, secure tunnel with no worries about traffic was almost hypnotic. Their big truck cruised effortlessly. The powerful engine hummed contentedly. Jan lay back, her eyes closed.

Close to the intersection with Oregon Highway 53, several deer appeared in the culvert on the left. Joe noted them. Normally, they would be frozen by the high beams and wait for the truck to pass.

Not tonight.

Several white-tail deer bounded up and across the road directly in front of the speeding pickup. They showed no hesitation or concern for the rapidly closing headlights. They ran as if pursued by a predator. Joe jammed the brakes and wheeled to the right. Jan flew up, restrained by the seat belt as they slued down the road. Joe managed to miss the deer by about the width of the hair on their backs, but he wound up at a right angle in the road, headlights pointing up a gravel driveway built over the highway culvert. He sat with hands tight on the steering wheel while his hammering heart slowed and the smell of burned rubber dissipated.

"What happened? What was that?" Jan was fully awake, shaking off the shock of the sudden stop.

"Deer," he said.

Joe was taught at an early age that sometimes in life luck is required. Sometimes, skill is required. Sometimes both. Joe was just lucky.

Soon, a lot of skills would be required.

Live or die.

Joe quickly pulled the pickup off the road and over the culvert onto the driveway, one of the few on the highway. He intended to turn around and pull back onto the road. A car passed by without slowing, creating a moving light show that flickered through the forested tunnel.

While Joe waited, he saw a car around the slight bend in the driveway, about 100 feet from the road. Its passenger's door was open, and the dome light was on, dimly lighting up a body a few feet from the car. As Joe pulled in farther, the pickup's headlights showed the body in bright relief. A man was sprawled near the yard of a small house. The lights were on in the house, and the front door was open.

"Oh my God! You killed him!" Jan said.

"Not me. Stay here. I'll check it out." Joe was winging it, running on the adrenaline rush. The fallen guy might be hurt and need help he thought. Or he might be dead from natural causes. Or a crime could have been committed, in which case Joe could contaminate the scene. Yeah, he thought, just like Law and Order or CSI.

Or the crime could be in progress. In which case, Joe was in way over his head, having been a civil engineer for the last twenty-one years and never the victim of a major crime.

Another car passed, again without slowing.

Joe thought for a moment. "Hand me the gun, will you." Another piece of luck. The Smith and Wesson 357 firearm and a box of ammunition were in the truck because, although they were never robbed at their house in Portland, the Jones preferred to keep the firearm with them when they left home. TV sets could be replaced and were not normally used to rob or kill people. Jan's eyes narrowed, unsure of what he was doing. She was right, but he tried to look sure of himself anyway.

"Better to have it and not need it than to need it and not have it." She got it. The gun was always loaded. Five in the chambers, none under the hammer.

Luck? Later he would question: Why did he really take the gun out just then?

Now the skill part. Joe could shoot. He had been shooting since he was thirteen. He claimed no special power or skill, but through no extra effort of his own, he was a "natural." He could hit clay pigeons on the fly with a 22 pistol when he was fifteen. He could hit swinging bottles at thirty feet with the 357 when he was twenty years old. Without using tricks, like using birdshot. More like Annie Oakley when she shot the ash off Wilhelm's cigar. He could not say how he did it. He just did.

As Joe stepped down from the four-wheeler, a sense of unreality gripped him. The adrenaline was wearing off. What the hell was he doing? Not only the suddenness of the event but also the surreal setting made him feel uneasy. The dark green fir limbs overhead were illuminated by the pickup's headlights, which reflected off the little red car. The trees swayed in a gentle evening breeze, and soft sighs came from the moving branches. The air was cool and moist as it moved along the forest floor, smelling of the earth, moss, and mold. Except for the deer and the bodies, the scene would be calming. *Yeah, except for that,* Joe thought.

The deer had run into the brush on the left side of the house. Now, they reappeared and bounded across the front yard and driveway. Then, they stopped, turned in a tight circle like cattle being herded, and ran back across the road. They paid no attention to Joe. He had never seen such a display in the years of driving this highway, but he had seen how deer act when a predator is near. They usually just avoided cats, and there weren't any wolves were to herd them that way. These deer were confused with no predator in sight. Not that Joe would have seen one even if it were there. Yet he knew that no natural predator had caused their actions.

He kept the gun ready. Maybe something was really out there. Or maybe an earthquake was imminent. He waited for the shaking. Nothing.

He approached the body on the drive, gravel crunching softly under his shoes. As he neared, Joe could tell that the man was dead. He once had seen a pedestrian hit and killed on a road in Portland. Dead is dead; it looks the same every time, apparently. Strangely deflated. Inert.

He bent and placed two fingers on the man's neck, feeling under the jaw for the carotid artery. This man was dead, for sure, but he lacked any sign of trauma. No visible blood, no bent or broken limbs. He looked like he had just laid down and gone to sleep. But he was dead. No breathing, no pulse at the neck, and he was cooling fast.

Joe looked up at the house. The front door was open, and the light spilled out onto the porch, illuminating another body. A woman sprawled over the three steps, apparently as dead as the man in the driveway. Joe did not approach. It was time to leave.

As he turned, he began to notice a sound—a subliminal thrumming wave, like an impending earthquake. Joe knew about earthquakes; this was the Northwest, after all. Part of the ring of fire.

But this was not an earthquake. It was something else. He heard a faint rumble underfoot—a hissing, seething. Coming from nowhere and everywhere. Definitely not an earthquake. Something was very wrong.

Joe looked back at Jan's face, which was illuminated by the dome light. He knew her look was on his own face. Fear. But she was looking past him toward the house. Joe followed her stare.

At first, nothing seemed further amiss. Then, a shape rose up from the left side of the porch. If the light had been off, he might not have seen it. It looked like a black basketball on three crab-like legs, maybe three or four feet tall. It moved in a jerky but somehow determined way, right toward him. He did not wait to see what it would do. After all, two people were dead. Retreat seemed the best option.

As he turned toward the pickup, another shape rose from the side of the red car, and not twenty feet away, another one rose from the side of the body on the drive. If they had been there before, he had not seen them. Yet another rose, this one near the pickup, lit a dim red by truck's taillights. It moved in that jerky, purposeful way toward him. It could beat him to the pickup's door.

More were rising, visible all along the road. Without thinking, Joe cocked the pistol, aimed, and fired. The firearm rocked back solidly in his grip, an automatic response, like shooting a clay pigeon. As always, the sharp report was muted to his ears. It was an easy, direct hit. A thin trail of transparent liquid spiraled out of the aberration lit blood-red by the taillights. The thing tottered in a circle and sank to the gravel.

The night had moved quickly from relaxing to frightening. More things were rising up, coming right out of the ground, shedding dirt, gravel, pine needles, and leaves. Joe sprinted to the truck and climbed in just as one hit the door with a thump. In the headlight, the Jones saw more—maybe twenty or thirty more—seemingly appear out of nowhere. Another hit the door on Jan's side. She jumped but did not scream. The shapes seemed to rise out of the ground everywhere. One, then another, bumped under the truck.

"What the hell is going on?" Jan asked in a low, shaky voice.

"I don't know. But we need to get away. Get somewhere we can alert the authorities."

They needed to get to safety, to the police. Jan dialed 911 but got a busy signal. "It's busy. How can that be?"

"Don't know. But we need to do something."

"The closest civilization is a market at the junction of Highways 26 and 53. It's just a mile away. Let's make for it." Jan said.

Joe backed out and headed slowly east. These things were rising up all along the road. Some were wandering into their path. The truck bumped them out of the way.

The market was on fire. Someone had hit the gas pumps, and the entire lot was burning. The fire was spreading to the market. A few people were running toward houses across the road. The things blocked them and touched them. It was like some sort of evil magic; whoever was touched simply dropped. Joe instinctively knew they were dead.

"These things seem to be everywhere." He turned back on 26 and headed west. "Back on the Oregon Highway junction, there's a roadside country store and motel. Remember? Just across from the Sea Breeze Restaurant and a 7-Dees garden shop. Just eight miles away. When we passed it earlier, it was open. Maybe that one survived. If not, we try for the Seaside police station." Joe headed toward the island of civilization. Jan was silent, watching the ground emit things all along the road.

What was normally a ten-minute drive max took thirty tense minutes.

The black blobs Joe began to think of as "Bugs" were popping out everywhere. Some emerged right through the edge of the blacktop on the road, apparently having no problem penetrating through hard surfaces.

The Bugs also had no mouths, ears, noses, or any recognizable features other than the three articulated legs. These legs were narrow, triangular-shaped bars that ended with a spade-like pod. Even in the terror-filled night, Joe noticed they sat or wandered in random paths until they sensed a human. Whenever they neared, the Bugs started toward them, rising up as the truck got close. The truck easily bumped them out of the way. In the rearview mirror, Joe could see them sink down into a squatting position.

Another herd of deer ran across the road. Joe slowed even more to avoid them. One doe actually bumped into a Bug. It simply bounced off and continued toward the humans. The deer was unhurt.

Joe drove even more slowly. The Bugs were everywhere. They bounced off the pickup at low speed, and he did not want to see what would happen at high speed. They felt very solid. If he sped up past fifteen or twenty miles per hour, they tended to bounce up onto the windshield.

One unlucky family seemed to think speed was safety. They passed the Jones going maybe sixty. Bugs were bouncing off the car body until they hit one dead on. The black basketball smashed the sedan's windshield. In the pickup's headlights, the Jones saw clear liquid splash into the car. The people inside were dead within seconds. The car swerved off the road into the culvert and rolled several times before coming to rest.

The Jones did not stop for them or any of the other wrecks they saw. Nobody touched by a Bug was alive. They made the trip to Lake's Roadside Market and Motel without getting killed.

When they got over the interchange to the motel/market, the parking lot was crammed with several randomly parked cars and one monster recreational vehicle. The gas pumps were intact. No fire here. Three sodium vapor lights on twenty-foot poles cast an orange glow over the lot. A State Patrol cruiser sat near the pumps with its light bar flashing.

Joe paid serious attention to the building for the first time. It was about 150-feet long with 10 motel units on the highway side. The market itself looked substantial and like it had been added as a side business after the motel was built. The entire building was raised on pilings four or five feet off the ground. Concrete block skirts covered the gap. The steps were concrete and maybe five feet up to a flat pad and the double-wide door.

And there were dead people—perhaps five or six bodies, mostly next to open car doors. And more Bugs, a lot of them. As the Jones approached, a young couple pulled in just ahead of them, parked outside the gas pumps, and made a break for the market door.

From a dormer above the lot, a sharp flame spat down simultaneously with the report of a short-barreled rifle. A Bug behind the couple fell.

Another round caught another Bug, not five feet behind them. The door opened, and a uniformed trooper appeared. He shot yet another closing Bug. But there were too many. Some were between the couple and the door. Neither the trooper nor the sniper in the dormer had a line of fire that didn't include the runners.

Joe quickly weaved the big pickup through the congested lot, pulling in at a ninety-degree angle between the couple and the Bugs near the door. The trooper closed the door. Joe rolled down the window just enough to aim the pistol. Keeping his hands inside the cab, only the muzzle pointing out, he shot the three nearest Bugs with three quick shots, aiming for the place where their legs attached to their bodies. This brought them down without spilling their guts all over the place. The through rounds sparked off the macadam fifty feet away.

The door opened. The couple ran in between the two cars blocking the steps, dodging the rolling Bug bodies. They raced into the building, past the trooper. The door closed. Bugs shambled into the void.

Joe backed up and then pulled up to the door as close as he could get. It was not close enough. Two cars, an Audi and a Buick, were parked bumper to bumper, parallel to the building; they blocked Joe's access to the steps up to the entrance. Bugs on both sides weaved around the truck.

Luck. A beautiful thing about driving a big V8 4X4 crew cab with a winch-strengthened bumper and a canopy is that it probably out-weighed the two cars put together. It had pulled a thirty-foot trailer without problems for several vacations since the Jones had bought the truck years ago. It was used when he bought it, and the previous owner had outfitted it extensively. At first, Joe had worried about the gas mileage, and his friends had teased him about it. But right now, he was happy for the power. To hell with the mileage.

Joe selected the four-wheel-drive low gear and pulled back, moving up on the Audi's rear bumper. Bugs bumped insistently against the truck. When the bumpers touched, he gave the pickup half throttle. They began to move. The Audi was in park, and its rear tires screeched and juddered as it moved up on the Buick. When the Audi hit the Buick, Joe gave the truck all it had, keeping the momentum. All hell broke loose. The pickup's all-weather tires ground and shuddered, and the Audi and Buick screeched back. Smoke billowed up. The whole mess moved under violent protest until the pickup's passenger door was even with the steps to the market door. Now, it was the Jones's turn to make the leap.

The rifle in the dormer opened up again, clearing out the Bugs behind them. Jan had the Smith and Wesson reloaded, and Joe leaned over, reached through the window, and shot the four Bugs between them and the door at the joints where the legs attached to the body. The reports were louder than he remembered. It was close shooting.

He had a good angle from high up in the cab, and the through rounds impacted the steps with small puffs of powdered concrete. The Bugs went down without spilling any liquid and bounced under the truck to the macadam. The door of the market opened. The trooper opened fire with what looked like a Glock 17. Several more Bugs that were closing around the truck collapsed without exploding. The trooper had learned about the joints. And he was a good shot.

The Jones jumped out of the passenger side, slammed the door, and lumbered up the steps into the market, a few paces ahead of the pursuing Bugs. The market door slammed shut. The momentary silence did not last long. A second later, a Bug hit the door with a thump. Then, the Bugs began bumping against the door and floor of the building. Death pressed all around. Someone began to cry. It sounded like a young girl.

Joe looked around and counted fourteen people altogether, including two teenage girls. They were all gathered in the market checkout area. He and Jan shakily held on to each other.

The trooper gave Joe a hard look when he entered. "You got a permit for that?" He pointed at the warm Smith and Wesson in Joe's hand. The trooper was a big man, maybe six-three with a large frame running to the heavy side. He was probably thirty-five or forty and had chocolate skin and fathomless coffee-colored eyes. The name tag on his uniform read "T. Streck." He looked like a career officer of the law who wasn't interested in promotion. *Just doing my job, sir.* Now, he was making sure a crazed lunatic had not just entered the room.

"I do if you think that matters right now."

"We'll see. Put it away. What's your name?" Joe introduced himself and Jan. The trooper looked at him. "Joe and Jan Jones? Hmm." He turned to talk into the mic attached to his shoulder strap over a protective vest. One of the men came over to Joe. He looked like a salesman, maybe five nine and heavy, with light brown skin. He was wearing expensive but casual clothes.

"That was my Audi you hit. You have insurance?"

"I do if you think that matters right now." For God's sake! Didn't anybody grasp the situation? No, of course not, they were in shock or denial or something. Thinking about it, he probably was too. Joe wondered: What were the stages after a tragedy? Denial, arguing, bargaining, depression, acceptance? *We are in denial now,* he decided. The Audi owner glanced at the pistol Joe still held and confirmed Joe's diagnosis, mumbling something about waiting until this blew over.

The room was thirty by fifty, full of grocery racks. Behind a counter in the back was a display of firearms. The checkout stand stood on the wall to the left. A staircase ran up the back wall over a small unisex bathroom. On the west side, a door opened to a storeroom that apparently had not been compromised. The far back wall had a door opened to a loading dock. The dock had a ten-foot-wide steel folding door. It was holding against the steady pounding.

Everyone except Joe and Streck was attempting to contact family and friends on their phones. Joe's phone was in the truck. Jan eventually gave up. She and Joe sat on the counter and watched the people who had managed to get inside. Voice and text messages were sporadically being sent and received by everyone. From the general tone, Joe gathered that the stories from outside were not good. He looked at Jan. She shook her head.

He watched the salesman for a moment, who was looking at his small screen. A look of fear and dread passed over his face. He staggered and sat heavily. Something bad had happened.

During a lull, one of the teenage girls shakily asked, "What are those things, anyway?" The question was aimed generally at the room.

Joe thought he may as well put a voice to his first impression. They needed to put a name to these things. "When I first saw them, they reminded me of bugs."

"Bugs, huh! Mighty big bugs," said Streck. "Sounds good. Bugs." He looked around. Nobody had anything better, it seemed. "Bugs it is."

CHAPTER 3

Saving Wanda

A voice came over Terry's mic, "Terry, you there? It's Wanda." There'd been no police com traffic for several days. Everybody in the room could hear.

"Yeah, I'm here." Terry did not try to keep it private.

"I'm not going to make it. Too many of those things around. So thirsty. So tired. Tell my husband I'm sorry, will you? I'm going to lay down for a while."

Terry was instantly attentive. "No! Don't give up. Just a little longer. I'm coming. Just a little longer."

"I'm sorry." Wanda's voice faded away.

Terry looked at the room full of the Survivors. They were a mess. They stunk. They were tired. They were sad and angry. But they were the Survivors. He needed them.

"All right, I need to get her. She is in the Oregon State Police headquarters in Warrenton. How the hell am I going to do that?" No one wanted to ask why. But the concern was there. Terry read it on their faces. He was surprised Devon didn't question this. "Look, she is my dispatcher. And a person. I can't just let her die. I have to try."

"What about us, Terry? What if you die trying?" Mary asked.

"You are important here," said John.

"I'm no more important than anyone else. Let me ask you. If you could save anyone's friend or family, would you risk it?"

That did it. "Our families are too far away. Yes, if it could be done, I would go myself," declared John. Most in the room nodded. John had some grit after all.

Bill Morris was again the first to offer a thought. "Well, look, you can't just waltz across the twenty-some-odd miles to your headquarters. But if you could get into Joe's pickup, it would probably get you there. It got him and Jan here. It's situated where we can access it with some ingenuity." Bill was so young, yet full of calm, analytical leadership. And married to another calm, logical person. This was a good thing amid their chaos.

"OK," Dennis said. "In the service, we had drills for poison gasses. We had suits we wore similar to the rain gear I see on the hardware shelf here. If we could tape you up in the gear, maybe it would protect you long enough to get to the truck."

"You can use my Ford," said Joe. "Just bring it back. It's all we have now."

"How are we going to get him to the pickup without letting them in here?" Devon asked. Terry read the fear on his face. That fear was not reflected in the Midders. The Morris' looked on with curiosity. Sally had the look of a scientist evaluating an experiment. Terry looked at Joe and Jan. He saw concern but no fear. He looked at Dennis and saw a hardened Ranger—no concern, no fear. He looked at the owners and saw that Joan had a concern. Stan looked like he was considering a problem, and then offered, "Maybe we can do something with the leftover plywood and studs."

"You have that material?"

"Yeah, in the back storage room."

They pulled the wood out and surveyed it.

"Let's get the suit and those two-by-fours and the leftover floor plywood," said Terry. "I have an idea."

They cleared out the entryway, pushing the display cases aside, and used the leftover sheets of heavy plywood and two-by-fours to make two walls that would serve as a protected pathway down to the truck. Joe counted the steps, flinching as Bugs bumped the glass, trying to touch him. The window held, and the liquid from the Bugs dried immediately, leaving no trace. He assumed an eight-inch rise and ten-inch land per step and then calculated the angles, accounting for the triangular gap at the step edges. Joe guessed the height of the truck's door panel to make a barrier in case the Bugs could crawl under the truck. They went to work.

Stan, Bob, and Dennis knew their way around woodworking tools. Joe measured and marked the wood to the guessed specifications. They cut the ends as best they could to the angle of the concrete pad and steps and the contour of the truck. They used the two-by-fours to brace the walls against the pressure of the Bugs. Through the dust and noise, the Survivors were unified. They had a goal now.

When they were finished, they tested the strength against the pressure of the men, two on a side pushing hard. It held. The men then lined the walls up with the truck door as best they could from inside. Their construction was heavy and awkward and came within an inch of filling the double doorway. The Bugs would not be able to get past the gap. A hinged flap was added to prevent Bugs from spraying inside.

Then Devon noted a problem. The doors opened outward. That would never work.

"The building code at the time required it," said Stan. "Some sort of fire code. The market doors had to be opened outward so a crush of people trying to leave would not trap them shut. It apparently applied to us because we could have more than so many people in here at a time."

"Anybody got any idea how we are going to get this contraption out without trapping the doors outward? Terry asked. "Once the truck leaves, the doors will be open. Even if you could pull this monster back, the area will be open during the time we are trying to lug it back."

"We could make this thing into a hall, with a door at the end. Leave it permanently," said Jan.

"That would leave the top and us open to the elements," said John. "There's not enough plywood left to cover the top."

"Make a second set of plywood doors for inside," said Mary.

"We need these doors. They have protected us so far. We have some heavy-duty hinges in the back. We can fix them to the doors from inside and then cut the outside hinges and jams with a metal cutting saber saw," said Stan.

"I vote for the hinges. We might need to use this thing again," said Terry.

"Terry will have to wait in the truck while we relocate the jams. We need a plan," said Bill.

They agreed. They planned.

When everybody knew what to do, they went to work with lots of worry, but even more courage.

And skill. When they were ready, Bob leaned out of the second-story window and shot the closest Bugs. It took several rounds to clear the steps. The Bugs did not respond; they simply imploded and sank to the ground.

The Survivors were set. Now they needed to move before more Bugs could take move into place.

"Go!" Bob yelled.

Live or die.

The plan went forward before anyone could have second thoughts. The girls opened the rehinged double doors inward. Cool, vaguely fetid air blew in. Before the Bugs could close in, Terry, Stan, Dennis, John, Joe, and Bill pushed the heavy connected plywood walls through, hurriedly bouncing them down the steps. Jan stood by with the 357, just in case. Bob came down. Joe checked his design. The walls reached the pickup with a bang and a narrow gap. The angle was good. The fit was not perfect; Joe could see daylight through the barrier at the landing of some of the steps and the truck. They waited with concern, ready to close the doors if any Bugs got through. But the Bugs could not crawl under the truck or through the gaps in the steps. *Now to test the function*, thought Joe, remembering the old engineering mantra "form, fit, function, and finish."

Terry went through, carefully scraping the carcasses down the concrete steps and under the truck with a snow shovel. Bob continued to watch the Bugs, who drew closer as they sensed people. The wall worked. Terry managed to get into the truck from the passenger side without getting touched by a Bug. The Bugs were slow to react and could not penetrate the makeshift wall.

The flap was retracted. Terry waited while the jams were refitted. Lots more noise and dust. But the doors were reversed. They closed behind him, and makeshift stops were drilled in at the top and bottom. Then, Terry folded the passenger-side rearview mirror back. The fixture still would not clear the wall, so he broke it off. Now he could drive away without it snagging on the construction. Joe winced. Jan said, "It's all right, Joe. You never used it anyway." Nervous laughter from the group.

The Survivors had accomplished something. They had faced danger and survived. A little pressure was released. They sat back and waited. Terry was on his own now.

"What if he doesn't come back?" asked Devon.

"He will make it," said Joan. "We'll have another Survivor soon. Let's see about the plans. We surely do need more room."

Luck for Terry. It was a sunny day, with a steady light wind from the north—another rarity in October on the coast. The low slanting rays gave the hope of summer warmth without delivering. Bugs covered the lot, spoiling the light, eagerly rising to touch the human they sensed. The truck started, and Terry backed out to the highway, threading in reverse the direction Joe used to come in.

The truck handled well; Terry liked its power and size. The Bugs seemed to bounce off with no effect. But there were hundreds, thousands, maybe millions between the Survivor's motel and Warrenton. On the highway, Bugs filled the road as far as he could see.

Passing through Seaside, Terry looked at the roadside houses. He saw the broken windows of some. Bugs were not crowded around them; there was nobody alive in those houses. But, in some places, Bugs gathered around, waiting, like those outside the motel. What about the resort hotels? He let it go. Even if there were people in them still alive, he could not get to them, and even if he could, what would he do then? There was no way to get them into the truck. There was no room at the motel. Damn! He quit thinking about it. One thing at a time.

The smell of rotting meat was sometimes bad at the motel when the wind came from the north, but here, somewhat inland and in populated areas, especially near Seaside and Gearhart, the stench was horrendous. Terry fought the need to vomit.

Out on the coastal highway, past the towns and on Clatsop Plains, Terry saw a continuing sea of black blobs. Not too many had cratered the road here. Most were inert; only when they sensed him did they rise. If it were like this everywhere, there would be few, if any, other survivors.

The trip to Warrenton took over an hour. The Jones had filled the fuel tank before they left Seaside, and the Ford had an auxiliary tank that held thirty more gallons. Terry had plenty of gas. He had to maneuver around a few accidents. Since the rising happened late on a Sunday night, there had been a minimal number of vehicles on the road, and most had swerved off. But the Bugs were continually getting in the way.

He saw no other living beings, save a few horses, and some domestic cattle in a field. The Bugs did not bother them. Man appeared to be their only prey.

He could not and did not care how any of this could be. He was thinking about how to get Wanda out of the reception booth. It was apparently secure, and the glass was bullet-resistant. All communication with people who entered happened through a louvered voice vent. The booth was off the reception area, immediately behind the main entrance doors on the west side of the building.

He turned at the Dolphin Avenue junction and made the short trip to the station. The area around the front door was littered with rotting bodies, shell casings, deflated dead, and live, rising Bugs. The double doors were not open. Bodies of officers he knew but could not recognize were lying in the entryway. He knew the back had a door leading to the interrogation rooms and offices and another leading to the locker room and a holding cell. The room Wanda was in had a door that opened to the office area but had no access from the lobby. The room was walled with a glass viewing front and a cashier's style tray for the exchange of paperwork. The door in the back led to offices. It would have to be shut tight for Wanda to survive.

Terry had brought the battery-powered drill and saber saw with the best bits and blades from the hardware section of the Survivor's store. He had spare battery packs. It was a simple plan: drive the Ford next to the booth wall; park the cab close enough so a Bug could not get between the cab and wall; open the rear window; use the saw to cut through the steel-studded, sheet-rocked wall; pull Wanda in, and back out. *Simple*, he thought. *Right?*

The sky clouded over, making the headquarters look sad. It was a relatively new building that had replaced the old tsunami inundation zone headquarters on Gateway Avenue near Pier Two on the riverfront in Astoria. As Terry sat idling in front of the building, it seemed he had spent a lifetime in that building. A lifetime ago. Men and women he had known for years were dead outside and inside. They came at Wanda's call and died fighting; the lot littered with their spent casings that reflected what was left of the weak sunlight.

Terry mentally slapped himself. Reflection was not helpful now. He maneuvered through the blockade, chose the lowest four-wheel gear, and eased the pickup past the entrance steps. He moved forward, the truck effortlessly pulling toward the building.

Now came the disgusting part. He pulled slowly forward over the rotting bodies of men he had known, men who had died guarding the door while the enemy tunneled within, taking them from behind. Bugs swarmed the truck, sensing the human inside. Thank God they could not climb.

He maneuvered the big truck into the entryway, jacking forward and back until he had the truck's side pinned against the dispatch wall. Some Bugs were smashed as he pulled up, and Terry enjoyed that small victory. He sat for a minute, feeling the insistent bumps from the Bugs, but none could get between the cab and the wall. They were inflexible. They seemed to have a hard inner shell covered with fur, like a hard medicine ball.

Then he saw how the Bugs got in. The concrete floor was breached by many holes. They had not heaved up the concrete but appeared to have turned it to powder and gravel. They had missed the small area where Wanda was. He could not imagine how, and again, it did not matter.

Looking in through the glass as he maneuvered, he could not see Wanda. She must be on the floor. With a sinking feeling, he hoped he was not too late. He slid over, rolled down the window, and took out the saw. It did not take long to cut a hole in the steel-studded, sheet-rocked wall. Through lots of noise and dust, Terry pushed a three-foot square section of the wall into the office. It landed with a crash. He peered through the opening into the room.

Terry was a veteran. He had witnessed just about every degrading human condition possible, including drug addicts and HIV victims. He had seen the aftermath of accidents: torn bodies and blood. He had seen puppy mills and neglected animals. But what he saw startled him. This was something else. This reminded him of an animal trapped in a cage when its owner had died. He had never seen a human reduced to such degradation.

Wanda cowered in the far corner, a small jumble of knees and elbows. The empty thermos sat forgotten in her lap. Filth was piled in the opposite corner. The stench and the sight of Wanda were more than Terry could handle, and he was sick in the narrow space between the wall and the cab.

He spit and steeled himself and looked in again. Wanda's eyes had the look of hollow, terminal terror. The look of the damned. She cowered away from the hole he had cut like it was the opening to the pit of Hell. He called to her with no response. This was going to be harder than he expected. He thought she would come over and crawl into the cab without prompting. Not today.

He let the motor run, set the brake, and moved to the window. He couldn't get through with the rain gear on. He struggled out of the bulky gear, except for the waders. It was easier to move now. He was sweating profusely. He poked his head in again and tried to call Wanda over. She was still catatonic.

He could not pull the truck far enough back to use the crew cab window. The Ford's bumper was pressed against the concrete inner wall as it was. He moved the driver's seat back as far as it would go and moved the steering wheel forward and up as far as it would go. The brake was a floor mount away from the window, so if he had to force Wanda through the hole, she would not accidentally release it. The gear shift was on the column, so it was at risk, but the brake should hold while the engine was at idle. He did not want to shut down, even with the fumes building up.

He was ready.

He forced his way in headfirst. The drop to the filthy floor was just four feet, and he managed to land on his hands and knees on top of the cut section without injury and fairly clean.

Now came more uncharted waters for Terry. He approached Wanda slowly, talking in low tones. "It's me—Terry. I've come to get you. It's OK. It's going to be OK." Over and over. When he reached Wanda, she was hot and stiff and shivering. She cowered away fearfully. He stroked her matted hair and soothed her as best he could.

"We need to leave; you need to get up." She had not spoken until now, but a sound came from her, a forlorn combination of hope and despair. It started at an inaudible range and rose in volume until he made out the words.

"Help me!" over and over.

It kept rising until it became a primal scream. Then it stopped. She looked at Terry through red, teary eyes and gave a deep shuddering sigh.

He took hold of her arms and said, "Yes, I'll help you. Get up now, and we'll leave here." She was slick with sweat and grime, but he held her to himself and helped her to the hole. "Stand here!" he commanded quietly. She was more compliant now and shakily stood as ordered, a blank dull stare replacing the hollow terror and fear.

Terry climbed back into the truck and then reached back through and pulled her up and across his lap. She immediately crawled into the passenger's footwell and curled up like an injured animal seeking shelter. He slid over to the driver's seat, opened the bottled water he brought, and offered it. She grabbed the bottle and began drinking greedily. He thought about warning her about too much too fast, but she wasn't going to pay attention to that. After a minute, she threw up most of the water and immediately drank the rest. It stayed down. He managed to maneuver back out without further damaging the truck.

The sky had turned to a gray, hazy overcast. The wind had shifted to the west, reducing the smell. The drive back was slow and tedious. The Bugs bumped off the truck like thrown medicine balls. One tall one rolled over the hood. Wanda cried out and shrank further into the footwell. The Bug hummed like a beehive as it sprayed liquid that streaked the windshield and then immediately dried off.

Terry needed some diversion. He found some CDs in the center armrest. Country and Western, fifties and sixties vintage, for God's sake. Who the hell were these Jones, anyway? He found a Willy Nelson cut about Georgia and played it. It was soothing, apparently. Wanda seemed to relax a bit. A song about "always on my mind" followed. Wanda relaxed a little more. Old Willy was useful for something besides promoting cannabis after all. The twenty miles back took another hour, and Wanda didn't make conversation.

When they reached the Survivor's motel, Terry saw that the plywood aisle was still up. But now several Bugs had crowded around the door. If he pulled in, the Bugs would be between the cab and the door. He knew the Jones had safely shot them, but he had Wanda in the cab. What would she do? There was no angle from the dormer now. He reached for the cell phone to see if it still worked. Maybe those inside could do something. Then, small arms fire erupted from a shooting port high above the doors. Standing on chairs, Joe and Dennis had drilled two ports through the wall above the doors where the Bugs could not reach and were now clearing the steps.

Terry edged forward as the Bugs imploded and through rounds sparked off the cars abandoned in the lot. Bugs fell, releasing their poison. When the steps were clear of animated Bugs, he pulled the truck as close to the aisle as possible without knocking it aside. He sat for a full five minutes to make sure the Bugs could not get between the plywood and the cab. He felt them try repeatedly. He also wanted to make sure that the ones that fell were dead and that the poison was dried up. When he was as sure as he could be, he slid over Wanda and opened the door. She let out a cry, sounding like a wounded cat, and compressed further into the footwell. Open doors terrified her. This was still not going to be easy.

The door to the store opened, and a figure clad in rain gear and waders came out, armed with a snow shovel. He carefully pushed the deflated bug carcasses down and to the side, under the truck. Terry climbed out, still in his waders, and grabbed Wanda before she could scoot away. He was a strong man, and Wanda was weak from hunger, but it was all he could do to hold her while he climbed the stairs.

When he was inside, Terry put Wanda down. She still looked like a trapped animal, eyes darting left and right, looking for a way to flee. But only for a minute. Then she seemed to recognize that these were people and she was not in immediate danger.

The Survivors saw a terrified, shivering woman. She had dark matted hair, deep blue eyes, and tea-colored skin. They waited for her to understand where she was. When she finally did, she broke down in great, wrenching sobs. Joan approached and held her, cooing soft assurances. Along with Jan, the two older women took her to the upstairs bathroom to clean her up. Then, they wrapped her in a blanket, and she fell asleep in the Lake's bed almost immediately.

The raincoat-covered man was Bob. He pulled Terry up and into the shower, where they rinsed off any poison that happened to get on their waders. When they shucked the gear and were back in the room, the group gathered around.

"How did it go? Anyone else make it that you saw?" asked Dennis.

"Nobody. It's a wasteland out there, filled with Bugs and bodies. It smells. It's . . ." Terry could not continue. Everybody was silent. "You know, there could be others in places like Wanda was, but . . ."

"You can't save them all, Terry," Joan said.

"We can't even save ourselves. We need God to help us," Devon suddenly interjected. The Survivors remained silent. Each wondered if that were true and if Devon were sane.

"We are still here," said Terry. "Let's save the theological discussion for another day. Right now, we need to get some space for ourselves."

Devon looked like he wanted to say more. Instead, he turned away, went to his area, and bent down in prayer.

CHAPTER 4

Adapting

Stan determined that there was no danger in cutting a hole above the counter wall between the store and unit one, followed by a door—if the unit was clear of Bugs. The door would be close to the outside wall, allowing for a narrow passageway to the next unit. Then, they could cut similar holes and doors in a straight line through all the units. Stan marked the location with chalk outline, and Dennis cut the first exploratory one-foot block, high above the floor. He poked it out and peeked in. The door and windows held. No Bugs. They cut a doorway directly below through the wall. The Survivors looked in and collectively sighed relief and hope. The unit had a bed and a functional bathroom.

Dennis cut another hole to the next unit. It was clear as well. One by one, they opened up the ten units, each with a working bath and queen beds with linen and towels. The Survivors laughed, happy for the first time since the day of the Bugs. Even Devon smiled. The only thing that concerned Terry was the distorted floor in unit eight where dirt had built up underneath—enough to place the floor within reach of the Bugs. But it held, and no Bugs came through.

The units were divvied up quickly. Each couple—Terry and Wanda who would not leave his side, Bill and Sally, John and Mary, and Joe and Jan—had a unit to themselves. Bob, Dennis, Devon, and the two girls each had separate units. Blankets and rope were used to create a hall so everyone could get to their unit without invading anyone else's privacy, at least by sight. It wasn't perfect, but it was better than what they had before.

The store still had some packaged food. All the perishables were used up. A cafeteria-style eating arrangement was set up. Life was at least possible, if not good. The Lake's apartment held a washer and dryer, which were kept busy. Joan became a sort of grandmotherly persona, calming tension, and dispensing wisdom. Her husband kept to himself.

To keep busy, Dennis, Joe, and Terry set up an exercise room on the back dock. Stan, Bill, and Devon set up a card and gaming area in the space vacated by the depleted frozen stores. Jan and Joan tended the eating arrangement. Mary and John set up an entertainment center using a TV and the DVDs and books from the store displays.

Then, the natural gas feed quit. No more hot showers.

Stan found some forgotten Sterno in the storage room. Since the hot water was heated by gas, disconnecting and capping the useless gas lines and burning Sterno under the tanks were simple. It was a slow process, but warm showers were possible again—one positive note in a depressing existence.

Life was not pretty, but tolerable.

Wanda recovered physically but remained attached to Terry. There was not much room, but where he went, she went, always within reaching distance. Terry did not discourage her, and eventually, she regained some autonomy. Gradually, the hollow look eased, and Wanda began talking. The story leaked out.

During the re-telling, Wanda became more animated and confident. But there would always be the hidden scar. That memory of being alone in the dark with no food or water, surrounded by faceless things trying to reach her, wanting her death. It was as close to Hell as one could get without dying. The Survivors could empathize. But they at least had each other.

Gradually, they began to wonder about other survivors. Each knew their family and friends probably did not make it, but they held out hope. Surely others had survived. After all, they did, and the President and Congress had secure military bunkers. And real survivalists, now proven not so paranoid after all, had bomb shelters. And there were the lucky ones, such as themselves.

Terry called a meeting in what was now a common room in the original store. The empty racks and stands were moved to the storeroom. Folding picnic tables were set up. Plastic chairs from the storeroom were set up.

"Let's discuss where we are now. What are the chances there are other survivors?"

"Well, let's think about it," Bill said. "The Bugs came out of the ground pretty quickly and at the same time all over the world. To survive, people would have to get to a protected place where all needs were supplied for at least a month now, and probably for a year. That place would have to be stocked with food and water, and it would have to be Bug proof. Most importantly, people would have to get there quickly. Anybody on foot or in a car, or office . . . Well, you get the picture . . ." he trailed off. The odds were small indeed. All their loved ones were in that boat. And their odds were getting pretty small, too.

"We have survived," said Terry. "There must be others." But they knew the odds. It would still be a while before reality set in. "We have food and water and shelter for the time being. I can't think of anything more to do. Suggestions?"

"Not much we can do," said Bill. "The electrical grid is down; no chance to contact anybody now. Maybe plan for when our food runs out."

Joan said, "That's for the future. Maybe the Bugs will die before—"

"Maybe. Hope for the best, plan for the worst," said Dennis.

"When the time comes, the truck will be our saving grace," said Jan.

Terry saw Devon recoil. He was wound tight about something. Was it the reference to saving grace? Terry knew it was not going to be good when it came out.

Fall arrived in full rainy force. Winter was coming. It would get colder. Near the forty-fifth parallel, the Oregon coast was considered a moderate climate. But forty degrees was cold without heat. And it had been known to reach ten degrees before, with blizzard conditions. The store was heated by a gas furnace in the attic; the units were heated by electric baseboard. No natural gas was available. The electrical grid had failed. The generator quit for reasons unknown. The Sterno was used up. Accessing the generator was discussed, but no way was found. They would have to survive without heat and hot water. No fun. But they could.

Life became a monotony of board games, and discussions carefully avoided talk of family. Each Survivor kept a slim hope that somehow his or her family had survived. But they all knew the truth. And sleep was no escape. Dreams turned to nightmares. Death stalked them, waiting patiently.

That which does not kill you will try again.

Still, they survived.

In late November, Joe and Jan lay in bed, surrounded by the darkness of a cloudy and moonless night. The wind blew smattering rain against the building. Without man-made light, the dark was deeper than anything they had known, except for an occasional power failure. Even then, artificial light from batteries and generators had powered the homes around their house. The backwash of civilization reflecting off the clouds lit the night better than the stars. Now, they were in the last room at the end of the motel. It was as dark as the bottom of a grave.

Aside from the sounds of rain and wind, the silence was also a new thing for the Survivors. All the previously unnoticed hum of appliance motors, traffic, the bustle of life, even far off airplane noises, were gone.

Now, there was no artificial ambient noise. No artificial ambient light. The sounds of nature were small and unnoticed. *It will change with time, but for now, it's a little like death*, Jan thought. She spoke in soft tones so as not to disturb the others. "Joe, what do you think is going to happen to us?"

Jan was a strong, wise woman who previously held her marriage together through sometimes turbulent times. She had raised two healthy, good children. Now she was lost.

"Good question. I don't know. If I had to guess, I would say we are going to survive. We have to!"

"Can we outlast the Bugs?"

"It will take some doing, but I think so. We'll need to get more food at some point. If we ration, we can last maybe another month on the stock here. We all are losing weight, anyway; that's good, right? We're lucky this store was used by locals as a supply. Probably the truck will be used like you suggested—like Terry did—to go to a store somewhere."

"You know, we're damned lucky, really. If those deer hadn't stopped us and got us turned around, we'd be among the people stranded on the road. Or trapped in our house. Here, we have a chance, anyway."

Joe was silent for a moment. "You know, sooner or later we'll need to confront the possibility, the probability, we're alone here. That we all are without our kids, parents, brothers, or sisters. Friends. Maybe anyone else. We could be unique here."

"What about our children? What about William and Janette?" Jan asked, her voice breaking.

Joe didn't know. He lay looking through the dark to the future. He shuddered. Jan began to cry, he held her and then he did too.

CHAPTER 5

Celebrating

The late December afternoon was gray and cold. It had been raining off and on for two days. A south wind was blowing at gale force. The sound of the howling wind and the heavy drops beating against the walls, pattering off the roof and puddling under the eaves, became monotonous and depressing. The parking lot dully reflected the light that escaped through the scudding somber clouds. The black Bugs sat wet and still. Waiting. Inside the Survivor's motel, there was little talk. They also waited. Who or which would last? Them or the Bugs? Life or death? That question had a sure answer in the future.

The Survivors sat in the common room, talking in low tones, reading, staring at the rain. There was a silent, growing feeling of pressure, of impending doom.

Teressa looked out at the wet Bugs. At least they did not rise whenever someone looked at them. Then, she suddenly said, "Hey, it's nearly Christmas! We missed Halloween and Thanksgiving. We need to do something." She ran to the storeroom. Vanessa followed.

Mary watched at her daughters running like sleek greyhounds. Teressa and Vanessa were almost twins. They were born within a year of each other. John was in a hurry. Well, she was, too. Now they were beautiful teenaged girls. Slim in the way only teenagers can be. In the first days, they were fearful. But now, they were resigned to waiting it out. They were sure as only the young can be that this would end. All would be well.

Mary was not so sure.

While the girls rummaged through the storeroom, each Survivor thought of their memories in silence. Their memories of Thanksgiving, Christmas, and New Years were softened and sweetened by time. Sadness replaced the memories. There was no way to get back to the festive, friendly feeling of the season.

Since the day of the Bugs and the demise of the electronic gear that kept track of time and date, no one had paid much attention to the passing days. "Look," Teressa said, returning from the back. "Here's a calendar I found in the back room. Let's try to guess the date."

Devon knew the date. He felt now it was going to be his responsibility to keep track of important dates. He passed on Thanksgiving because he saw no heart for it in the Survivors. Plus, it was not actually a Biblical holy day. It was something George Washington dreamed up to ease the aftermath of the Revolutionary War, and Lincoln made it a national holiday to ease the tension of the Civil War.

Now, Teressa had breached the gloom. Devon was waiting for the actual calendar date to ask for a celebration, but it was close enough to traditional Christmas. He knew Christ's actual birthdate was probably in spring, but it had been changed by those in power at the time to co-opt the pagan festivals of light. He also believed that the sacred date was corrupted by commercialism and greed. Santa Clause gave children gifts for behaving. What about Christ? And he knew none of that mattered to the Survivors. What mattered now was to guide the Survivors in the way of God. To draw the wayward people back to the basic truth.

"It is really the twenty-third today, but it's close enough," he said.

No need to guess now.

Silence. There was no Christmas tree. No ham, turkey, stuffing, mashed potatoes, or gravy. No pumpkin pie. No presents. No stockings hung by the fire. They were suddenly depressed again.

Devon felt the need to take the lead. He had to bring the Survivors back to God—one step at a time. He also had to respect any feelings against himself. He felt—no, he knew—he was looked upon as a zealot. He had done that to himself. He could correct that.

He broke the silence, "Let's think about this." The imitation of Bill's mantra drew some smiles. "OK. We are in a bad spot. Out of respect to our non-Christians, I am not going to push for a traditional Christmas with prayer, praise, and reflection. But we need something here. We are in a bad time. We need to help each other out. We are the Survivors. I suggest we each tell a story of our happy times. That we listen to each other with sincerity. I don't want to go forward into what awaits feeling like . . ." He faltered for a moment. "Feeling like we have been abandoned. I believe we have not. Or we abandon hope. Or, at the risk of being preachy, we abandon God."

There was some doubt. Where was this going? But no one argued.

"I will start if it's OK?"

A low chorus of cautious assent followed as the Survivors gathered around the tables.

"OK!" Devon gathered himself. "I remember just this last Christmas. On the eve, my family went to midnight mass at the Catholic church in Forest Grove. It was so beautiful. Candlelit interior softly showing the holy stained-glass images. The congregation was so reverent. Friends and neighbors together in peace. The story was so beautiful. The songs so moving. I remember the best ones, 'O Holy Night' and 'Silent Night.'" Devon was lost in reverie. He caught himself before he started singing. He smiled in a shy and embarrassed way. "Anyway. The next morning, we opened presents under the tree. Later, we had a wonderful turkey dinner made by my wonderful wife. That night, we sat by the fire and had eggnog and roasted marshmallows." He took a breath.

"Now, before I get lost in the past, let's set sight on the future. We will get through this. There will be Christmases in the future. We are the Survivors here and now. We are in a dark time. And I have to say it will not last . . . God will show us the way. Now, we need another good story."

Devon had started something, something that took hold. The day seemed brighter. The mood was lighter. The girls jumped at the chance to tell their stories. They took turns telling of a Christmas at their grandparents' house in Maine. Sledding, a real horse-drawn carriage, and nights by the fire. A real snowy Christmas with a tall, sparkling, fresh-cut tree decorated with hand-made ornaments.

"There was a big hill in the back yard," chirped Teressa, reverting to her childhood. "We sledded down and pulled the sled back up a hundred times. It was so fun. Then we got tired and came inside. Mom had hot chocolate ready."

"With marshmallows! We made a big snowman with real coal eyes and a carrot nose," added Vanessa. "We didn't have a top hat, so we used one of Dad's baseball hats."

"Grampa had a sled and horse. We got to ride through the forest."

"We got to hold the reins of the horse. He was so big and gentle."

"There was a big bonfire at night. Everybody sat around it and sang about Rudolph, the Drummer Boy, Frosty the Snowman, and the baby Jesus."

"And in the morning, there were scads of presents. I got just what I wanted. So did Vanessa."

"There were lots more Christmases, but that was the best."

"Yes, it was a good one," said Mary, smiling at her daughters. "But our first one, the one with just your father and me, was also magical." She turned to the Survivors. "We were just married, right out of college. No jobs, no money. Crushing student loans. We managed to get a rent-controlled flat in a six-story walkup in New York. We got some ham and potatoes with food stamps. Cooked them in an antique oven that had no heat control. On or off. We laughed and watched it closely, running back and forth, turning it on and off. We ate a delicious meal." She laughed. "We decorated with colored paper leftover from my art classes. We lit candles and sat on the ragged couch and listened to carols over a scratchy radio. Then, like magic, some carolers from a nearby church began singing just below our flat. We went out onto the cold fire escape and listened. God, it was beautiful. Even from six stories up it sounded like they were in the room. I know it was because we were in love, but..."

"She is right," said John. "It was more than magical, more than being in love. It was like a gift. A gift without cost. That was our first Christmas, and one I remember most. Except for the Maine one, of course."

It was getting dark inside. The Survivors lit some candles, which almost made the room seem warm. "Wonderful," said Devon. "How about you, Dennis?"

Dennis stood uncertainly and looked around at the expectant faces, at the altered market room. Then it came to him; his best memory was right here. He told of his last Christmas before deployment. "It was here at this place. I decorated the thirty-foot fir at the south side of the store. It was lit up with lights and could be seen for almost a mile up 101." That was good, but he needed to describe the warmth of his grandparents and their worry about his deployment.

"There is no way to tell the joy of having grandparents like these. My folks passed away in a car crash when I was six. They took me in and treated me like their own. Here on the coast, there's not a lot of snow, but the year of my deployment, we got a few inches. It was beautiful. I remember during Christmas dinner they asked God to protect me during Operation Inherent Resolve. At the time, despite what they told me, I did not believe God took sides." He smiled a knowing smile. "And maybe He doesn't, but there are no atheists in a foxhole when incoming is shaking the ground." Dennis shook his head.

"The next Christmas was filled with homemade cookies and foot powder," he laughed. His grandmother smiled. His grandfather was stoic, trying not to become emotional.

"As Teressa and Mary said, the one before deployment was the best."

The candlelit faces glowed.

The storytellers were animated now. Wanda stood without prompting and told of her Italian family's feasting and hugging. "My father was a baker in Portland when I was young. The family would get together Christmas day after church services. Most of us were thoroughly Americanized. We were also a big family, and some were not too far removed from traditional Italian Christmas. It's a major holiday in Italy, and some family members carried on older traditions. Children received gifts on Epiphany night from la Befana and on Christmas day from Babbo Natale. It was a good time to be a child." She became wistful.

"But the best was the food and the setting aside of family feuds. All were welcomed to our home. No animosity was allowed. All were embraced. It was a taste of what Eden must have been like. And the food—like heaven. Christmas Eve was lighter fare. No meat. But Christmas day . . . aah . . . I cannot explain how magical it was. Mama and Papa cooked and baked all day. Tons of fish. Tuna, salmon, smelt, calamari. And spaghetti and baccala. The entire family was welcome, even neighbors and passersby. And the pastries! The pies! The gelato! But mostly, it was the feelings of friendship, joy, and peace. I thought as a child it should always be that way." Wanda came back from her reverie. "Now, here, it is similar. There is no la Befana, Babbo Natale, or Santa Clause. But, I don't know why, I feel a friendship, joy, and peace that I can't explain. We will survive as a family." Although Wanda was still trapped in the motel, she was moving past her time alone in the booth. Here, she had friends.

"Hear, hear," said Bob.

"How about our hosts?" asked Devon.

Joan stood and told of her Christmases past. "I was raised in Texas during the oil boom. Father was a rigger. I remember the smell of oil on him. He was a big man and tried hard to provide for us, me and my two brothers. We lived in Humble, Texas, while Dad chased pocket reservoirs in the Humble oil fields to the south." She sighed. "There was nothing humble about Humble. The town was full of itself." Again she sighed. "But that's not what I wanted to say. We celebrated Christmas reverently. Sundays and Christmas were some of the only days Dad got off. We made the best of it. We decorated a stunted pine, and we opened presents our parents thought they had hidden." Laughter. "We feasted. It was southwest fare. Roast chicken, baked glazed ham, mashed potatoes with butter and whipped cream—the real stuff. Corn on the cob. And mom baked an apple pie that was so crisp and sweet," she sighed again. "We listened to songs on the record player: 'Silent Night' and 'Do You Hear What I Hear.' Just being in our small house with the smell of cooking—without the smell of oil—was magical." Joan got a wistful look, and her eyes filled. "And now, here, I think I can feel some of the same."

Silence. The Survivors reveled in Joan's reverie. An imagined chorus of "Silent Night" filled the room.

Stan stood next to her. "Joan and I have had many Christmases. All were filled with some joy. Now here with a group of strangers—Survivors—there is something special."

"That was—is—wonderful. We need another," said Devon, looking at the Jones.

Jan stood and told of their trip to her grandparents' place in Colorado when she was a young woman. "The family gathered to hear about our heritage. I won't expound on our ancestry. Save our grandparents came from a war-torn Europe with nothing. They managed to survive and then thrive in America. That Christmas, when the family was gathered together at our ancestral home, the one my grandmother's parents grew up in outside Denver," Jan choked, bowed over, and then straightened. "They both died. It was Christmas, and they died!" She again fought back tears. "We found them in the morning, sitting on the freezing porch, a quilt in their laps, nestled together in quiet repose. No one heard them exit the house."

She steadied and continued, "Like Joan, that's not what I want to say, because there was no sorrow. Only a joyous reflection on well-lived lives. Ours was not a big family. Grandma had only one child, my mother. And I . . . we have had two children." She stopped, not wanting to make this sad by mourning her children.

"Anyway, we celebrated. We had a big, beautiful noble fir that grandma had decorated with memorabilia. Grandpa had strung lights over the house. In the snow, they twinkled merrily." She thought for a minute. "It may seem strange, but because of the way they sat, so serene, literally frozen in time, we left them there while we celebrated."

Jan sat down, seeming to fold in on herself. Then she straightened again. "Despite the tone I think I gave, that was the best Christmas I think I ever had. Certainly the most heartfelt."

Joe held her. "My turn," he said.

"I was there for the Christmas Jan just told you about. It was everything she said. She neglected to say that both grandparents had terminal cancer. In my mind, it was a blessing to the family that they passed that way, instead of in a sterile hospital somewhere, apart from each other." He looked at Jan and smiled. "Now I have to go back further in time." Joe told of a specific Christmas Eve and day he spent as a boy. "Ours was a large family in Vancouver, Washington, and I was the middle boy. We always hunted up the largest tree we could find in the local lots and then laughed while my father tried to set it up, the top scraping the paint from the ceiling. The best Christmas was when I got my first gun. I was thirteen. I remember that when I opened the case and saw it, I almost jumped for joy. Father watched closely as I examined the pistol. The first thing I did was as I was taught: to open the cylinder and check for loaded rounds. Several spent casings fell out. I looked at my dad and smiled. He nodded. I was ready in his eyes. I saw pride." He thought for a second. "Not the traditional gift, but the memory was of my father's pride. It was memorable."

Dennis looked at him. "I've seen you shoot. It was a good gift. It was good for us here, now."

"Yeah. Anyway, we ate until we were ready to pop. Then the pies came out." Laughter. "It was after that I knew I had a talent." He trailed off. "The best talent I had, though, was for finding love. Because I met this lovely woman here. Christmases became our family doings. Except for the one in Colorado. And now the one here."

"Ha! You think?" Jan said, "It was I who found you."

"Next. Save me," said Joe, laughing.

"Bob to the rescue. While we are talking about guns, I'll go next." He took a breath, looked concerned, and then started off with a strong voice. "There was a time in the David Douglas forest. I was camping alone in two feet of snow at twenty degrees, hunting a rabid bear. One that was not hibernating and was terrorizing the local hamlets.

"*Christmas!* I suddenly thought. Without family, I lost track of time. I ate a Christmas dinner of Spam over an open fire. And slept in my pup tent, in a sheltered area under a tree, the flap open so I could see the stars through the trees.

"I'd awoken in the night, not sure why. All was quiet. No sound at all. The starlight gave a ghostly glow to the fresh snow. I felt somehow calm. Then, even at peace. When I remembered the date, I felt the need to say something, and in the middle of the night on Christmas Eve, I said these words: 'You know God, I have not led the best life. I am divorced. She was right to do it. I am a loner at heart. But I did love her and the boys. Now I am out here in the middle of the forest, hunting a rogue bear. He should be in hibernation but . . . Well, that's not Your concern. I just wanted to let You know. I appreciate the gift of Christmas.'

"I started to go back to sleep when I heard the crunch of heavy footfalls, and a large, dark form moved toward me. I was wrapped in this sleeping bag and could not move quickly. My rifle and my dart gun were out of reach, sheathed against the cold snow. I didn't move; I didn't call out to God. I was surprisingly calm. I couldn't say why. The form coalesced into a bear. Perhaps 300 pounds. Underfed and under-weight. Slavering, long loops of thick saliva drooling a silvery color in the meager light."

Everyone in the room leaned forward to hear Bob. He spoke lower and lower, almost talking to himself. "I should have been terrified. This was a large rabid animal within a few feet of me. But I wasn't. The bear snorted, made a sound like a long, sad moan, and looked straight at me as if I was—I dunno—God. Then he laid down and died. Right there in front of me. I will tell you, I cried for him. And I actually asked God to take him home." Bob stopped. There were tears in his and the Survivors' eyes. A rabid bear had died, and the Survivors mourned it.

"I didn't want to be sad now. This was actually a joyous feeling for me. I don't know why, but I felt closer to God then than at any other time in my life."

There came some amens and comforting sounds. Then quiet.

The newlyweds stood together. Sally started off, wiping away a tear. "Sorry about the bear. But I bet your hope was realized. Now, we will tell of our first Christmas together. It was before we were married. Our families got together in my grandparents' house. It was a big, older home with lots of room. And we needed it all. My father had passed away the year before. But there were thirteen of us there. Bill's parents, my mom, three sisters—two were married. And Bill's brothers, one of whom was married. We were still a young family, so no grandkids yet."

"We were also very traditional. Everyone ensured that me and Sally were kept apart at night," said Bill.

Sally smiled. "Well, that was not a bad thing, just hard."

"Anyway, we did the traditional things. The tree, gifts, feasting." Bill smacked his lips. "But the best thing was sitting around the fireplace in the living room with hot cider and maybe a rum eggnog, listening to her grandparents tell of Christmases past. I cannot describe the reverence these people had for the tradition. And I don't mean the tree and presents."

"They were very orthodox," Sally said. "It was not superficial. It was deeply felt. And they conveyed that well. We left feeling somehow reborn. Free of guilt and need. It faded over time. Now I feel a little of it again. Like those stories before, it was the best Christmas ever."

"Wonderful. How about it, Terry?" said Devon.

Eyes turned to Terry.

He shook his head. While the stories told here were nice, they were not his. He suddenly realized the difference between his background and the others. There had been no white Christmas, no Santa Clause, no midnight masses in his childhood. And for sure, no rabid bears or frozen parents. Indeed, his early life wasn't anything like theirs.

"Come on, Terry," said Teressa. "You have to have something."

"I don't have memories of Christmas like you all."

"So what? You have some good memories of something. Family? Friends? What did you do at this time of year?" she said, instinctively negotiating the racial issues that popped up.

Terry thought. Where he grew up, the streets of the neighborhood were not safe. Drugs and gangs were everyday hazards. His parents did a good job of keeping him and his brothers out of trouble, and he thought he did a good job with his own children. When he was married, they moved to Astoria to a new job with the Oregon State Police. They celebrated Christmas with food and presents along with the city and fellow troopers, but it was somehow perfunctory, without true joy. Christmas was not theirs.

He thought hard. There had to be something. Then it came to him.

"There was one time." Terry started, watching the Survivors for judgment. He saw only curiosity. "A long time ago. It was close to New Year's. Our family—my mother, father, brothers and sisters, uncles and aunts, cousins and some I didn't know—came to our home in South Los Angeles. I was fifteen. Turning into a man. My grandparents were dead by then. We did not have Santa Clause. We had an Elder. And Kwanzaa. It was a new thing for us." He looked around at the faces watching him. There was still no judgment. Still, merely curiosity.

"For the turning of the season, we exchanged handmade gifts and feasted on what I was told was traditional fare, including something called Groundnut stew made from peanuts, yams, and chicken. It was good, but I didn't pay much attention to it. By seventeen, I was in the service and didn't look back." Terry sighed and continued. "I regret that. But like those before me, that's not what I want to say. At that time," he looked at Teressa, who had mentioned "time," and winked, "our Elder, who was a wise man, taught us a song. It was a traditional seasonal song from Nigeria. It was a call for peace and good crops. The Elder translated it into English for us. But he sang it in Hausa, one of many languages spoken in Nigeria. I remember it. It was sad and hopeful. It was uplifting and grounded in reality.

"Now, I was a terrible singer. The family insisted everybody sing, and most were good singers. It was a beautiful sound. I was embarrassed and mumbled a lot. But like I said, I remember it. It makes me happy to remember."

The girls chimed in together. "Sing it. Sing it. Sing it!"

"I can't sing."

"Bullshit," said Bob. "Neither can I, but if you start off, we can follow."

"Yes. Yes. Yes!"

"All right, but you'll be sorry. I only hope I can do this well enough for the feeling it gives." He took a breath, stood, and began. He was right; he was not a good singer, but the song in Hausa carried through. About halfway through, the girls began to accompany him. They had surprisingly mature, clear, well-modulated voices. Terry raised an eyebrow and continued. Others began to pick up the cadence. As he said, it was a simple tune that was full of emotion. Terry reached the end, but animated, he continued anew. More Survivors sang. Bob was also right; he too was a terrible singer, but he had the emotion right.

They got to the end. Terry stopped and looked around again at the smiling faces. Tears welled up and rolled down his cheeks. "Thank you," he said.

"That was beautiful," Devon said. "Can I sing the song I remembered from our last Christmas?"

"Go ahead," Terry said. "If I can get through it, you can too."

Devon started "O Holy Night" in a clear, clean tenor. It was a song most knew, even Terry. The Survivors quickly caught on, and the song wafted out into the growing dark. No one noticed Joe stumble over the "fall on your knees" passage.

No one wanted to break the ambiance. They sat and talked for a while, like a big family at a Christmas feast. Joan brought out some chocolate mix, and they warmed it with water over some candles.

Devon wanted to press for prayer, but seeing the joy, he decided not to. Inwardly, he saw a positive step. He could save them yet.

Merry Christmases were exchanged, as well as handshakes and hugs. The candles were extinguished. They quietly moved to their rooms. The dark closed in.

The cold rainy winter passed slowly. Temperatures dropped below freezing for only a few days. It was uncomfortable, but the Survivors endured, bundled up, watching the condensation of their breath when they talked. Now, it was March. The rain was getting warmer. The Necanicum flooded twice. The Bugs just squatted, held on, and endured, waiting.

Flora and fauna were prospering. All kinds of carnivores and carrion eaters had preyed upon the bodies that were left to rot. The bears, mountain lions, and coyotes had thrived. Now they were back to being themselves. The resultant stench was almost gone, swept away by the continuous wave of storms blowing off the Pacific Ocean. Cockroaches, flies, molds, and bacteria had peaked and ebbed. Opportunistic plants thrived. Scotch broom, ivies, and blackberries ran amok.

The Survivors, though, were not thriving. The feeling of Christmas had dissipated with the supplies. The stores were depleted. Rationing helped, but there was no food for several days. The Survivors were beginning to starve. They were that lucky water was gravity fed and that the reservoir held. But showers were cold, and electronic devices used up all the batteries in the store and died. No more video games could be played. No more diversions. Joe had religiously started the Ford once a month to keep the battery up. Bugs crowded around the makeshift hallway each time.

Terry called a meeting and asked for suggestions, first on how to get food and medicine and then maybe to get the generator going. "What're we going to do now?"

Bill said, "Well, let's think about this. It seems from the info in the tweets from before everything went dark that the 'fuel' in the Bugs can last for about a year. That means we need to survive until the end of summer, at least. We need food now. So, the method Terry used to get Wanda should work to get food. The local Safeway in Seaside will have canned goods that will keep for years. Someone," he looked around the room at Terry and Dennis, "will have to drive there and then drive through the doors into the store, and somehow seal off an aisle, get the canned goods, and drive back out."

"Sounds easy, but that will be risky," said Dennis.

"OK. Does anyone remember the Safeway layout?"

"Yeah, I do," Joe said. "The Ford will fit through the doors and, I think, the aisles. We sure as hell can't walk inside. The bodywork has taken a beating now, so anymore is inconsequential. But it cannot be immobilized, or we are kaput."

"If we don't get food, we are for sure kaput," Jan said.

"The Bugs could be dead tomorrow," Sally hoped.

"We have to risk it," Terry was pragmatic.

"Yeah, we do. We have to chance it," Joe said. "If the Bugs are gone tomorrow, so much the better. We can probably push through the south doors. The aisles for goods are aligned east/west. I think the truck will fit down the aisles. Even if it doesn't, we can risk knocking over the displays and doing a smash and grab. There will be Bugs inside. There will be shooting required."

"The best bet will be to use the truck to seal one end of a row," said Dennis, "Kill the ones that remain. I don't know how to seal the other end. The display cases are probably bolted to the floor. The floor is probably reinforced concrete."

Bill said, "OK, let's think about this." Half of the Survivors mouthed the words as he said them. They still had some life in them. "Ha, ha.

Anyway, perhaps it would be possible to drive down the aisles and reach through the crew cab windows."

Terry said, "Good idea," and then looked at Joe. "Can it be done?"

"I don't know, but we have no choice. I will drive. Dennis?" said Joe.

Dennis said, "Let's go! Hoo-ah!"

"Hoo-ah!" echoed Terry.

Everybody chimed in. "Get some toilet paper, get some coffee, get some books, batteries, DVDs, beer, wine . . ."

"Don't forget the Spam," said Bob. Laughter.

Terry said, "OK, relax. Get what you can without getting killed, for God's sake. Also, for what it's worth, when I was coming back with Wanda, one of the Bugs bounced over the hood. When it got close to the windshield, I guess it sensed me there. It hummed like a beehive and sprayed poison. Watch out for that. I don't know the range, but it seemed to blow it out about a foot. Let's get you suited up."

Looking like paranoid beekeepers, Joe and Dennis went carefully through the doors and the makeshift aisle to the truck.

Once again, the Survivors shared a feeling of loss. What if something went wrong? What if Joe and Dennis didn't return?

"They will return!" said Jan, answering the unsaid questions. "My Joe will return!"

"And our Dennis," added Teressa and Vanessa together. Mary looked at them. What was that all about? But she knew. She was young once, too.

Joe carefully drove over Junction Road onto 101, north past Circle Creek Campground, which was now littered with a few empty recreational vehicles, scraps of tents, and clothing, and on into the Safeway parking lot next to a MacDonald's and the Town Hall. The parking lot was surprisingly empty. Most people who were in their cars had tried to make it home. Those in the store didn't. But on the night of the Bugs, there had been just a few people shopping.

The south doors were the sliding kind that opened on hinges if the power went out. Joe drove the truck through by pushing the doors aside with the now-damaged bumper. Inside, it was surprisingly dark. He turned on the truck's lights. To the right were the remnants of the produce display. Nothing but rotted bananas, melons, and other unrecognizable vegetables remained, along with lots of ants and roaches. The meat section was a mass of maggots and flies. Thankfully, they were confined to the meat and vegetables.

The main aisle in front of the checkout stands was littered with dropped groceries and carts. The stench trapped in the building was almost unbearable.

Just a few desiccated human bodies and no rising, animated Bugs were inside the store. The ones that got inside had left to hunt other humans when finished. But more were following the truck inside. The main aisle held kiosks for papers, batteries, and DVDs. The aisles, except for those steel posts that held up the roof, appeared wide enough for the truck. Joe found the aisle with the most cans—soups, beans, chili, and such—and K-maneuvered the truck to back in. He knocked aside the checkout stands and then risked a short trip outside the truck to grab the batteries before the Bugs could navigate the door. He just threw the whole kiosk in.

Dennis climbed out the back window and opened the canopy door. The bed was higher than the Bugs, but they remembered what Terry said about the Bug's spraying. When Dennis indicated the optimum position for gathering food, Joe locked the brake and climbed out the back window into the truck bed with Dennis. Bugs had rounded the aisle from the open end like ants to sugar. The shooting began.

Joe was the shooter. Using a semiautomatic 22 caliber short-barreled rifle with short ammunition to minimize the sound and poison leakage, he cleared the area and kept it clear while Dennis loaded cans and plastic bottles full of juice. Dennis threw the groceries in through the canopy doors. It worked. Then, they repeated the strategy on other aisles. They collected canned meats, beans, chili, tomatoes, preserves, coffee, toilet paper, cereal, powdered milk, prepackaged dry dinners—everything they could think of. When the bed was loaded, Dennis started throwing the lighter packages into the back seat of the cab. For a while, they labored under warlike conditions, expending lots of firepower. Joe went through three 25-round mags. The 22 shorts did not splatter the Bugs. They simply fell. And when one fell, there was always another.

They got enough food to last quite a while. After a couple of hours, they were swimming in nonperishable food. Joe was running out of ammunition. They closed the canopy door and climbed back in over the mass of food and headed back.

Away from the stench, the drive back felt good. Like returning home.

As before, when they arrived at Survivors, the ports opened and the steps were cleared of Bugs. Joe got the Ford close enough to keep the Bugs out. He and Dennis got out and shoveled off the carcasses, got out of their Bug-proof gear and then began the job of carrying the goods in. For that, there was lots of help.

Their bellies full and feeling better, the Survivors sat around the common table that night and talked again about other possible survivors.

Bill said, "Well, let's . . . here is my thinking. With the first conditions we talked about, now there is another. Can anybody have enough food and water for a year? I'd say the odds are slim for anybody except survivalists, and even those people would have to get to the bunkers fast. Even then, the Bugs would get in if the floor wasn't steel-reinforced concrete."

Terry said, "OK, we all have loved ones out there. It's sad to think about them, but we need to be strong. Let's get through this, and then we will search. Another few months. Be strong."

"Be strong?" said Devon. "We need divine intervention to survive. We need to call on God. Obey His laws or He will punish us like He did to the others." After the Christmas stories event, it seemed Devon had found his way. He had been calm. Now, for some reason, he was animated, almost panicking. He could not let the Survivors drift away from God.

Terry was suddenly equally adamant. Up until now, he also had remained low-key, staying calm and logical for the sake of the group. Now, he spoke through gritted teeth, barely controlling his anger. "What you did for us last Christmas is not forgotten. But there's no need to panic. Now, we will survive or not depending on our abilities. These abilities came from God. We'll use them the best we can. You all can deal with God on a personal level. Me? I am going to do what I can to survive. Does not include begging."

Joe felt his anger rise along with Terry's. What was it about fundamentalist religion that set him off? Jan grabbed his arm as a warning. He did not feel it. The others watched with sudden fear.

"Don't let arrogance cloud your mind. We cannot survive without God." Devon was genuinely worried.

"I stand by my statement. God helps those who help themselves. In this case, it's us helping each other. I don't know God's will. Only my own," asserted Terry

"Surely you know God punishes people who disobey Him," said Devon.

There it is, thought Joe. What was hidden in most religions of the time. Intolerance. Guilt. Judgment. Punishment. The seeking to impose, by force if necessary, some sort of divine will. The cornerstone of all religions: My way or the highway straight to hell. But it was men who made religion what it was. Not God!

"You mean the God of Israel? The God of the Old Testament? The God who demanded burned offerings, sacrifice, and blood? The one who ordered Abraham to sacrifice his son? I do not see that as what the real Creator wanted," Joe growled.

"Do not blaspheme. We are in peril."

"Yeah, we are. But we survived. Each of us needs to pick their own path. I will not dictate . . . nor will you! Understand?"

Terry has it right, thought Joe.

"Yes. And I fear for our souls."

"Fear for your own, not mine," interjected Joe. He could not understand why Devon was suddenly so adamant. He could not punish. *But he could guilt us into his way,* he thought. The stink of religious judgment was strong. *He is blaming us for this.* Joe started forward. "You will not tell me what to do or believe!"

Jan grabbed him, held on. There was no reasoning now.

Stan and Joan suddenly stood up. The action caused Joe to look at them. John and Mary also stood. "Then let us leave it at that. And plan for another day," Joan said, looking at Joe with sad eyes. The sureness in her voice and being filled the room. Calm emanated from those who stood.

"Stand down, Joe," Stan said. His voice was low, but it carried authority.

The Survivors went silent. Devon was thoughtful, and Terry and Joe were still agitated, but calm was returning. Jan kept hold of Joe. Wanda moved and stood in front of Terry. The rest were in various states of confusion. The tense air began to clear. Joe's look went from angry to sorry. Terry now looked conflicted. This was a fundamental problem. One that needed closure. But the people involved seemed to be at an impasse. Each Survivor thought about it differently. With different levels of concern. But all saw the danger of a physical fight.

Slowly, the Survivors retired to their rooms to ponder the conflict and to continue the long wait. The discourse was put on the back burner by most. It was not forgotten or forgiven by one, though. Terry knew it would be discussed again. He saw the way Jan looked at Joe. Soon.

Very soon.

"What the hell was that about?" Jan demanded. They were sitting in their room, but she was being loud enough to be heard throughout the building. "If you got some bug up your butt, get it out now. We don't need that stuff here and now."

Joe thought, *yeah. Tell it!* Then he responded, "I don't know. I don't want to bring God into this. Religion caused enough problems in the world. We don't need it here."

"That wasn't about religion. It was about God. We can debate without putting our hands on each other, you moron!"

"No, it was about religion. Devon's religion. That and God are two separate things. But you are right. I overreacted. So did Terry. I will take it down a notch."

"You will take it off the chart! Apologize to Devon! Now!" A demand.

"Jan, that's too much. I will apologize for my actions, but not for my beliefs. Devon can have his. But he will not tell me what to do or believe. He can't tell me God is going to punish me, or you, if I don't bring Him a burned offering! Can't you see that?"

"Joe, I'm sorry. I don't want to fight. But we need to keep it together here. Can't you see *that*?"

"Yeah. I think everybody got it." He called down the hall, "Sorry, Devon."

"Terry?" called Jan.

There was silence for a moment then, "All right. I should not have jumped so hard. Let's leave it alone. Stay out of each other's faces. Respect mine, I respect yours. OK?"

"Devon?" called Jan.

"Agreed. I just want to protect us. But I won't be so vocal. I will pray in secret, as the Lord taught. And for the record, I don't do the burned offering thing." Devon went from serious to almost amused.

"Maybe you should spend some more time with the New Testament," offered Mary.

"Maybe I should."

"Everybody OK with this now?" Jan asked.

All, of course, were listening. Assents were given and received, all without a face-to-face meeting. A new thing for Jan. She was sort of proud of it.

But the rift remained.

CHAPTER 6

Freedom

One spring night, a mountain lion screeched out by the river. Vanessa asked her dad, "What was that?"

"Nothing, don't worry about it."

"Oh, for God's sake, tell her the truth," said Mary. She was wise about religion, but tempers were short about most other things. John just did not know what it was.

Bob took up the role of peacemaker. "That was a mountain lion, Vanessa. Probably testing its territory. Maybe making little lions." He winked at John and Mary. "Your father is right. No problem for us."

"Sorry," Mary said. "I didn't mean that."

"I know. Just a little longer, Mary. We have to keep it together for the kids."

"We're doing OK," said Teressa. "We'll be OK." The family came together, seeking comfort from each other.

They'd been cooped up for ten months. Talk was rare now. The other Survivors did not pay much attention to the exchange. They were turned inward, shielding themselves against the dark.

Later that night in their room, a candle pushing back the seemingly relentless dark, Joe and Jan talked in low tones.

"We can't go on like this," said Jan. "We are headed for a major confrontation. A severing of relations. This is like a big family that can't get along, with nowhere to go. We can't get away from each other. There will be an explosion of sorts. We—you and I—must be ready."

"Yeah, I see it coming. So do all the others. There is nothing to be done, though. Just hold on and last it out. The Bugs can't last forever. In fact, probably only another month or two."

"But can the Survivors outlast the Bugs? That's the real question."

"We will or we won't," said Joe. "The problem here is can we outlast each other? Terry and Devon . . . and me. They . . . we . . . are at odds over how to . . . believe, I guess. I sided with Terry, but Devon has a point. If we look back at how we all got here, there is a lot more to it than luck."

"But you were right, too. We don't know God's will. He does what He wants. And we do too! If He wants to save us, great. If He wants to destroy us, well, we won't know, will we? It will just happen. The door will break, and the Bugs will get us."

"You're right. We just have to persevere. It is in our nature."

"You know what?" Jan said, changing the tone. "I've been thinking. There is a lot of time for that after all. We've talked about spirituality like this: I have a body. I have a soul. I have a spirit. I have a mind. Each of these statements supposes 'I' own these things. If that is the case, who am I? Who or what is the entity of 'I'?"

"Wow! I never thought of it like that. As they say, that's above my paygrade. But I think the soul and spirit are the same. Like how Jung postulated the anima as our incorporeal essence—that which animates us. That which is us. Crap! Did I really say that?"

"Yeah, you did. And you're right. Sort of. Also, most world religions postulate multiple gods or at least some sort of pantheon. Angels and demons, or something similar. The first part of the Bible in Genesis says man was made in God's image. In fact, the plural was used when referencing God. We could quite possibly be godlike, be our own anima," Jan said.

"We're all over the place. Ouch! My brain hurts."

"Ha! Do you really own your brain? Or in your case, do you even have one?"

"Hardy-har-har. You drop this esoteric bomb and then run away from it. We ought to drop it on Devon and see what happens."

They quietly laughed. Joe said, "It is something to think about."

"Yes. But we have each other for the time being."

"Yes, we do. And I'm damn glad for it. You keep me grounded. I think without you I would have hit Devon."

"You came damn close. Let's sleep on all these thoughts. We have a long way to go."

"Why have we not talked like this before?"

"Well, because we haven't been in this position, I guess."

"Let's hope we get out of this before..."

"Yeah, let's hope."

They fell asleep in each other's arms. The night was calm. Tomorrow was a new day.

In their room, Terry and Wanda also talked in low tones.

"Terry, you need to do something. The Survivors are losing hope."

"What can I do? These people can handle it themselves. Let Devon raise their spirits."

"From what I saw, you are the one who held this together at first. You say we should stay out of each other's faces. But we need hope. Devon will want us to call on God. I know you will not beg. That will just cause more problems."

"Yeah, you're right. Truth is, I didn't know what to do at first. I was just winging it. And I don't know what to do now."

"Well, you sure did it right for all your not knowing. Let me make a suggestion. When you saved me, that was you doing the right thing. Acting, doing—that's you. Now, how about calling a meeting? Saying we are almost done. Just a little longer. Let's start thinking about what we will do when the Bugs die."

"All right, let me think about it. Tomorrow, we'll do something."

"Thank you. You're a good man."

"We'll see. I don't want to start Devon and Joe up again."

"And you, too. It's got to be handled sometime before something bad happens."

"Let's sleep on it. I'm getting an idea."

They snuggled against the cold and drear.

During the siege of Bugs, Wanda was mostly catatonic, terrified, and then needy. Her first night at the motel was spent in the Lakes bed, away from the bumping devils. The women tried to help her. They assured her she was safe. She did not believe it. The second night they gave her a room of her own. She was so afraid, she snuck into Terry's room and curled up in a corner.

Terry of course knew she was there. He got up, came to her, picked her up, and put her in the bed. He then climbed in and turned his back and went to sleep.

Wanda nearly melted. A feeling of safety came, then a feeling of betrayal. What about her husband, her children. She then cried-loud. She wailed, she screamed, the bed shook. Terry lay still. The Survivors heard but did not react. Gradually she slowed and then as if by a miracle, slept.

It was not until after the Christmas celebration that she actually turned to Terry in bed. He hadn't tried to take advantage. She knew like Bob, Dennis, and maybe Devon; he took care of himself when the need arose. But she knew that was a distant second best for men. And she was right there. It must have been hard for him. "You sure?" he'd asked. She pulled him to herself and kissed him. "Yes."

Terry was a considerate lover. She felt him trying not to be too rough. But she also knew when it came to making love, for Terry she could have been any woman. He loved her in his way, but sex for him was just that, sex. Eventually, she learned to accept it and enjoy sex as he did.

That morning, the Survivors sat around the common table after a breakfast of cold cereal and reconstituted milk. Terry said, "OK, we made it this far. There is just a little more to go. Now, Wanda and I have been talking, and I'm sure all of you have, too. So, Wanda will now share her ideas."

Eyes turned to Wanda, who looked aghast at Terry. He was grinning like a Cheshire cat.

"Um. Well . . . I kinda thought we could talk about what we're going to do when the Bugs die . . . God, Terry, way to put me on the spot."

"Your idea, Wanda," Terry said, still grinning.

"A good one, too," said Bob. "I've had enough Spam. I'm gonna get us some fresh dinners. Salmon, crab, beef. Hell, I'm making myself drool."

The Survivors perked up. Started thinking.

"Plant a garden."

"Walk on the beach."

"Find some blackberries for jam."

"Find some new clothes."

"Repair the generator."

"Sit in the sun."

Thoughts continued around the table. Wanda was smiling. Terry was grinning. The Survivors were alive again.

As before, the glow faded with time. And each new day dragged on and on and on.

The answer about who would last would come in another couple of months. For now, the Survivors turned inward again. The silence was pervasive. Interactions were at a minimum. Even couples were solitary. They were trapped in what amounted to a dark, airless prison. But they were the Survivors. The remnants of Devon's Christmas and Wanda's hope pushed back against the dark, keeping them away from the abyss. Keeping them hopeful and sane.

Summer arrived. The sun made things seem better.

Then, one cool sunny day in the middle of September, after a mild, wistful, and hopeful summer passed, Vanessa let out a yell. "Look outside! Look! Look!"

Joe was sitting at the window reading a novel for the tenth time, looking for some nuance he might have missed. He put it down and looked at the parking lot. Something was different. It took a minute for him to see, to believe. The Bugs had seemed to be dormant for about a month, no longer rising when a Survivor went to the door. Now they were decomposing, melting back into the earth from which they came. The Survivors watched like it was a movie, a reverse time-lapse of a blooming flower. At the end of just one day, no trace of the Bugs remained. In one day they arose, and in one day they sank.

They had survived! They had outlasted the Bugs! It was time for celebration, for the Survivors to emerge. But first, they needed to be sure they were safe, that the Bugs would not rise again. How to do that? It became a topic for discussion.

"Any ideas?" Terry asked the assembled and newly animated Survivors.

"Well, let's think about this." Bob's standard response got a little laugh, the first in nearly two months. "We know they arose from the ground. We know they targeted humans and were very toxic. We know how we survived—by being close to a safe location. We know they killed using poison and they needed to be close or touch the victim. We know they are not very mobile, relying on numbers to do the job." He paused. "What we don't know is why. Why were they engineered and distributed? It is relevant as to how we proceed."

There was a flurry of discussion. The consensus was that some force wanted to destroy humanity without otherwise affecting the ecology. The unimaginable arose as probable.

"Aliens! It is the only possibility. No one on earth could engineer and deploy the Bugs," blurted John.

"Why? For God's sake," asked Devon.

"Because they want this world—without us in it. That's the only explanation. Unless they are just psychopathic," said Bill. They all thought for a minute.

Then Bill had the final thought. "And if that's true, in either case, they'll be back to finish the job, will they not?"

"Well and good, but let's get back to the question. How do we assure the Bugs are really gone?" Terry was again being pragmatic. "One problem at a time."

"Somebody needs to put on the raingear and take a look," said Joe. "We need to set up a killing zone and take a short hike. I will do it." Jan looked at him like he just volunteered to go on a suicide mission. But she said nothing. This would wait until she could get him alone.

"Hah!" said Dennis. "Not a chance. You are too valuable. I will go."

There was suddenly a lot of crosstalk. Me. No, me. No, me!

After a lot of calculation, it was decided the two best pistol shots would go—Joe and Terry. Dennis and Bob would stand by to cover with rifles.

"To hell with privacy." Jan buttonholed Joe before they could get set. "If you don't come back, I will kill you myself." She spoke loudly enough to be heard all the way out to the parking lot.

"For you, I will return, even if the gates of Hell open up. Anyway, there is no danger now from the Bugs. We can tell when they're coming by the tremors in the ground. Remember, I was out there when they arose. I know the signs. It gives enough time to get back here. I think the aliens are now our biggest worry."

He did not know how wrong he was or how right.

Jan said, "You better." And kissed him.

Joe and Terry got ready.

The paranoid beekeepers left the barricade up just in case and crawled out through the truck. Out to the highway and back, skirting the cars and remains of those who did not make it. No Bugs appeared. Nothing moved. All was quiet on the skeleton-littered pock-marked parking lot. They moved a hundred yards up and back on the highway. Nothing. No sign of the Bugs remained.

The next day, they did it again, walking the north field. Nothing. Then again.

A week later, they took the barricade down and moved the truck. They were free!

The Bugs had disappeared. They had decomposed into their original elements and were washed away by the Oregon rains.

By the end of September, no Aliens had appeared. No Bugs had appeared. It was time to clean up. As before, when the Bugs hit, the Survivors went to work without direction.

Bob and Dennis found some plastic sheeting in the store, and together, they moved what was left of the bodies who were killed trying to get to the store, to a patch of ground behind the building. They carefully found each person's identification and placed it on the shrouds.

Joe, Bill, John, and Terry set about clearing the derelict cars and motor home. Jumpstart batteries were found at the Seaside Auto Parts store and charged from the generator. They were easier to work with. After a bit of work, they managed to move the vehicles across the road, out of the way. The motel now looked better.

The rooms were sealed off from the makeshift doorways. Now they had true individual rooms with doors that opened to the deck.

In the soft evening of the fifth day of freedom, the Survivors finished cleaning the area around the motel. They ate a common picnic of barbequed salmon Bob had caught. But the glow of freedom waned. The future was waiting. And it was not promising.

"We need to honor the dead somehow," suggested Devon. The shrouded remains were still laid out behind the motel. Time to tread carefully here.

"What do you mean? There are probably billions dead." Joe was wondering if this was going to be another confrontation. The table went quiet.

"Yes. But these people could have been us. I am not asking for a funeral or a 'religious' ceremony. Just to commend their souls to God."

"I think that happened a long time ago," Joe dryly mumbled.

"Then let's do it for us. I think it will be beneficial."

Joe could find no artifice; Devon was sincere. That was the problem. He was always sincere.

"How do you propose to do this?"

"A simple statement. By name. I know it's late for commending them to God. I think we should do what we can for them. And perhaps add something for the other billions."

"What?"

Jan butted in, "Can it, Joe. This can't hurt. Let's do it. What do you think, Terry?"

"As long as we don't go begging."

"Done," said Devon. "I will not insult anyone here." He was beginning to see a path here.

That evening, as the sunset, the Survivors stood over the dozen graves. The bodies were laid in. No crosses were made, just plaques with their names carved in.

Devon read the names and tossed the IDs into the graves as he did. "God, we commend these souls to your care. We know you have already received them and perhaps billions more. As much as we can, we commend those also." He then began to shovel dirt over the bodies, tears in his eyes. He had not asked for anything from God, and somehow it felt good. The others began to help. Both Joe and Terry noted that Devon had not asked for anything. The others were caught up in the sincerity of the moment and were quiet.

"Joe?" Jan said.

"Devon, that was good. I thank you."

"Terry?" Jan said.

"Yeah. It was good."

There was a consensus-building. Devon could be the Survivor's "spiritual" leader. But there would be no "begging."

The alien problem was not forgotten; it remained in the background of their thoughts. The memory of the Bugs remained. Everyone moved about armed. Dennis and Terry gave a short instruction in pistol firearms. The store had enough for all. Targets were set in the field.

Eventually, most were thoroughly shredded, and all could shoot if they had to. The women shot with a sort of glee. Jan, Joan, and Wanda each had some training. They helped the others. The men were, of course, stoic. Even Devon took it seriously.

"Damn, that felt good," Mary said, as her smoking pistol locked open and the target showed a nice, tight grouping. "Why haven't I done this before?"

"No need before," said John. "But you're pretty impressive."

Mary smiled. It did feel good to be capable, to not need others for protection. Her daughters could shoot also but did not have the glee of their mother. There were no police or army here for protection. Even Terry seemed to be one of them—a Survivor, not an authority. She and the Survivors were their own authority, their own protection. She went to clean her weapon.

Regular runs to the local Safeway and the Walmart and Costco in Warrenton had kept up with the basic needs of the Survivors. The clothes at the local stores were a godsend. The generator was repaired. The gas heaters were swapped out for electric. They had hot water!

They were happy Bob knew his way around the beach and forest. They ate fresh crabs, clams, and salmon. The Seaside beach was loaded with clams. The Necanicum estuary had crabs and a late run of salmon. Bob caught the fish. Since no authority made it difficult, he simply waded out and netted what they needed. He taught the Survivors how to harvest the fish.

Domestic cattle had gone feral. Bob and Dennis slaughtered one away from the motel, out of sight and mind of the more sensitive Survivors. Steaks and hamburgers were still good.

Fall was on the way. Mother Nature was busy working on man-made structures. Pacific storms rolled in, one after another. Jan remembered how many repair jobs they used to see in Seaside. Without regular maintenance, rain and wind would degrade the wooden houses quickly. Better-built high rises might last hundreds of years, but in the end, all would yield to time and weather. The motel began to suffer. The Survivors pitched in and repainted it with the most expensive paint they could find at the home improvement store across the way.

They sanded and resealed the deck and carefully dismantled the gas pumps. The pumps would not work without electricity, company programs, or credit cards. The web was toast. Gas from the underground tanks was pumped by hand.

They were making the motel their home.

At another common dinner, Bill put forth an idea. "We need to rethink how we keep track of date and time."

"Why?" asked Devon. "Surely we can keep the Lord's calendar."

"Well, that's actually the Gregorian calendar. Remember, the months all came from the names of Roman emperors who fought about who had the most days. The years are from a guess at Jesus' birth. Anno Domini. It was a convenient way to date history. Even the makers of the calendar did not foresee how far back it would need to go. Or when it wouldn't matter anymore. Sooner or later, it will be inaccurate without some tinkering."

"You're right about the guess and months, but what do you propose?"

"We've thought about this," Sally said, indicating Bill. "The Bugs came near the autumnal equinox. This can be the start of our new year. Year One of the New Beginning. We can keep the old calendar for reference."

"What about the months?"

"Same names but using the sun's height as a guide. A sundial!"

To most of the Survivors, this was a non-issue, but Devon wondered, "What about birthdays, anniversaries, Christmas?"

"Transfer them as we go."

"You're going to have to explain how this works," said Terry.

They did. Taking turns, the Morris' explained how the new calendar would work. They would make an area completely flat with the gnomon set at forty-five degrees, pointing at the North Star. "The longest and shortest shadows will then be divided by twelve. Equal months, with the equinox in the center. The method will work forever. No leap years. Our new calendar. Year One for the Survivors. The sundial will be like the one on the Prom, remember? We are lucky to be at about the forty-fifth parallel. There will be not much distortion, said Bill."

"We know the forty-fifth parallel is actually just north of Lincoln City, about ninety miles south. But what the hell, it's close enough in geophysical terms," said Bill.

CHAPTER 7

Year Two

Searching

The year turned. The seasons passed. The new sundial was calibrated. Thanksgiving and Christmas were marked and celebrated. Thanksgiving dinner was an eclectic batch of ethnic food and spices. Each Survivor spent a lot of time scrounging through the local stores, and each brought a cooked meal to the table. Joe and Dennis found a couple of stoves from one of the big boxes. They set up another generator, both working hard keeping up with the cooks. Bob brought Spam. All got to see and taste what had been reminisced about while they waited for the Bugs to die.

For Christmas, they decorated a real tree. Ate more delicious food. And shared presents. Even Terry went along with Santa as played by Stan. They sang the songs in memory. In the spring, they celebrated Easter, the vernal equinox, in a nondenominational way. Devon waited patiently for Christ to be recognized. He thought he saw God at work here. He waited.

Terry remembered another springtime Hausa song about crops and planting.

Bob was still a terrible singer.

In the middle of a wet spring, the Survivors decided it was time to check for other survivors. Surely, there had to be some who managed to meet all the requirements of a safe place, proximity, supplies, skill, and luck. And, against all odds, they wanted to check about their loved ones. They met on a rare sunny day on the back deck. The damp air was fresh and clean.

"I think it's time for us to see if there are any other survivors," Terry started. "Any ideas?"

"It's going to be a mess out there. Time and weather will have degraded the roads. We need vehicles that can rough it," said John.

"I know there're some Humvees at National Guard Armory," said Dennis. "We will need to jerry-rig them, but I think we can get some of them to run."

"Let's get them." Dennis and Terry went to work.

The vehicles were diesel-powered. It took an effort to drain the sour fuel and replace it with stabilized and biocide-treated diesel. In the end, three rumbling Humvees were ready with extra fuel cans aboard. These vehicles did not get good mileage.

"What are these things?" asked Teressa.

"They are high-mobility multipurpose wheeled vehicles. Humvees for short," said Dennis. "They will handle almost all road conditions. And they are armored in case there are heavy-duty predators out there."

"What?" exclaimed Mary.

"That's a joke. These vehicles are just what we need to handle adverse conditions."

"What?"

"Quit digging, Dennis," Terry laughed. "Look, there's no danger in this search. If there's any problem, we turn around, agreed?"

After a brief discussion, it was decided that Terry would go south on 101 and cut across the low Cascades into the Capitol at Salem at the best route and opportunity. Wanda would go with him. She was still seldom far from his side.

Dennis would go north through Astoria and make for Washington's capitol at Olympia using the best possible route. Teressa wanted to go with him, but both parents said no. That was just a little too much. Teressa was a little put-out, but she knew why they said no. She felt the ache of becoming a woman. She instinctively knew Dennis was a man and, as such, could be manipulated by her. That would probably not end well. Still, it was hard not to argue.

Joe would go east on Highway 26 through Portland to Mount Hood to see if altitude and temperature had any effect on the Bug's lethality. Jan would stay and help with the gardening. The truth of the matter was that she did not want to see the aftermath. This motel was now her home.

Bill and Devon would do some shopping in Cannon Beach. Bob and Terry had opened the road using chain saws, clearing a landslide that had pulled down some fir trees. That area had not been tapped by the Survivors yet.

"Go armed," said Bill. "We don't know what may be out there."

"What?" said Sally.

"That hole is deep enough, Bill," laughed Terry. But Sally was right to worry.

Joe had his 357. Terry had his Smith and Wesson 9 mm. Dennis had his M17 from his grandfather's store. Stan had managed to score some Army surplus guns. Dennis was happy about that.

Bob would stay and guard the gardeners against predators with his 7mm magnum hunting rifle.

Nobody in the motel knew yet what the real predators were.

They decided four hours out, four hours back would be the rule. Less but no more was to be the guide.

The addresses to check in Forest Grove for Devon and in Portland for the Morris' and Midders were given to Joe. With any luck, he would bring back the people or let the relatives know where they were. There was no expectation of success. The real aim was to see if any authorities survived. They left in the morning, which was overcast with little wind from the northwest. The day would clear up in the afternoon and be rain-free. The treks would take about five to eight hours, depending on road conditions. The worst problem would probably be landslides and wrecks. If anyone met impassible conditions, they would return. No one was to be gone overnight or do anything stupid.

Priority one: Check for survivors. Two: Check for anything they could use when the supplies ran out. There would come a time when they would need to be self-sufficient. All rudiments of civilization would eventually decay. Cars would break down and would not run. Gas would become stale. Even canned goods would spoil. All manner of machines would rust. The basic infrastructure had failed long ago. The rest was headed downhill.

CHAPTER 8

South Jetty

Four hours out, four hours back. Less, but no more. Dennis followed Highway 101 north. The Humvee bounced noisily along. The road still held a few weathered potholes from the Bugs, mostly on the berms. Everywhere else, the marks had been erased by time and weather. The fields and beach grass had recovered well.

The Young's Bay Bridge was clogged with a dead semi that had stalled near the bridge's narrow lift. The cab was tilted at an odd angle. It looked like the driver might have gotten out to see what he hit. He didn't get back in. Dennis managed to squeeze by, scraping the tires on the lift structure.

In Astoria, the going got a little complicated. Dennis had to maneuver around an accident on the 101/30 traffic circle. He passed under houses from various movies he saw years ago that were now showcased in the silent Oregon Film Museum, housed in the old Clatsop County Jail—*Kindergarten Cop, Short Circuit, The Goonies*. He finally managed to get to the massive ramp leading to the Astoria Megler Bridge. From a ways away, the bridge looked like it was constructed from an Erector Set. It appeared insubstantial from a distance but was significant up close.

The four-mile-long ramp and bridge over the mouth of the Columbia River from Astoria into Washington was remarkably clear. To the east, up the river, several empty cargo ships sat at anchor, slowly turning as dictated by the wind, river-flow, and tides, waiting in vain for a load of containers or wheat. Washington Highway 401 was a different matter. The two-lane highway had a landslide and washout mess he had to work around. He managed to skirt it and caught Highway 4 at Nacelle, where he headed for Raymond. The road was better, with less wear than in the lower gorge. He saw signs of the recovering wildlife population; deer and elk wandered the forests off the road. Herds of cattle roamed, and once, a small herd of horses crossed the road ahead of him. The stallion watched him carefully. Dennis idly wondered where it came from. Probably a stud from an outlying ranch. He was sort of happy to see that.

He made it to Stony Point on Willapa Bay, where the Willapa River flowed into the bay. He stopped pushing through the brush and sat looking out over the bay toward the passive gray ocean. A sudden sadness and loneliness filled him. He shook it off, got back into the Humvee, and headed farther north to the town of South Bend. It was dead.

Up to now, he had been intent upon survival. Now, apart from the Survivors, he felt the terrible loneliness rise again. He stopped at a coffee shop parking lot and gazed out over the river at nothing. He put his head on the steering wheel of the Humvee and silently cried for all the lost souls. For his family. For his brothers in arms. In all the time he was in Iraq, he had never felt like this. War was chaotic and miserable but also filled with comradery and heroism. And hope. Here, there was nothing. Absolutely nothing. This must be a taste of Hell, he thought.

He pressed on. Then, for some reason, he turned at Highway 107 toward Aberdeen instead of Olympia. Again, he looked out at Grays Harbor toward the depressing sea in yet another dead town.

He could go no further. There was no point. He was a Ranger, and he knew when to cut his losses. There was nothing left. He turned the

Humvee around and headed back, retracing his path, operating on re-mote. Numb and resigned. When he passed over the Astoria Megler Bridge again, his eyes finally cleared. Out west, six miles away, and al-most out of sight, he noticed a large cruise ship.

He stopped at the top of the bridge in the overhead superstructure. Got out. Looked through his binoculars. The ship had to be big to be seen over the dunes. It had floundered on Clatsop Spit and was listing badly. It looked out of place, a ten-story floating apartment sinking into the sand. Another tragedy on top of all the other individual tragedies. His eyes watered again, then dried. He steeled himself. Damn it, he was a Ranger. Rangers lead the way. He was a Survivor. His head cleared.

He was interested. For some reason, he wanted to see the wreck close up. Curiosity? He had no reason, just an urge of some sort. He could still see the top of the ship from the 101 bridge over Youngs Bay. He took East Harbor Drive to Highway 104. Lost sight of the ship because of heavy tree growth. Found the turn off for Jetty Road and then the beach access. He pulled down the eroded path to the beach. Now, he could see it just a quarter-mile north.

He stopped the Humvee and got out, looking through his binocu-lars at the sad wreck. It was a massive ship, still held together and rock-ing gently in the rising tide. It was hard aground on the sandy beach, waiting to be slowly torn apart by the relentless sea, like the *Peter Iredale* whose skeleton he was next to. Just another tragedy. What was he doing? There was nothing here for him. He turned to go.

As he did, he spotted movement on the tilted deck out of the corner of his eye.

Something moved! He took out his binoculars again and scanned the deck. Nothing. Perhaps an animal had gotten aboard. Then he saw it again. A human! A woman! Alive after all this time? How? He got back into the Humvee and headed onto the beach toward the ship.

The figure watched as he drove toward the ship. He closed to within shouting distance and got out of the vehicle, but he was suddenly at a loss for what to say. From 100 feet away, they looked at each other as if each were an apparition, a figment of their imaginations. Dennis found his voice. "Hello, can you hear me?"

The woman was probably mid-thirties, slim, almost skinny. Her hair was black, long, and dirty. Her clothes were soiled and worn. There was something feral about her.

She stood transfixed for a long time, and then she reacted. He spoke English; this must be America. "Are you real? Are you real? Say you are real!" she cried.

"I am real. Who are you?"

"Help me! Help me!"

She was on the lowest deck cabin balcony. Nevertheless, it was twenty feet above the beach.

"Who are you?" Dennis needed to open a dialog. This is what he had been taught in military classes designed to help men who were traumatized in battle.

A time passed; he saw she was thinking. Trying to remember? "Alima. Alima Hosni. I am Alima Hosni from Manila. Praise Allah." Then she straightened and said, "Who are you? Are you Allah's *Malak*?"

Dennis had seen her look in the faces of children in Iraq, the children desensitized by the insurgent's brutal tactics of beheading those with whom they disagreed. They were taught that the path to paradise was through pain and suffering. Mostly someone else's, they hoped. Being only property, women need not apply for paradise. Death was an end for them. Sometimes a blessing. Now for her, there was some hope leaking through.

"I am Dennis Lake. I am a survivor of the . . ." He started to say Bugs, but she might not understand. He fumbled for words. ". . . invasion. There is a group of us to the south. We offer safety. Can you get down from there?"

She looked over the railing and nodded. She turned back inside and returned with a nylon rope. *She's been thinking about this*, thought Dennis. She tied it to the rail and slipped over the side. Holding with feet and arms, she lowered herself to the shallow surf. Dennis stood without moving. No sudden action. Showing no threat at all.

She approached like he would disappear at any moment. Slowly, step by step, until she was within a few feet. Then she collapsed.

He was afraid she might have died right there in front of him. He went to her. He did not touch her, though. He remembered his training before he left for Iraq. She had praised Allah, and to touch her was forbidden. She would not understand. But she breathed, she lived. He knew how to treat battlefield injuries and some types of traumatic shock, but this was new. He waited.

After a few minutes, she roused, confused for a minute. Looking around at something other than ship and sea. Then, her brown eyes fixed on Dennis with a look between disbelief and hope. "You are safe," he said. "Let's find a place to talk for a minute. I saw a picnic table a little way back. I have coffee we can make over a fire." He didn't want to go too far from the ship. She might be emotionally attached to it.

She stared at him uncertainly, then nodded. She got to her feet carefully, watching him now with curiosity. This Malak seemed tentative. Had she offended Allah? What was going to happen now?

"Will you get in the car with me?" Again she nodded. He opened the door for her. She recognized a military vehicle and was worried but climbed in. They set off to the bench he had seen. The machine noise seemed to bother her, and he offered the ear protection headset. She declined.

He found a campsite and made a couple of cups of cowboy coffee over a small fire in his tin pot. He did not want to go too far from the ship in case she was attached to it. He did not ask anything and simply waited, trying not to stare at this lost and frightened girl.

In the silence, Alima began to talk without prompting. This Malak seemed to be waiting for her. She now must explain her actions to Allah. She would do her best. Her story came out like a jigsaw puzzle spilled out of the box, a disjointed and randomized account of over a year-and-a-half at sea in the liner—alone. Dennis let her talk. As she did, he began to put together a harrowing account of loneliness and deprivation. And survival.

The luxury ship *Wave Dancer* was at berth in San Diego. It was brand spanking new. Which Dennis figured was why the Bugs did not get her. The "seeds" were sown before the ship was assembled. Thus, the Bugs did not grow inside the ship's waste systems.

Alima was working in the galley, inventorying the stores with a fellow crewman prior to the maiden voyage. Just a skeleton crew was running checks on the ship's readiness. The captain was on the bridge with several techs, observing as the systems were brought online and tested. She did not know it, but it was her greatest piece of luck that the tests were just completed and satisfactory when the *shayatan* appeared.

Her first hint that something was wrong was when the captain came on the intercom and, in a calm but tense voice, ordered the mooring lines to be cast off and the ship to be underway. All personnel were to secure all ports and doors and await further orders. A second message stated that the emergency protocol for pirate evasion was active. Alima's crewmate opened the door to the galley to see what was happening. A shadow passed by, and the man she knew as Astride dropped to the floor, falling against the door and shutting it against whatever was outside. She went to his side, but he was dead. There was no mark on him.

She looked through the door portal. When she got close, what appeared to be a faceless, black shayatan hit the glass, leaving a smear of liquid that quickly evaporated. She recoiled. A numbness set in. She sat at the crew's mess and went blank for a minute.

The ship lurched. She heard commands from the captain to get underway. The helm answered, and she felt the great engines engage. She felt the forward motion of the ship. The com stayed open. She heard the hurried orders to steer port and starboard in rapid succession. She could feel the impacts on the hull even through the insulation of several decks. Then, the ship straightened and went to full power. Alima sat and wondered what would happen to her now. The ship plowed on.

Then, there was no more maneuvering. She figured the ship cleared the harbor. The captain came on again and stated he had set a course for Hawaii. Stated that there appeared to be an infestation of some type of bio-robot, lethal to people—all across the world. Some of the robots were onboard. Crewmen were advised to stay inside. He thought maybe Hawaii would be safe. It was the last she heard from any living being until now. But she knew these were not robots; they were shayatan. *Iblis* had managed to reach into this world. Was Allah displeased?

Crying and shaking, she instinctively managed to get the body of her crewmate into the walk-in freezer. Then, against all reason, she slept, curled up in the corner as the ship plowed toward Hawaii. When she woke, it was dark. She found the light switch and turned it on. She was alone. There was food, water, and toilet facilities available. Her immediate needs were taken care of. But she was alone with a shayatan stalking her. She prayed to Allah. *Deliver me, please!*

That was not to be for a long time.

Life became a blur. Inside the galley, there was no real sense of day or night, just dark and twilight. And the relentless, subtle movement of the ship. She did not know it then, but by the fifth day, there were no more other live people left on board.

She also did not know it when, after days of solitary confinement, the ship neared Hawaii. It finally ran out of fuel 100 miles to the east. It had not been fully filled at San Diego. The emergency generators kicked in but failed shortly thereafter. The lights went out. The refrigeration and air conditioning failed, and food in the galley began to spoil. It began to stink. If something did not happen soon, she would starve to death in the awful loneliness, or the shayatan would kill her.

Then, something did happen. A hurricane spawned in the southern Pacific near Baja California, followed the trade winds north and west, and found the ship. It was a category three when it hit in the middle of a dark night. The ship was rudderless and drifting. Her first hint the storm was coming was that the yaw and pitch increased, then intensified. She felt the battering as a muted howling and knew the sound as a typhoon.

Fifty-foot waves and fierce, wind-driven sheets of rain washed over the ship, covering the decks and scouring off anything not secured. There were no open ports, but the relentless Pacific bashed aside some outer cabin deck doors and washed into the lower deck cabins. A service entrance was breached. Alima felt the water blast through the hall outside the galley. The ship rolled broadside, fore and aft, port and starboard, with Alima grimly enduring in the fetid dark. Stumbling on the heaving deck, she needed something to hold on to. She heard the spoiled food shifting in the closed refrigerator. Heard the putrid mass pushing against the door.

She waited alone in the shrouded galley, and the room seemed to compress. She found the sink and held on for dear life while the storm tore at the helpless ship as if trying to drown it, and her. She was trapped. She was abandoned. Was she to be drowned when the ship went down? Was this the shayatan's doing? Iblis? Alima shivered and cried. In the nausea-inducing, violent movement, in her delirium, she thought, *Is this Hell? Am I dead?* Yet she yearned to live. Then, she steeled herself.

There was nothing to do but persevere. The doors were holding; the ship was staying afloat. The shayatan could not get to her, no matter what it did. There was a reason for this. She held on and prayed. She did not know it then, but her prayers were answered—in a way.

The engineers and builders had done their jobs. The *Wave Dancer* stayed afloat, even as the storm raged for several hours. The ship finally went calm. Alima found the strength to peek out the portal into the dim light of the hall, ready to jump back if the shayatan appeared. It did not. She waited for a long time, watching. No shayatan. At last, she had to leave the galley. The stench was becoming unbearable, and she was thirsty and hungry. She could wait and die here or take her chances. She gathered her courage and opened the door into a deserted hall. Then, she carefully stepped out into a clean promenade on a calm, sunny day.

The shayatan must have been washed away by the storm. She fell to her knees and praised Allah.

But what to do now? Surely, any food topside would be spoiled. She prowled the decks. Nothing. The pumps for the fresh water were down. Was she spared the shayatan only to die of thirst or to starve to death? She felt despair. She prayed again. *Help me, help me!* But there was no answer. Or was there? It hit her like a beautiful sunrise. The lifeboats. They were stocked prior to the shayatan plague. These were thirty-man boats, each with prepackaged meals and water for a week. There were twenty boats. Enough to supply her for a long time.

But she was still alone. *No*, she thought, *Allah is with me!* She would be delivered. She waited for a sign. She made sure she told the Malak of her faith in Allah.

"Allah saved me. Alou Akbar," she said to Dennis, her big brown eyes exuding sincerity.

She continued her story. Life blurred again. She set up in one of the luxury suites. She watched days string by and the seasons' turn. She wintered in the North Pacific, huddled in supposed topside luxury, shivering as the temperatures dropped and rain and sleet peppered the ship. She gauged the direction of the drift and the seasons by the sunrise and set. At night, she watched as the stars turned with the ship's movement. She figured the ship was moving north, then west, then south. She knew the Japanese current would eventually push the ship to Alaska, Canada, and then the Pacific coast of America. It was her last hope that she would get close enough to make it to land and, possibly, civilization. If not, the cycle would start again. She would not survive that. She studied how to manually deploy the lifeboats.

What if the shayatan were there on land? She became afraid. But there was nothing she could do about it, so she waited. She was delivered from the shayatan and the typhoon. She would be delivered from the ship.

The ship ran aground on a spring day after the wind had blown it south and west for three days. During a high tide and a low Columbia river current speed, the *Wave Dancer* was pushed past the jetties and run aground on the Clatsop Spit, not far from the south jetty. Alima was asleep when it hit. The lurch and grinding awoke her. The ship rolled, and she was thrown against the wall. She scrambled to her feet and looked out over the slanting veranda at some sort of observation tower on the sandy and green shoreline, not a hundred yards away. She recognized a jetty. But she did not know where it was. And worst of all, she did not know if shayatan were waiting on land. She again prayed to Allah to be delivered. She waited for several weeks as the ship was carried, grinding over the sand, closer and closer to shore, listing further and further, not knowing what to do.

And now, her prayer was fulfilled. Allah was good. A Malak was sent to find her. She took the earmuffs, curled up in the front seat, and breathed a great sigh as Dennis drove her to her new home.

Dennis knew from her tale that she was a Muslim. He tried to remember his history. Manila had a Sunni sect, he thought. He remembered the word "shayatan." He did not know the precise definition, but he knew it was derogatory. He heard it used to describe himself when he was in Iraq. He had no animosity toward the locals for that. The country was a mess, and foreign men with guns and armor were patrolling their streets.

He did not know how her arrival would affect Devon. So he would say nothing. If she revealed it herself—well, he'd just see how that would go.

CHAPTER 9

Portland

Four hours out, four hours back. Less, but no more. Joe managed to get to Forest Grove after working around a couple of slow-moving slides on the summits of the Coastal Range. Once, he had to cut through a fallen birch tree he could not skirt. The Humvee performed as expected.

Joe marveled at the highway's ability to endure. Without the thousands of vehicles pounding it every day, it remained quite serviceable. The valley highway was actually passable without much maneuvering around vehicles. Only once did he have to use the shoulder to move around a truck jack-knifed across the road.

Devon's address was in an upscale community off Highway 8. As he neared the town, Joe noticed scraps of clothing and bones. Human bones. Skeletons. In the ditch, yards, and sidewalks near the parking lot of a fraternal house. The faded sign in front advertised a Bingo game. The time noted was the same as when the Bugs rose. Most remains were disturbed by animals. He saw none, though. What was a boom in carrion now was a bust. The wildlife had returned to normal. He hoped.

He parked in the yard of Devon's home, got out, walked up to the porch, and looked through the grimy front window. Clothed bones sat on the couch inside the neat clapboard ranch-style house. They looked like three bodies nestled together. Bones and the hide of a loyal dog lay at their feet. Holes permeated the floor. *No survivors here or anywhere,* he thought.

Joe pulled out on Highway 47 to Highway 6 and then to Highway 26, headed east. It was mostly clear, but as he got closer to Portland, the road was a mess. Luckily, the road to Portland was mostly four to six lanes with wide shoulders and a wide median. With a little jockeying, he made it to Portland at ten.

As he drove east past the Portland Zoo exit in the west hills, he saw his first living thing in the city. There were cattle and horses in the fields in the Tualatin Valley, but nothing like this. It ran across the four lanes 100 feet in front of him in a shambling lope. At first, he could not put together a thought. Then it hit him. It was a jackal! A jackal, for God's sake! Then, another rose up over the berm and followed the first. Both looked at the Humvee with interest, but with no fear. Joe thought about the zoo and what happened to the animals when the Bugs came. To be trapped in a cage with no food or water—he stopped thinking about it. Apparently, some of the more agile ones had escaped. Perhaps the electronic/magnetic locks had failed when the power died. Maybe the keepers had opened the gates. Then, he realized the more agile ones were mostly predators—the canines and felines. Jackals and lions. Joe moved along quickly.

The big city was as quiet as a tomb, littered with clothing scraps and bones. He managed to get over the Willamette River using the Marquam Bridge. On the east side, he encountered a setback. The off-ramps to I84 and Highway 26 were hopelessly blocked. He got off on Water Street and tried to get up Broadway. This too was blocked. He found no sign of human life. One good thing about being the only moving vehicle was that he did not need to obey any traffic laws. He reversed course and headed back up the off-ramp and back over the bridge the wrong way.

Nobody stopped him. He managed to get over the river using the Ross Island Bridge.

Joe made the rounds of the homes he was to check. His heart ached. There were no survivors. It was beyond depressing. There were no words to describe his feeling of loss. He passed by several burned-out houses. Some had used fire as a defense or to warm themselves before . . .

His last stop was his own home. It was overgrown. Sad. Decaying. A wave of sadness washed over him. He sat and shivered. He sat until he was spent of all hope. He turned the Humvee to leave. His eyes watered, and he was barely watching the street. Then, he saw something in the parkway. The median was overgrown with weeds and ivy vines, but there was movement—something. He slowed and saw a tragedy taking place.

Several animals looking like coyotes, yet somewhat larger, had surrounded a dog. The prey was a matted and thin retriever of some sort. Its hind leg was at an awkward angle. It was dragging its way in a circle, bearing its teeth at its attackers. But it was hopeless. The band darted in and out, biting at its nose and flanks. It was just a matter of time, and not much was left.

Joe made a decision. He did not know exactly why. The retriever needed to be saved. He drove over the curb toward the pack. They did not disperse. They were not afraid. But they stopped the attack long enough for Joe to get within shooting range. He stopped, opened the door, and shot in the air. The band was startled but did not run. He shot at the ground in front of the biggest one. It jumped sideways and looked at the ground where the bullet hit, curious but unafraid. Then it looked at Joe.

There was no mistaking the look. It was a predator's stare, yellow eyes sizing up a meal. The band turned, almost as one. It was the last thing they did while whole. Joe shot the big one between the eyes. It dropped like a marionette with the strings cut. The others stared uncertainly. Joe shot the next one as it sniffed at the dead one. That did it. The rest scattered like leaves blown by a sudden gust of wind.

The injured dog tried to rise but could not. It was spent. Joe reloaded and cautiously approached. The dog watched him with big, soulful eyes. As he got close, it growled and showed its teeth. Joe stopped and kneeled down. He talked to it in a normal voice. "It's OK, pup. I am going to help you. You remember people, don't you? It's OK." He drew closer. The dog tried to run but fell with a piteous yelp. Joe noticed the band was still within eyesight and focused on them.

"OK. We don't have much time here," he held out his hand, palm down. "Sniff this, pup. I'm your friend." The dog licked its lips and whined. "Good dog, good dog." Joe put his hand on its head. He saw now that it was a female. One hind leg was broken. There were other bite marks on her flanks and nose. She shivered. "I have to carry you. Do you understand?" He put the Smith and Wesson in his holster and carefully reached under the animal. This was dangerous. He would have to trust the dog not to bite his face. It was going to be close.

Slowly and awkwardly, he got his arms under her and lifted. She was painfully light. No more than twenty-five or thirty pounds. He guessed a retriever of her size should weigh maybe fifty. The band was closing again. He started back toward the idling truck. If they struck now, he would have to drop the dog to get his gun and shoot. He did not have to. The band stopped at the two dead and began to feed.

He managed to get the dog onto the passenger seat. It lay shivering and whining so low he could hardly hear it. He climbed in, closed the door, and opened a bottle of water. He reached over and pressed it to the dog's mouth. At first, nothing, then she licked at it. When she figured it out, she wolfed down a half pint while he held it for her. Then, she curled up, and with her head pointed at Joe, she closed her eyes and slept.

She did not move while Joe drove the noisy vehicle back to Seventeenth, over to McLaughlin and the Ross Island Bridge, over the Sylvan Summit and on to Survivors Motel.

CHAPTER 10

Salem

Four hours out, four hours back. Less, but no more. Terry and Wanda had a somewhat difficult time getting to Hebo. The highway was very curvy. Terry thought he maybe should have taken 26 to 15. But since he did not have to worry about traffic or speed limits, he could use the whole road. They made good time, even having to work around a rockslide south of Cannon Beach and a washout at Arch Cape. And the ever-present Bug holes on the roadsides. They continued through silent coastal towns.

At Highway 22 West, the going got easier. On farmland and open areas, some domestic cattle and sheep were grazing. It seemed bucolic at first. But they noticed the animals seemed wary and on edge. More feral than tame. The cattle watched the Humvee with interest. They passed the dead Spirit Mountain Casino and got into Salem with minimum problems with blocked roads.

Salem was a ghost town. Nothing but a few rags and bones remained of the people who once lived there. Nothing was moving; nothing was alive. Even the beasts avoided the area. The Capitol was deserted; if there were anyone inside, they were not coming out now. No luck.

There was some time left, so they moved on. They turned south on I5. The going got rougher. The freeway was a mess of cars and trucks, and several times, Terry had to use the median. Lots of broken windshields and crashes. At highway speeds, Bug collisions were deadly.

They stopped at an interstate wayside on I5, near a water tower. Terry tested the water at the spigot and found it was still operational. After running the rust out of the pipes, he filled their canteens. Over a year had passed, yet the tower still had water in it. Someone knew what they were doing when they built it.

He used the facilities; the toilet actually worked. But there was nothing for them here. It was time to go back. When he returned, Wanda was staring at something around the corner from him. He walked over and looked.

The building had shielded the view: across a field was a lion. It was an African lion. Not just a lion, but a hunting lioness. And not just one, but three of them. Terry knew there was a Wildlife Safari at Winston, but he had not thought of it. The animals there must have broken out. And there were more open zoos around the northwest—a new thing to watch out for. Maybe the hole Dennis and Bill were digging was real. But for now, he needed to get Wanda to the Humvee.

Wanda was paralyzed. First Bugs, now lions. For Terry, it was definitely a new feeling to see lions without bars or a moat between them. The lions were sitting on a dead cow, apparently waiting for the male to arrive. No wonder the cattle they saw seemed wary. They watched Wanda with piercing yellow eyes. They made no move toward her, but their body language said, *Mine! Beware! Danger! Do not approach!*

If they decided Wanda was either a competitor or food, Terry could not stop all of them—probably any of them—with his sidearm. The Humvee was on the other side, away from the lions and their kill. He would not be able to see them once he got Wanda to back away.

Terry softy called, "Wanda, back away to me, slowly. No sudden movements. Keep your eyes down. Back away, one step, now another, another." The lions' ears perked up.

Wanda was compliant, doing exactly what he said. She was scared, but she trusted Terry explicitly. He saved her from the Bugs; now he would save her from the lions.

He saw her shaking but moving steadily back. Another five paces. There! He touched her shoulder. She twitched but immediately relaxed. It was Terry, her savior. She was safe now.

Terry said, "OK, easy now, we're going to circle around to the car. OK? Stay with me. Here we go." He needed to be able to see the lions if they decided to see if Terry and Wanda tasted good. Wanda could feel his tension. They were not out of danger yet.

The three lions watched as one. Each head turned, their movement in perfect sync. Their yellow laser eyes intently focused. Terry and Wanda were within twenty feet of the Humvee when all three rose, their eyes suddenly fixed on something to their left. Terry risked a glance. It was the male. He was padding toward the kill, hopefully, intent on feeding. Terry and Wanda were forgotten for the time being. If the male didn't care, the lionesses didn't either.

The male was aimed at the kill as if he had not seen or was not paying attention to the people, as if they were of no consequence. Terry didn't for a second think the male didn't know they were there. The lion simply did not care. He was not concerned. He was the king here. The memory of man had disappeared quickly.

Out of the lions' sight now, Wanda and Terry reached the Humvee and got in, glad the vehicle was armored. Maybe the hole Bill and John were digging was not so deep after all. Wanda was breathing like a racehorse. Terry waited for her to calm down. "You OK now?"

She was shaking but answered, "I think so. Lions?"

"Probably from the Safari Park in Winston. God only knows what survived without man to keep them." Was a damned rhino next?

They started back. Terry cut back to 22 then to the coast road. He did not want to meet anything else. *At least,* he thought, *the coast road is lion-free. For now.*

It was certain the coast roads would, within a few more years, be impassable. Maybe with some heavy equipment, they could make some roads useful, but travel was going to be hard soon enough. They saw no indication of any survivors or any more lions. They got back in the late afternoon.

CHAPTER 11

Marauders

While the searchers were out, Bob watched the two girls and their mother run the big John Deere tractor over the ten acres they gleefully plowed. They were happy to be outdoors and operating the tractor and plow John and Stan got running. Jan was fixing dinner. John and Bill were working on installing a wood-burning stove in the common room. The Lakes, Alima, and Devon were upstairs.

The girls were ready to sow the field with the seeds they'd collected from various plant businesses. It was a little late in the season, but what the hell. They had to get started sometime. It was late afternoon, the sun was westering, and the air was calm. The girls stood in the middle of the field and talked, pointing. Deciding where the seeds for the various vegetables would go, Bob guessed. Getting ready to call it a day.

They had decided that Bob would watch for dangerous animals. This was a smart and lucky thing. Bad luck was coming. Skill would be needed. During the absence of man, various carnivores had become bold. Especially black bears and pumas, and sometimes coyotes. Bob had stood with the women for a while but decided to get some coffee. Nothing was moving out there now. He settled down about 200 away, but he had a clear, unobstructed view of the field where the girls were and the surrounding area. He sat comfortably with his coffee.

Like a sniper, Bob was just a dot on the motel deck chair at the back of the building with a good line of sight. Through the Leopold scope, the girls looked close enough to touch.

The low sun shone, and the air was sweet and clear. Birds flew. A deer appeared across the river chewing on a young fir tree, seemingly unafraid of the farmers. Suddenly, it bolted into the trees. Bob noted the movement and wondered what was up. He scanned the tree line. Nothing. Why did the deer bolt?

And then he knew why. From behind him, a full-size motor home came down from the highway interchange—one of those made from a fifty-foot interstate bus chassis, like the rock stars used when traveling. It was shocking. Bob started to get up out of his chair, but something made him stop. Something felt wrong. It was disconcerting.

The mobile home drove on the 101 Highway apron over the Junction Road past where Bob sat, came into the field, and stopped just past the girls. Three men appeared from behind the motor home and approached the girls. At first, it looked like they were just talking. Bob picked up the rifle and sighted through the scope. Nobody looked his way. He apparently had not been seen. It seemed OK.

Then Mary suddenly struck the tall skinny man who was in front of her.

Instantly, the other men grabbed Vanessa and Teressa and pulled them behind the bus. Mary fought the skinny guy until he hit her and she fell. Bob went prone, the coffee cup and table knocked aside. He watched through the scope for a chance and saw it when the skinny guy started for her. The reticle crosshairs centered on the guy's chest. Bob pulled the trigger. The jacketed 7mm magnum bullet made the 200 yards in the blink of an eye. The skinny guy collapsed, exploded pieces of heart and blood, forming a pink cloud behind him.

Bob worked the bolt and scanned for another target, but there were no others left. He did not think of the consequences. Of the accountability of his shooting. Nothing except to somehow stop the bus. If he could. He would kill the men inside. Why he immediately tossed aside a lifetime of civilization to become so barbaric, he did not care. He did not think of the law. There was none. None except what came from his rifle. Bob was ready to kill any who showed. There was no inhibition now. The law was what he made it.

He could not shoot directly into the bus; the girls were inside. But he could shoot at the tires. They could not take the girls. The bus lurched forward. It had eight rear tires, four per side. The left front tire was his first shot. The bus swerved and continued. He switched his aim. He had just blown the rear left outside tire when a volley of fire erupted from the bus windows. Bullets filled the air with a singing whine. They impacted the deck and walls, sounding like a carpenter's air hammer. Two wet smacks. Bob was hit.

Hearing the shooting, John ran out with his sidearm aimed. He was hit, as well. He went down hard. Bob fought through the pain and managed to hit another tire. Operating on rote memory, he loaded a spare clip. The motor home bumped up to the highway. For a moment, Bob had a shot at the driver. He settled the crosshairs on the bouncing window. He almost pulled the trigger, but the face he saw in the driver's side window was Vanessa, held there by a hand wrapped in her hair, her eyes wild, her mouth open in pain. He shifted his aim before the bus pulled up onto the road and headed north. Working the bolt action desperately, he got off 3 more shots at about 300 yards and hit the back where he supposed the engine was. Then it was gone. Gone with the two teenage girls and an unknown number of men.

He had failed.

CHAPTER 12

Joe

Joe returned in the late afternoon. He immediately knew something was wrong. No one was outside, and the motel was closed up despite the warm air. When he got out of the truck, Jan came out and ran up to him, grasping him like the end of the world was near. "Marauders!" she cried. "They took the girls."

The story came tumbling out. Some men in a motor home had kidnapped the girls. Mary had a broken nose, and John was inside suffering from serious gunshot wounds. Bob was also wounded.

Bob yelled from inside. "Get in here! We need to talk."

When Joe got inside, he was stunned. John was sitting up but had blood leaking from holes in his leg and abdomen. He was pale and shivering but still held his gun. Devon was probing his back, looking for a bullet that was still inside him. Bob was lying prone, and blood leaked from his buttocks. Joe noticed a new face but did not ask. Time for that later.

Bob said, "Not as bad as it looks. Just can't sit up. Hit in the ass, for God's sake. But that's not the point. Dennis arrived a few minutes ago and set out immediately. You need to go, too. Look for a luxury bus with flat tires. I'll tell you this, there are at least three, and maybe more got away. I killed one in the field. The others were behind the bus. And at least one of them can shoot. They have automatic pistols, like Mac 10s or something. As soon as I hit the one, someone inside the bus picked me out pretty fast from 200 yards and put a burst of 3 right in my circle. Hit me twice. I was prone, if I was standing . . . The other shooter just emptied his gun in a spray and hit John. I told all this to Dennis. You got to go help him."

Joe looked at Jan. The air was thick with fear and worry. "You be careful," Jan said. "I can't go with you to reload." She handed him a box of shells. He put them in his pocket. "Make your shots count." Joe saw the look of a vengeful mother then. Jan wanted him to kill the marauders. He would do that.

"I will. First, you have to take this dog I found and see what you can do for it." She did not question him. Time for that later. She cradled the limp dog. "Find them. Kill them! Bring the girls back," she confirmed.

"I will. I'll be back with Dennis and the girls." Joe checked his 357 and added a round under the hammer. Six had better be enough. No AR 15s. They could not get into a long-range firefight with the girls near. And those rounds would go through walls. He got into the Humvee and sped off north on 101. It was a good thing it happened quickly. If he had time to think, he was not sure what he would have done.

Joe sped up 101. At the Seaside Chevron gas station, he smelled the burned engine and followed the smeared tire tracks onto Holladay Drive. Then, up Avenue G. He caught up with Dennis just over the Necanicum Bridge. The kidnappers had driven on their flat tires and burned engine up to the South Prom a few blocks from them. It appeared from the faint smell drifting in from the ocean that the engine was shot. They were stranded. By the time Joe got there, it was time to move.

"We can't wait for dark. We can't drive up there. We have to be quiet," Dennis said. "They will hopefully be drunk. They've had time to do their worst by now. But we can't allow them too much more time with the girls. It's been over an hour now since they got away. Since we don't know where they went exactly, we can spot them by the sound or light they use. We'll check the motor home first. If they are not there, we'll look door to door. They'll be close."

The early evening was cooling, and mist from the sea was condensing on derelict cars, making them seem almost new. Joe and Dennis made their way up through the beach houses south of the ocean-front condos. The motor home was dead. Inside, it was smoky. The marauders had left it.

"Look for the light or sound from whatever room they have. We are going to penetrate and kill them all. Watch for any guards. Be quiet. If we spot a guard, let me take him out. Watch your line of fire. The girls are there." Dennis was not just an Army Ranger now. He was fueled by an ancient drive to protect one's own—the tribe, clan, the family. The light of revenge burned brightly in his eyes, a long knife in his hand. "These are men, not targets. Can you kill a man? We can't flinch now."

Joe felt the same drive, and a need filled him. A primal, raw, savage-driven need. A need to lash out, destroy. He said simply, "They are dead men."

Dennis nodded in the cloud-diffused sunlight. In that thin, pale, copper light, his blue eyes looked lit with fire. He turned and went over the seawall onto the grass-covered sand. Joe followed.

They were just over the seawall when they spotted light in a window of a house. The marauders were in a hurry; they picked the closest place. If they were going to kill the girls, it would be after they used them. From over fifty feet away, Dennis and Joe could hear their coarse laughter in the still twilight.

Dennis was silent for a minute. "Looks like three in the main room. Nice of them to pick such a close place. Let's go." They moved around to the backyard. Dennis scanned the area. "No guard. Let's go in the back door quietly. In fast. Kill them all. Anyone standing, sitting, or lying down. We don't know who is who. Kill them all. No mercy. No wasted bullets." Dennis went into a combat stance. Joe copied it.

Joe did not need to answer. Dennis had seen him shoot. Joe's heart pounded and his mouth was dry as he followed Dennis up the silent concrete steps, through the broken door, down the hall a half step behind. He heard a muffled grunting from behind a door and the louder laughter of the men coming from the front room. Someone said, "When we're done here, we go back and see about any other women. I need to gut the sombitch shot out the goddamn bus and killed Floyd." It fired the need to kill that rose in him like a flood of vengeful lava.

Then, a door opened from his left, and Joe looked into the face of madness. A man was lit by a battery-powered lamp in the darkened bedroom. He wore an expensive shirt and pants, but only blood covered his naked genitals he was putting back. He had a black beard and was tall and angular. His eyes were lit with psychotic dementia, and his mouth curled into a snarl. He screamed out to Allah sounding like a devil and started toward Joe, a long glittering knife appearing in his hand.

CHAPTER 13

Mustofa

Mustofa felt like he was in heaven after being in hell. This was a taste of what Allah promised for His faithful through his prophet Moham-mad. After spending endless months trapped with those barbarian in-fidels in that warehouse, this was a just reward. He understood in the true heaven in the lap of Allah that the *houri* would be more compliant. They would obey his every wish. This infidel whore had fought like a she-cat. He had finally stunned her with a blow to the head; it was the only way to properly enjoy the union. He was happy she bled; it showed she was a true virgin. He was contemplating sending her ahead to his own harem in heaven, but the others would not like that. They were infidels and were treacherous. Especially the tattooed man. He did not want to meet Allah yet. The other whore was used by the tattooed man first, but she might be amusing yet, later.

It had been a harrowing time for Mustofa. He had been trapped in the supply warehouse with other convicts who were considered too dan-gerous for the California State prison system. They were being transported in a federal van to a maximum-security prison somewhere he did not know or care when the *daeva* of *Ahriman* emerged.

As the daeva erupted, the guards had been ordered to move them into some sort of military warehouse until the powers that be figured out what to do. As it turned out, there was nothing to be done. Several federal Marshals had been following and preceding the van, but none survived. Of the state guards in the van, the first guard was killed hustling the prisoners into the side door. The second, when he tried to see what was happening by looking out the window in the makeshift office. The glass was broken and a daeva touched him. He fell almost instantly. The daeva had tried to climb in, but the tattooed man pushed the dead man into the window, stuffing him in tight. The last was killed when he opened the door to see what was happening. Something bumped him, and he slammed the door and laid down and died. The prisoners were smart enough not to try that again. They found a sheet of plywood and pushed the dead man out of the window with it. They held it in place using an empty rack.

He did not know any of the others except for the bald tattooed man who had killed someone in a drug deal. The man was in the California State Prison for thirteen years. He was again eligible for parole but could not impress the parole board and had killed a cellmate for being an informant. Idiot. But he was dangerous. Mustofa could see the tightness and lethality in the man. The others were murderers of various sorts. Gang and drug-related, mostly. These animals were pathetic. Without the focus on the teachings of Mohammad and, thus, the blessings of Allah.

Mustofa had beheaded his wife for infidelity. For flaunting herself publicly, dressing like the western whores. To be incarcerated for that was an abomination. That he condemned the court for not complying with Sharia law probably added to his sentence. These infidel Westerners were weak and stupid. A woman was a man's property. Some of the other prisoners took a dislike to him because he beheaded her. He did not talk about Allah with them. He did not have to. He had the protection of the Islamic Brotherhood while in prison. Now he did not. And once again, he could not talk about Allah or Sharia.

Yet he had stayed with them. He had seen the large predators roaming the northern California hills. Without the mechanical abilities of the infidels, he would be on foot. Alone, he would stand no chance of ever reaching some civilized place. And perhaps he could return to Iran and sanity eventually. He was sure the Great Satan was the target for the daeva. This was allowed by Allah. For sure, Iran would be spared for the *Mahdi* to arrive. But first, he needed to survive.

Then they were left alone in the warehouse. It was a long, horrible time. It was good the warehouse was stocked with MREs leftover and/ or ready for the latest war and a working lavatory. The floor was reinforced with rebar. He saw where the daeva had attempted to get through, without success. Allah would have to forgive him if some meals had pork in them. He had to survive, did he not? And Allah had provided the food, after all.

One prisoner was killed when he went crazy. After about a week, the youngster who looked like he played one of those idiotic western games like football, but was really a sadistic child molester, had tried to flee through the door. He was a serial rapist who tortured his victims. He was psychotic and sullen. But he was no match for the tattooed man.

The powerfully built tattooed man had moved with an alarming speed and caught the boy by the door. The boy looked big and strong, but the tattooed man had killed him effortlessly with one motion that made a popping sound in the boy's neck. The second convict had simply laid down and died in the third month. A weak infidel without Allah. They had hauled the bodies to the second floor and tossed them out the windows so the smell of decomposition was not too bad.

Now, by the grace of Allah, they were here. Actually, they were here because the perverted one wanted to burn down the Astoria Courthouse, the one in which he was convicted of the strangulation death of his perverted lover. The others thought this would be fun. And there was nothing else to do. Mustofa knew Astoria was a port. Maybe there were ships there.

When they saw the women, there were six ex-prisoners left. The infidel who tried to catch the older woman was killed by a sniper in the building down the road. The tattooed man and the perverted one had opened fire, and the sniper and another was hit. But one still managed to cripple the bus as they fled with the girls.

Maybe they would go back and see if there were more women at the building. But for now, he had the whores in his power. It was good to be here now. The tattooed man was the first to taste his choice of the girls. But Mustofa was second. He did not know the tattooed man had already had them both.

He was spent after just a few minutes. He did not understand how the tattooed man could be in the room for as long as he was. But there was plenty of time to enjoy the whores. He opened the door to let in the next man and was struck by the vision of a gray-bearded man with a pistol staring coldly back at him. Another clean-shaven man was moving toward the other room. They had to be with the man with the rifle who had disabled the bus. This was unacceptable, but he instantly knew what to do. Calling to Allah for protection, Mustofa drew up the knife for a quick thrust.

But the pistol aimed with alarming speed. Just before a brilliant white light exploded behind his eyes and just before a terrible blackness covered the light, Mustofa had a sudden great fear for what awaited him.

CHAPTER 14

Joe

Joe shot the demon through the most convenient target, the snarling mouth. He watched detachedly as blood and brains splattered the wall and glinted dully in the lamplight. He turned quickly and followed Dennis past the kitchen into the main room, a step behind, his gun up and ready. He heard Dennis say in a casual voice with perfect clarity, as if he were hearing through a headset that blocked out all other sounds, "Die!" The gunshots were muted, insignificant. One marauder was already falling, bullet holes in his chest. The hot brass from Dennis's M17 tumbled in the gray light. The picture window glass on the west side cracked with pink spiderwebs from the through rounds. The man on the left was unarmed. One armed combatant remained. Dennis was lining up on him. Joe swung onto him also, a bald and tattooed man who was rising from a chair with some sort of machine pistol.

The man did not appear afraid or surprised, nor did he appear to be in a hurry, but he was very fast. He was close to beating them. His gun was spitting rounds into the floor as he raised it in an arc toward Joe and Dennis. Joe felt the wood floor chip and reverberate with the impacts. But he already had his 357 lined up. Like the clay pigeons he had shot years ago, he snap-shot at the most obvious target, the one which assured instant death. The machine pistol was within a split second of hitting Joe when his 357 barked. He felt Dennis fire, and at the same time, something hit him in the leg. Joe's round put a hole in the bald man's left eye. From the downward angle of the bullet, the brain base spewed from the back of his head, the man's bald head craned awkwardly to the right, all his effort ending instantaneously. The tattooed man slumped back into the chair, his useless gun slipping to the floor. Joe swung onto the last marauder. This short, scraggly, shirtless man was now fearfully backing away with his hands held defensively in front of him. Joe shot him through his hands into his chest. The hole appeared a split second before Dennis's round hit within an inch of Joe's.

A miasma of cordite and blood filled the air. "Make sure of the one in the bedroom," Dennis said as he shot the first man again. Normal sound was returning to Joe's ears. Above the ringing, he heard the reports of Dennis' gun and the sobbing of both Vanessa and Teressa.

He found the bearded man crumpled on the floor with a pool of blood widening beneath him. His heart was still working despite not being connected to a brain. The gunshot to the heart was loud, and Vanessa cried out in alarm. A new fetid odor assaulted Joe's nose. The man's bowels had loosened. He reloaded.

It had taken just a few seconds to kill four men.

The sisters were quiet now, huddled under the covers, blankly staring at him through tearstained eyes.

Dennis entered. "I count four here. There's probably more somewhere."

Teressa wiped her eyes, sniffled, and said, "The one they called 'queer' was supposed to be guarding against you."

"Thanks, Teressa. You both are very brave. Where is he?" said Dennis. Before she could say anything, they heard the answer.

From down the avenue, a burst of automatic fire and several shotgun reports were heard, echoing between the house and the neighboring hotel, past the bus and out to sea. Dennis immediately closed the door facing the backyard. They dragged the body out into the front room with the rest of them. "My guess is that was Terry and the queer. We have to find out what happened now. You are hit. Your leg. You stay here, protect the girls. I'll check it out. Hoo-ah!"

CHAPTER 15

Terry

Terry and Wanda returned to the motel shortly after Joe left. Jan took them aside and quickly explained the situation. After getting the story, Terry immediately left to go after the girls in the same mode as Joe and Dennis. Wanda gave him a kiss and said, "Kill them." Jan smiled.

"Bring back my girls," said Mary. "Bring them back!"

"I will." People were going to die by his hand. Never had he killed anyone in his life in the line of duty or any other way. Even in the service. But today was as good as any to start, and the marauders were as good as any to kill.

Bill and Stan took up their guns and stood by the windows. Death was in the air.

Tracking the burned rubber smears in his headlights, Terry found Dennis's and Joe's vehicles quickly. He was not into stealth. If Dennis and Joe had contacted the marauders, it would be over. Any marauder left would be his. He spotted the motor home pressed against the Prom like they thought it was a road. These were not locals.

He pulled around Joe and Dennis's Humvees, accelerated up Avenue G, and was closing in on the motor home when his Humvee was suddenly peppered with shot.

Skill and training meant everything now. Terry reacted on retained muscle memory, instinct, and drive. The side windows were open for ventilation. Terry felt the heat trails and heard the buzz of rounds passing through the cab. The back window cracked and spiderwebbed. The door reverberated with impacts. Terry stopped and was out the door before the barrage ended. He glimpsed the flashes north, from up the darkening Downing Street. He spotted the man a block away, just a dark figure standing in the middle of the street. The shooter spent an entire clip and was fumbling for another. Terry pumped the shotgun and fired three quick rounds of buckshot from over the hood. Twenty-seven 30-caliber lead balls hummed the air at 700 feet a second. The body of the marauder took ten of them.

Terry jacked in another round and started for the downed man.

Willy Wallace was different. He knew this for as long as he could remember. And others did too. He was in constant trouble for hurting things. He liked to hurt things. In the beginning, it was cats. He liked the sounds they made. By the time he was in grade school, it was other kids. Those sounds were even better. His parents were at a loss. They tried all they knew. Willy was counseled. He continued to hurt others. He was sent to reform school. He continued to hurt others. Finally, when he turned eighteen, he was tried as an adult and was sent to prison for hurting someone. In prison, it was he who got hurt. When he got out, he went on a spree.

The hurt he did then killed people. This time, he was sentenced to life. The psychologist who testified against him said it was a near certainty he would re-offend. He heard the words "sadistic," "sociopath," "psychopath." He did not care. He was sent to a prison in California and then put on a van to be transported to a maximum-security prison in Nevada along with the men he now traveled with. Then, the things appeared, and he was trapped with these hard men. It was like being in hell. But they had lasted, and they were free, and now he was still with them.

It was still a little like hell. There was no way to hurt these men. They were too hard. And he got used when they felt the need. But he stayed; he didn't want to be alone. At least he would be able to burn down that damned courthouse.

For now, he was supposed to be on guard while they abused the girls. He had no desire to fornicate with them. He would like to hurt them, though. He wanted to hear the sounds they would make. He was good at that, and it was the only thing that gave him some semblance of pleasure.

When they kicked him out, he went for some booze. He found a liquor store in town. It helped him still the need to hurt. If he turned on the men, it would be the last thing he ever did.

When he was near the house, he heard the shooting and wondered if they were killing the girls. Then, he saw the Humvee with the black guy in it pulling up the avenue. This had to be one of the people at the motel. Maybe he could just wound the guy. And then he could hurt him. The others would not care about this one. He opened fire.

He missed. He saw the rounds spark off the car. What the hell kind of car was that? He was fumbling for another clip when there was a booming sound, and he felt a terrible shock, like he had touched a live wire. Then hot pain. This was worse than anything that happened to him before. The sky got darker, and the street hit him in the face. He could not move.

He was barely alive when the big black man walked up to him. He felt a boot turn him face up. He saw the shotgun aimed at his face. He had a sudden wish to have never done what he did. He saw the flash, then nothing—ever again.

Terry heard a sound behind him. Before he could turn, someone said, "Hoo-ah!"

"Hoo-ah!" he returned, recognizing Dennis, who came out from behind a derelict car. "Hiding behind that chunk of junk, huh. Smart. I still have three in the gun. Never know what I might do when lead is flying." He laughed, then grew serious. "You're still alive, I see. What about Joe? The girls?" He was suddenly worried. Why only Dennis?

"Joe is with the girls. We killed those up in the house. Looks like you got the last one, according to Teressa. Let's go up and get them." Terry let out a soft breath. They left the bodies where they fell. They would become just another addition to the uncounted death toll.

CHAPTER 16

Survivors Motel

When they got back, Mary rushed out and held her daughters, crying but saying nothing. John and Bob both tried to get up, but Devon stopped them. "Let them come to you." They slumped back on their cots and waited impatiently. The rescue party came in. The girls were still numb. They huddled together with their parents, sitting with John on the cot. Bill and Devon helped Bob over. Then, cautiously, carefully all the Survivors joined in. As Vanessa and Teressa acknowledged each, one by one, all held them in a comforting embrace. The girls slowly began to stop shaking. It got dark. Candles were lit.

As Joe's wound was tended to, the men told their stories—without any bravado. There was silence then. The room was filled with wounded and damaged Survivors, yet it also seemed filled with some kind of peaceful healing. As the shock wore off, the girls began to cry softly, but without pain. It seemed to Mary that their hurt was somehow being exorcised. She could feel it. She looked around at the Survivors and saw the care and wonder in their eyes as well.

Devon was silent. He struggled to understand. *Why did this happen? Did we somehow offend God?* Yet he watched the Survivors' outpouring of love and protection of the sisters with reverence. He thought he knew God's love, but here in this room, at this time of violence, pain, and death, he sensed the feeling of true love. Love without exception. Without condition. Love without God? It could not be. Yet the Survivors didn't call on God.

He needed to pray. The Survivors must be brought back to God. This could not happen again.

The dog watched. This was to be her new pack. She smelled the residual anger of the male two-paws. The concern of the females. She smelled the damage to the two young females. It was not debilitating. She smelled the damage to the three male two-paws. She knew they would heal. She saw the females tending to the wounds. She felt the pack grow calm. Caring and praise were here. The pack took care of its own. They had tended to her. She felt the binding on her leg and knew it was good. It was good to be here. She limped to her new den, secure in knowing she was protected. Knowing the care of the pack.

Alima had held the girl's hands. She felt a love she did not know existed. But she also watched, first with a sort of wonder, then concern, then fear. What was going on here? Where had she been taken? She heard the description of the attackers and knew one was a Muslim because Joe told of the man calling to Allah as he charged. She felt the hate of him from the men. Would they hate her, too? She prayed again for protection. But Allah did not protect the Muslim.

The room became calm. Couples stood together. The Midders sat together, surrounded by healing protection. Then the spell waned—yet remained. Slowly, the Survivors broke up and returned to their rooms to rest. To heal.

Except for Terry. He had to check. He took a flashlight and went to the Humvee. He counted sixteen bullet hits on the beast. Many on his door. If this was a car . . . but this was an up-armored vehicle. The damage was minimal. The fool had spent thirty rounds, and none had hit him. But he remembered the windows were open. He remembered the buzz of death in his ears. He was ready to discount the accuracy of the marauder. But second thoughts crept into his brain. Was it a pathetic shooter, his luck—or something else? He went to Wanda, who was waiting for him. He needed comfort.

"Are you all right?" she asked.

"I don't know. That fool fired an entire clip but . . . nothing."

"Terry, listen for a minute. It was a brave thing you did. Now, at the risk of sounding like Devon, there was something special here tonight. I don't mean the attack. I mean the love, caring, compassion. But there was something else, too. When you described the shooting, I nearly cried. I came close to losing you, yet the fool missed. How? Why?" Wanda stared at the dark ceiling.

Terry was silent. Wanda continued, "There was something special besides the love. Some of us got hurt. But . . . there was no . . . damage. I don't know how else to put it. We are stronger somehow. You are stronger." She trailed off, lost in some sort of wonder.

"I feel it. But now I know there is danger in this new reality."

"Yes, there is. It can't be all perfect. So we get better. More vigilant. You are my—our—protector."

"Don't want that burden."

"That, my love, is what makes you good for it. And you have help."

"I'm going to need it, I think."

"Yes, you are. But not right now." She cradled his head. "Sleep. There's tomorrow to think about this."

He fell into a restful sleep. Wanda watched him and smiled. Then she too fell asleep.

That same night, Joe and Jan lay together in the inky blackness. Joe's wound through his calf was superficial and was bandaged tightly, throbbing with a dull ache. He had not lost much blood. He would be sore and limping for a while but functional. The rest had gone to bed, except for Bill and Devon. They remained awake and alert, watching for other marauders. Everyone felt there were no more, but who could guarantee that?

"You want to talk about it?" Jan asked.

Joe was silent for a full minute, and Jan waited patiently. "I don't want to, but I think you are going to make me." Before she could answer, he continued. "I think Bob, Dennis, and Terry are OK with the shooting. I am too, with shooting these pieces of filth. But I have a hard time with what happened to the sisters."

"You feel for them. But *you* just got through killing five human beings. That's got to have some effect."

"One and two halves by me. But who's counting. You know, I thought about it... after, while you were fixing me up. During the action, I felt nothing but this strange need for vengeance. It fueled me. I don't think I could have done it without that feeling. Yet I was calm. Without fear." He stopped, thought. "No . . . there was fear, fear I would fail. The need drove me through it. And I don't have a problem with that. I read somewhere about how to deal with killing. It was explained like this: Suppose we had an infestation of cockroaches. We would kill them with whatever means we had. Right? We would not feel bad for them. Well, cockroaches are just little bundles of DNA, doing what they are programmed to do. They have no choice in the matter. These marauders had a choice. They chose wrong, and it caught up to them. I feel nothing for them."

"So these people were cockroaches?" Jan said. "I called them marauders. I don't know why."

"Accurate name. Yes. They were nothing. In fact, they were less than nothing. They had a choice. They chose an evil path." But something inside him waivered. Did he do the right thing? Had he just blindly followed Dennis? Had he let hatred drive him? Had he thought for himself? He remembered the fearful, doomed look of the last man he shot.

"Yes, they did. Worse than nothing, because of their choice. They were less than cockroaches! I'm glad they're dead. I'm glad you killed them." Jan was deadly serious. Then softly, she said, "For what it's worth, my husband, I love you, and you did the right thing." And with that, doubt fell away from Joe.

"Thank you, my wife."

Then he had a stray thought. "You know, it's funny, but the girls credited Dennis as their savior. I was the one who shot the shit bag who was attacking them. Don't get me wrong. I am not jealous. It's just interesting."

Jan's eyes twinkled in the darkness. "You silly man. You are taken. Dennis is . . ." she thought, ". . . prime material. And available."

"Prime material? Of course. You would see that, wouldn't you?"

"I'd be blind not to. Remember, his voice was the one they heard when you struck down the marauders." She was silent for a beat. "But you are my man," she said softly.

"And you are my woman."

They nestled up and got comfortable, waiting for the new day.

No more was said, but Joe did not sleep well. He was restless. It was not the pain of the gunshot. A residual rising need, an anger, was kindled, eating at him. He could not name it. He knew it was not good. He worried he could not control it.

That night, Bill and Sally laid together, snuggling against the cold. "Do you ever wonder about the past?" she asked.

"Some," he said. "But not much."

"It was a terrible time compared to this. Even with the Bugs and marauders here. Back then, there was a continuous cycle of hate, murder, and revenge. It played out in real life and in movies, television, and books. And even now, I am glad we are here. If this had to happen, at least we were there for the daughters, along with the Survivors. Teressa and Vanessa seem somehow . . . unphased. God, they are beautiful women."

"It wasn't all bad back then. There were redeeming qualities. There was love and compassion. We had it. We still do. The daughters know that."

"Yes, we all do. But the majority of media was negative. 'If it bleeds it leads' seemed to be their motto. I sometimes felt we would eventually succumb to it. What would happen to the Midder daughters then?"

"Never! We would not give in," asserted Bill. "I know you. You are a beautiful person. Remember Christmas in the motel? The good times."

Sally responded, "And here it is. Here they are. Even with the bad happenings, we are happy. How does that happen?"

"Without a constant media barrage of negativism. We are Survivors."

"What about the girls? How can we help?"

"We already have. And we, the Survivors, will continue to offer support."

"What about a possible pregnancy?" Sally was suddenly concerned. "I personally would not want that."

"We'll see tomorrow." Bill was also concerned now. "I hope Devon does not become . . . Catholic about it."

"Me, too. Best be ready for it. I will support whatever the Midders decide, if anything."

"Shouldn't we bring it up if they don't think of it?"

"Wait and see. Wait and see."

CHAPTER 17

Healing

The day after the marauders were killed was damp and overcast, yet calm and mild. The sun would burn through the clouds in the afternoon. The Survivors gathered in the motel common room around two picnic tables, making room for all. An oiled tablecloth from a local outdoor store lay on the top, covering the blood-stains from the night before. They sat, except for Bob and John, who uncomfortably laid on cots. There were now sixteen of them. Alima sat with them, but she still had no idea of what was happening. There was a lot of discussion and crosstalk about yesterday.

Devon had turned out to be very knowledgeable medically. He had some pre-med training before turning to pharmaceuticals and then to medical devices. John and Bob would live. John had one bullet that had passed through his kidney and lodged near his spine. Devon had pulled it from his back with a pair of long-nosed pliers through a slit made with a razor blade. The disinfectant was hydrogen peroxide. John would be pissing blood for a while, but he had born it all with gritted teeth and sweat and without any opioid painkillers. Both John and Bob wanted to be alert if anything else happened.

The wounds were allowed to bleed for a while and then were bandaged. John was weak and pale from blood loss and pain. Bob's wounds were through without any fragments left. Bill had found the bullets embedded in the wall where Bob was hit. His holes were plugged and bandaged when the bleeding had stopped. It would be a while before either Bob or John would be functional again. Both needed rest.

Joe had the wound to his calf. It was bandaged and would heal OK. But it was still sore as hell. He wondered how Bob and John could handle the pain as well as they did. They were wondering about each other.

The dog was tended to as best as Jan could, her leg splinted with a dowel and then taped. The bite wounds were slathered with the antibiotic salve Jan had used on the men and then bandaged. The dog had suffered through it without complaint. Her big eyes focused on Jan like a babe on its mother. It drank some more water and lapped some broth and leftover stew. She would need real dog food soon. She looked a lot better than when Joe had dropped her off, and she hobbled around on three legs quite well. She sat under the table, feeling the protection of her new pack.

Terry called for suggestions, first for the treatment of the gunshot wounds, second for medical treatment for the girls' injuries, and third for discussion about the Survivors' defense. There were several suggestions. The best medical advice came from Devon. "We need to get to a pharmacy and get some Cipro or Amoxicillin antibiotics, bring all you can find. The Providence Hospital pharmacy will have some. I will figure out the dosage and expiration dates. John and Bob need lots of fluids. Find some canned juice if you can. They need some iron supplements, too. The girls just need some time and love."

Mary stood. "We need some 'morning after' pills, too." The Survivors went silent as they realized what this meant. Bill and Sally looked at each other.

"Add it to the list," Terry said to Bill and Dennis, the designated gofers.

"Wait a minute," Devon interrupted. "We should let God decide this. He will know best whether to allow a child to be born or not. To kill the unborn is a mortal sin."

"This isn't up for group discussion! We appreciate what Bob, Terry, Joe, and Dennis did, and you too, Devon." John was pale and bent, but he stood with his hand resting on his wife for support. "But we've discussed it within the family. We are in accord. We will not allow those bastards to further harm our children." His voice was pained but sure. There was to be no question of this decision.

"We need to know what we are looking for," said Dennis. "This is not something common, is it? Like RU-486 or whatever."

Teressa looked uncomfortable but spoke with conviction. "It is . . ." Then she stopped and said, "My sister and I agree with our parents. I don't want that monster to . . . to have a chance to continue . . . in me." She took a breath. "What you want . . . what we want to have is the prescription drug. It will be found in any pharmacy. It must be used soon. Today."

"Wait a minute!" shouted Devon. "Don't you see? We are the chosen people. We are the last people on earth. Like Noah in the Bible. God has wiped out all sin. He is starting over. If we disobey His Law again . . . then it will be the end." Devon had to bring the Survivors back to the laws that would save them. "This is a test of faith."

John was adamant. "This wasn't the work of God! And we don't know about other people. After all, the marauders survived somehow."

"No! They were the work of the Devil! We must remain pure to earn the protection of God. We are the chosen. We're here for a reason. We must not destroy life." Devon was panicking.

In silence, John just stared at Devon in disbelief.

"We don't know God's will," said Terry. "But I, for one, am not willing to subject or force my beliefs upon any here. Nor are you, Devon." He turned to Bill. "Get the medicine."

"Let's go," Bill said to Dennis and started for the Humvee.

Again, there was silence. Then Devon started off, "I have thought and prayed about this situation we are in for some time. My wife and children were sacrificed for the greater good. I cannot let their sacrifice be for nothing. If you are determined to disobey God, you are doomed. I cannot stay."

"Sorry for that," said Terry. "But I say again, this isn't God's work. By all accounts, this condition we find ourselves in is the doings of aliens and the marauders who came here. We will survive. We will protect ourselves. We will search for others. But we will not impose values on each other. What the Midders decide is between them and God. And they have decided. It's done!"

Devon stood. He could not allow murder. He could not allow the Survivors to be punished by God again. He turned with intent to confront the Midders. Joe moved and stepped in front of him, his leg momentarily forgotten. For the second time, he confronted Devon, feeling a need to protect the girls, even at the expense of violence. The "chosen" reference burned in his mind. Time stood still. Even Terry was shocked.

"You will not stop this!" Joe put his hand on his weapon. The thing he feared was here, and he did not try to stop it.

The dog watched and listened from under the table. She was unfamiliar with her new pack's hierarchy, but she knew a fight for dominance when she saw it. In such a fight, there was no right or wrong, only who won. She heard and smelled the aggression. The two-paw who brought her here was reaching for his noisemaker. She knew it caused the death of the coyotes. This would be a fight to the death if he pointed it. The other did not cower or roll over. Yet he was not in fight mode. He stood without threat. She had never seen the like. But she knew if a fight started, the pack would be one less.

Whining softly, she started limping back to her den, preparing for the loud noise.

Then the young female also started whining. The dog stopped, waited.

"Wait a minute, everyone!" Teressa's voice was small and low, but all heard the imperative need. The Survivors went still. "Devon? Devon!

You do not know. You cannot know. You are incapable of knowing. What happened."

"Teressa!" her father said. "You owe him nothing."

"No, Daddy!" Resigned, tears ran on her bruised cheeks as if to escape the hurt. "I owe it to myself, my sister, and all here." Her voice rose, got stronger. "My sister and I were raped . . . *raped!* You cannot imagine. The tattooed man was bad enough, but I can still see that monster, standing over me, yelling to his god, while he . . . *used* me." That image burned unbidden into Devon's mind. He shuddered.

The day grew grayer. The wounded dog whined louder. Clouds blew up over the Tillamook Head, dulling the sun's attempt to break through the overcast. Somewhere a crow called, and another answered. A soft breeze rustled the tablecloth through the open doors. All the Survivors sat quietly, hearing the pain and terror coming from this brave girl, hoping, knowing it was catharsis, the beginning of healing, and a rebuke to Devon. Or maybe a call for him to stay.

"When he finished, I saw the devil's look in his eye. He pulled out a large knife, and I knew he wanted to cut my throat. But something happened. He turned to leave and, God help me, for a moment . . . I wished he had killed me!" Her mother moved to her and held her, saying nothing. She continued, "Then I heard, as if from the voice of God, 'Kill him!' I knew it was meant for the monster. And so did the monster. He screamed horribly. And God's angel sent a thunderbolt that shattered his head. Something inside me rejoiced. There were more thunderbolts, and I knew God was destroying the evil men." She paused. "I know it was not actually God, but God's hand guided Dennis and Joe. Do you see? God saved us.

"But the hurt did not go away. Devon, I will *not* carry that monster's memory or life. You can reject me and leave if you wish, but I will not, nor will Vanessa, carry a monster. God would not want that. I think you should stay and help us all survive. But it's your choice to make."

There were tears in Devon's eyes.

Joe stepped back. The rage in him had died, killed by the soft voice of this child. Something he could not do himself was done for him.

They all sat down. "I am not a mindless zealot. I am sorry for your pain." Devon stopped to compose himself. "I am a Catholic seeking to find my way. Seeking to guide us in the path of righteousness. Lately, I have read the Bible extensively. As Terry pointed out, the Old Testament is full of God punishing those who disobey Him. I feared today He would punish us all for your actions. But until now, I have not had to make such a life-and-death decision. I, too, applauded the killing of the marauders. It was God's justice. You are right. God condones that. I myself called them the Devil's own. Yet I did not know the reality of the sin committed against you. I did not know." His voice fell, and he slumped in his chair. "I will pray on it. God will lead me on the right path. But for myself, I think forgiveness is required here. For me. I ask it from you and God." He put his head down and went silent. Then, he took a deep breath and said, "The pills you want are called Plan B. They have no side effects. They are the most effective and can be found in any pharmacy."

There were no dry eyes at the table. Both sisters leaned forward and said, "You have our forgiveness."

"See to God yourself," Mary said to Devon. The Survivors were quiet.

Stan Lake stood and cleared his throat. All eyes turned to him. He was not one to speak much, and the command for attention was unusual. "Now, I don't profess to be any more important than anyone else here, but I have been around the block—several times. I have a lovely wife of more than sixty years. I served my time in the army. Now, I have watched you and have seen something extraordinary happening here. The way things happened—the right people at the right time to survive the Bugs and marauders. Here is the way I see the God thing. I read the Bible a long time ago. I did not understand much of it except, like Devon said, it is full of God issuing laws and mankind breaking them. However, there is the Psalms and Solomon's Song." He smiled, sobered, and continued. "I saw nothing in it about abortion. That is, I think, a religious tenet. Then there is the New Testament. There is not much I remember there, either, except for one part, maybe Devon can pinpoint it, where Jesus says, 'Call no man Rabbi, call no man Father.' The teaching was to not let any man come between you and your Maker. To not let anyone tell you about God. It is up to you to reach out. For what it's worth, I think that should be our way. The past religions and governments have been both good and bad for people. But they stood between man and God. They have no place here. Terry is right. Nobody here should seek to impose his will or belief on another."

"That was from Matthew twenty-three, verses six to nine," Devon said. "Jesus was preaching against the Pharisees. It is, 'But be ye not called Rabbi: for one is your Master, even Christ; and all ye are brethren. And call no man your father upon the earth: for one is your Father, which is in Heaven.' I think Stan has the meaning right. I have tried to follow the will of God, and I will not become as the Pharisees."

There was a silent assent. Stan's wife stood with him and began to clap. Everyone joined in. Nothing further was said.

Bill and Dennis rose and went for the supplies and pills. The rest broke up into pairs and families and retired to ponder the events.

Alima did not know what to make of this. It seemed she was delivered from the shayatan into an infidel camp. The blond man she thought of as a Malak was just a man. As she heard the young woman tell of her rape by a Muslim man, she was conflicted. Hearing the pain of the women tugged at her soul. But was it not the right of the Muslim? She began to think she should fashion a *hijab* and maybe a *niqab* so as not to offend Allah. Yet was it not he who led her here?

Alima came from Manila, where Muslims were a minority. The majority were Catholics, like the one called Devon. She knew neither religion's practice was pure. Both believed theirs was the true path. Both only tolerated the other because of secular law. She believed each would destroy the other if given the chance. Yet her father was not radical. She could move freely within the confines of the Bangsamoro region. However, she had to wear a complete hijab when in the Catholic region. And be escorted by him or her brother. This was to protect her from un-wanted attention. She knew it just made her more of an attraction; she saw it in the eyes of the men she passed. The mystery of what lay beyond the garment was apparent.

However, her father was tolerant of her job. He was pragmatic when it came to money. And the money she earned went to him. The cruise ship company was tolerant of her request to wear the hijab as long as it was without the niqab. It reminded her of how the nuns dressed. They had something in common.

Here also, there seemed to be a need for tolerance. Unlike Manila, most here seemed to believe in a god but were without formal religious tenets.

The women here were friendly, but she was withdrawn. They waited for her to engage. They dressed informally but conservatively, preferring function over fashion. Unlike some on the cruise ship who flaunted their bodies, these women seemed natural and unconcerned. She knew Dennis had heard her call to Allah. But he said nothing. She suspected Devon knew as well. Alima did not know what to do.

She was given her own quarters. She was provided with clothing. But the hate for the Muslim man haunted her.

She would abide. Allah would show her the way.

Someone's way was coming. That was for sure. Bill and Sally saw it.

"There's going to be an explosion," Sally said. "I could see Jan get-ting ready to . . . I dunno, take Joe to task."

"Yeah, I saw it, too. Be ready. We may need to step in."

"How? If Jan goes medieval on Joe, how could we do anything?"

"Don't know. Readiness is all."

"Readiness won't be enough if Jan reacts badly. It could tear them apart."

"Not a chance. We're Survivors."

"I love your optimism. I believe it, too. But the test is coming soon."

"I don't think it will be too bad. Jan will yip at him for a while. He will say sorry and that will be that."

"It's going to be worse than that Bill. I saw the look in her eye. This could be a bloodbath."

"Joe can handle himself. I hope."

"Me too. Let's be ready to yell 'time out' just in case."

"Readiness is all."

"What about the others?"

"They better be ready too," said Bill. "It won't be that bad."

"I hope so," said Sally.

They settled down to wait.

CHAPTER 18

Confrontation

That night, Jan was silent, and a chill filled the air on the deck where she sat with Joe. The iciness Joe felt was not due to the temperature. He knew what was wrong. "I'm sorry," he said lamely.

"What is wrong with you?" For the second time she was loud enough to be heard by everyone. "Were you going to shoot Devon, for God's sake? You can't do that!" She was almost crying. "Who are you?"

"I don't know." Silence.

"Well, figure it out! You can't do that! I can't live with that!"

"I am not the same man since the Bugs and marauders. Something's changed in me. It's like I have this need to protect us, the girls, all of us. I'm not a loose cannon. If danger came to Devon, I would react the same to protect him." Joe came upon some truth. "And there is this. I have a violent aversion to religion. The thought that someone could tell me how to live my life and punish me or you if I don't do it galls me. I don't need that. I don't want that. It makes me crazy. I didn't know how deep that feeling ran 'til the girls showed it to me. It's gone now. Stan said it right. I know Devon is sincere. Doesn't make it right." He steeled himself. "Devon!" he called out. "We need to talk. Just you and I. Now!"

They were loud. The Survivors heard it all but remained silent. Devon stirred and went to the meeting room. Joe took a deep breath and started for the room. Jan grabbed his arm with warning. He shook his head. But she went with him. When they got to the room, Devon was waiting, sitting in the dark with his head in his hands, dimly lit by a guttering candle. Joe turned to Jan. "It will be all right." He then addressed Devon. "Let's go outside."

They went through the door over the deck to the picnic table. Devon sat across from Joe. They were now outside in the cool dark. Joe spoke in normal tones; there were no secrets here. "Devon, we need to find a way to get along. As you may have guessed by now, I cannot abide religion, or someone telling me what or how to believe. Now, I won't be so . . . adamant. The girls purged it from me. But . . . I won't be told by you how to act, to believe."

"Yes. I get it," Devon spoke dryly. "Yet we need God, can't you see? How are we to know what is right and wrong without guidelines? I saw the look in your eyes when you stood in front of me. It was not the look of the righteous. I was not afraid, though. I saw regret also."

"I think I agree about God . . . yet I think I know how to live without consulting Him. And how are we to know His mind, anyway? You can't tell me, and I can't tell you, and I sure won't let the Bible or any other book tell me." Joe paused, thinking. "And yet I see I'm telling you how to believe, even as I tell you not to tell me . . . God, what a mess."

"No, it's not a mess, and you're not telling me how to believe. You're just telling me to leave you alone. That you have your own way of thinking. Your own way of morality. I won't question it. Like Terry said, and Stan wisely augmented, each has to find a path for himself. I agree not to impose on others. As I have already done with Plan B. And I ask for you to not resort to firearms to settle disputes. There will be others." He smiled in the dark.

Joe felt a further lifting of the weight he carried. For all his preaching, Devon was a good man. "Done. It will not rise to that level again. I can't say we will not have disagreements, though."

"A good debate is always welcome. Even Jesus debated the Pharisees. But . . . He didn't use guns to make His point."

Joe looked at him through the dimness, searching for ridicule or deception. There was none. It was a friendly poke in the ribs. He laughed. "So be it. For the record, Jesus was concerned with the religion and power of the Pharisees. And he did throw the money lenders out of the Synagogue . . . with violence."

"This is going to be interesting. But I don't think there'll be any money lending here." Devon reached across, found Joe's hand, and shook it.

There was tattered clapping from the motel. A step was taken. There would need to be more.

Bill and Sally looked at each other and smiled.

Alima heard the exchange. This was more than forced tolerance; it was respect. Such a discussion would not have happened in Manila. She wondered how she should act with these—she wanted to say infidels—but instead, she could think nothing else than *people*. Joe had a violent reaction to religion, yet he had apologized. She felt no danger from him, like she had felt from some passengers on the cruise ships. She was still pretty sure most the Survivors did not know her religion. She awaited Allah's direction.

The next day, they met again at the common room picnic tables. The sun was shining more, but the air held a hint of rain to come. Terry brought up the defense motion again. But John interrupted, "There is something we need to address first, I think. From the conversation yesterday, it is apparent we need to discuss how we are to relate to one another. If it is true there are no more or damned few survivors, then we actually are part the beginning or end of humanity on earth. We need to agree on . . . how to live, I guess. How to go forward." His voice was stronger, and he was less pale. He still rested on the cot, but he was healing rapidly. In one day! Mary wondered how. Without doctors and a hospital.

"Good idea," said Terry. "What do you suggest as a starting point?"

"I don't know. Perhaps the tribal template is a start."

"What is that?" asked Devon. "Not some godless, hedonistic type of life, surely."

"Not at all. From my recollection of high school history, the tribal life is where each has a personal connection to God or the Great Spirit, not to be questioned or ridiculed. Where individual thoughts and actions are not judged unless harm comes to another. There is no central power. But there is a deference to wisdom gained through age and trial."

"Like American Indians," said Bob from his cot. He was propped up and leaning on an elbow. "But remember, the Native American was a notional man. They had enemies, and blood was often shed between tribes."

"True, but this condition is not like that. First, there may be no others. Second, we have more knowledge and quote wisdom now," offered Bill.

"All right," said Terry. "First, we seem to have determined that there are no other survivors within a hundred miles, save Alima, and that appears to be another miracle. The marauders' bus had California plates. They were talking about being held in a warehouse loaded with nonperishable food. Not the kind of miracle we wished for, that's for sure. Anyway, perhaps some seats of government exist somewhere, but not here. I'm beginning to enjoy the freedom we have here. We tend to forget the millions of laws that existed before—enforced by endless layers and supply of government officials. Of which I was a part. Confused by sociopathic lawyers and abused by the powerful. If what happened to the marauders had happened back then, we'd be facing vigilante charges, at the least. Let's let things evolve naturally, including respect for each other's beliefs." He looked at Joe. "In the meantime, we need to plan a defense."

"Well, we all know how to shoot," said Dennis, "except Alima. I'll teach her if she wishes."

Alima was being included. She did not know what to say, but she could not take the life of another. She gathered her courage. "I cannot kill." The Survivors looked at her. There was no judgment, just interest. She put her eyes down.

"That's okay," offered Devon. "We cannot force our beliefs on anyone." He sent a smug look Joe's way.

"Right. But we will protect you, Alima. With force, if necessary," Joe assured her, returning the smug look.

Amused silence. Alima felt a warm glow. This was not the stern protection of her father, who would punish her for transgressions. This was a protection without threat. She realized that if the girls had been in Iran or Saudi Arabia when this happened, they could have been stoned to death for being whores for what happened to them. Here, they were cared for and protected. This kind of care felt good.

"Let's set up a watch system. See if we can scrounge some more walkie-talkies," said Terry.

"Yeah. Sixteen of them. Two way, with open com capability, rechargeable," said Joe.

"Well, off we go again," said Bill. He and Dennis started for the truck.

The main room was dark. A glimmer of starlight filtered in through the open window. Except for the lookout, the Survivors had retired for the night. Joe was scheduled for first light in the morning. He sat with Jan in the meeting room, savoring the silence while the generator was off. It was something they had gotten used to—silence. Always before, there had been some ambient sound, mostly unnoticed. Cars, planes, appliances, the drumbeat of civilization.

And the dark—they had gotten used to the dark. Always there had been the glow of cities reflected off clouds or deadening the night sky through the haze of industry. Not now. They were adapting.

Actually, there did remain some sound. Nature's sounds: the sigh of breeze in the trees, the muted crunch of waves on the beach from over three miles away, birds, bees, and a soft symphony of lesser and greater sounds that had been lost before.

"What is happening here?" Jan asked. "I mean, there's no precedence. This group—us, these Survivors—have come together by accident, but we have cooperated naturally, working out a potentially bad problem without law or courts. Without a central government, a power telling us what to do, how to act. There's no structure." She had a legal background; this was unknown territory for her. "I see the sisters healing faster than would seem possible. It's due to the combined care of the Survivors, I'm sure of it. I still can't get my head around it. If this had happened in the past, there would've been investigations, trials. The girls would have been put through another type of Hell. Facing their rapists in court. We would have been unable to help. I . . ." she fumbled for a thought. "Well, it looks like God got this one right."

"Maybe, but Teressa and Vanessa were raped. Did it need to happen for us to move forward?"

"I can't say. That idea is beyond my knowledge." Then she had a strange thought. "Could this fall apart? Are we headed for a melt-down like those Armageddon movies we saw?"

Joe thought for a minute. "For the record, it was you who brokered the peace treaty between Devon and me. Like Stan said, you were the right person at the right time. I see the same thing with the sisters. Their recovery is like a miracle. You're right. I'm going to quit second-guessing everything." Then he said, "No way are we going to fall apart like those movies. That stuff is stupid. Made for entertainment, not for real. If you try to count the logical discrepancies they proffer, you run out of fingers and toes in the first five minutes. It required a willful suspension of disbelief to watch that drivel."

"Yet here we are. You got an explanation for the Bugs?"

"No. Maybe some of those alien movies were close to right." He smiled in the dark.

"I'll answer my question myself. I don't think we will fall apart. We are better than that."

"You're right. Actually, although this is not the way we would like to find out how it should be, I think it is the way it is supposed to be. The tribal template is worth looking at. But maybe there should be no template, no expectations. Our previous laws were written and instituted to codify moral behavior based on religious dogma. They were made to force acceptable behavior under threat of penalty—obey or get hurt. Now, here, we don't need the written part. The morals are inherent here. No one steals, no one harms another . . . because we need each other. Not just to survive, but on some deeper level. Actually, when you think about it, it's when people don't need each other that the morals break down. Plus, we talk and listen every day. No selfies, Facebook, Twitter, or any of that crap."

"Yeah. There are sixteen of us. We are a tribe, so to speak—a small one, for sure. Our continued existence is dependent on our skills. Plus, I think the trauma of the Bugs and marauders and discussions about the will of God," she smiled, "have strengthened our bond, so to speak. That deeper level thing you said."

"So to speak, yes," Joe agreed. They laughed.

"But what of the comforts of civilization? You miss any of that? Sooner or later, we will run out of preserved food. We can grow our own and hunt like you say, but with all the knowledge here we could not make a computer. We could not even make a pencil or paper."

"That's true. We can farm. We can hunt. We have a lot of stuff we can scavenge. We can't build a computer from scratch, but we can scavenge one and power it up using a generator. Libraries still exist. Knowledge is not lost. But I'm going to miss coffee and toilet paper when they run out."

"Yeah. Me, too. But there are bigger things to consider. The generator requires an energy source. Gas will deteriorate in time. Motors will break down. Books will rot. Pharmaceuticals will expire. We are headed for the bottom. Entropy. Gravity wins."

"Don't be so gloomy. We can always hand-crank. I read somewhere that gas and diesel will only last for a year, yet we are still using it. And we have plenty of supplies. We have enough for our generation. In the meantime, let's live as best we can. And yes, I miss some comforts. Like relaxing at a beachfront hotel, being waited on. Dinners at Pier 12 or Maggie's or the Wayfarer's in Cannon Beach. Baseball or football on a Sunday. But I don't miss a lot of it. Like wars and lawyers and politics. And I sure don't miss taxes!"

Teressa and Vanessa drifted over, small pale ovals in the night. "We couldn't sleep. What are you guys talking about, anyway? So seriously." Joe spotted Mary watching from the hall. She did not come in, though. She just listened, watching out for her children.

Jan again marveled at their resiliency. In another time and place in the past, she might have said, "Nothing you need to worry about." But here and now, in the post-Bug/marauder era, she said, "You know, we were discussing our future. The future of us Survivors. It's not a rosy picture."

"You worried about more bad men?" Teressa said without fear. *God, how beautiful, how wonderful are these children*, thought Jan. Yet they were not children now.

"A little. We are prepared now, so if there are more, they will not be a problem. More than that," Jan said. Suddenly, a thought surfaced. What was lurking in the background during the time of the Bugs and marauders? "We may be the beginning of a new world. Or the end of it. Are there even enough people here to repopulate?" She had read somewhere that, to keep a viable population, it was necessary to have at least 250,000 people. Then she thought, *Yeah, some pointy head had done a genetics study*. But how did modern man start, some 100,000 years ago? It sure wasn't with 250,000 Homo sapiens to begin with. Did they just materialize out of thin air?

Teressa had the answer. "If Adam and Eve could do it, we can, too."

"We are maybe going to find out," said Joe.

Jan changed the subject before it could get complicated. "What about doctors and dentists? What if someone gets sick? What about toothaches? Don't you miss being able to listen to good live music when we want?"

"We did pretty good with the gunshot wounds. Devon seems to know his stuff. And you did the dog well enough. We can fire up a stereo with some CDs still."

"You going to learn how to fill a tooth? Huh?"

"I'll bet we could pull one with a little ether."

"How about an appendectomy? Cancer? Heart attack?"

"Slow down! Yeah. There're things we probably can't do. But we can weather them. Or die trying. The only difference from before is that there will be no one to prolong life. When you think about it, the end is the same."

"That brings up another point. What about procreation?" Jan dove back in. "To prevent inbreeding, there has to be a . . . variety of mating." Jan was worried. "I theoretically could have another baby. I haven't gone through menopause yet." Joe suddenly thought about that. Was she offering to be impregnated by another for a variety of mating? His anger flared and then settled. No, not that.

"Let's not get ahead of ourselves here. A bomb like that could set off another confrontation with Devon. Are we going to pick and choose mates for Teressa and Vanessa? What about their parents? And any other potential mothers? Are we going to require babies? Not a chance." Joe glanced over at Mary who remained at the door.

"Right now, it looks like most of the Survivors are already paired off. Terry and Wanda. Bill and Sally. John and Mary. The Lakes. You and me." Jan though a minute. "I've seen Dennis eying Teressa. Devon eying Alima. That leaves Bob and Vanessa." Jan did not see Mary.

"You sound like a matchmaker. This is *not* a damned TV series. Let's let things progress naturally."

"Calm down, Joe. I bet others are thinking about this, too."

"We can't bring this up out of the blue. There has to be some sort of natural way to breach it. God help us when it comes up!"

"It'll work out," said Teressa. "Us Survivors are the best. And I couldn't do better than Dennis, and Vanessa couldn't do better than Bob." Honestly said. Jan again thought it was both a miracle Teressa had recovered so quickly and a shame she had grown up so quickly. Jan could not stop wondering. If the rape had happened in the city, there would have been police, doctors, and lawyers involved. The comfort of the Survivors could not have been there. It would have been clinical, sterile, impersonal. Then, the long painful process of trial and testimony—possibly months or years long—dealing with their rapists, who would be well cared for, well represented, and secure in the knowledge they would be free one day to do it again.

And the media. They would seek a story. They would tell a story. The rape would take on a life of its own. How would all this affect their family?

How would it affect the sisters? Jan knew it would not be good. It was sad it had happened at all. But if it had to, this was the best way. The marauders were dead. The sisters cared for. By a family, by the Survivors.

Mary listened and felt concerned. Her children were hurt, yet they seemed so calm. It made her wonder. The scenario Jan wove seemed real. Again, she wondered. Could she allow that? She went back to John, who rested uneasily. Her daughters went to their room, softly talking.

"You OK?" asked John.

"I think so, and our daughters are better than could be expected. How can that be?"

Without thinking, John said, "We are the Survivors."

She could not think of a better answer. "Yes, we are."

She slid in with him, and he immediately felt better. She did, too.

Later, after the sisters went to bed, Joe said, "I need to talk to Devon."

"Why? What about?" Jan sounded worried.

"His family. When we first got to the motel during the Bug infestation, he seemed heartbroken. Remember, he said his family was sacrificed. Later, we had the marauders incidence before I could tell him. I did manage to tell the Survivors generally that I found no one alive. They knew the odds. But I actually looked into Devon's house. I need to tell him. I need your advice."

"That depends on what you found."

"I saw the family in the front room. They were on the couch together. There was a dog at their feet. There were holes in the floor. The windows were broken."

"The Bugs got them."

"Yes. They died painlessly like all those we saw. But the dog . . ."

"Oh my God. So sad. It would have died of starvation."

"Yes. How do I do this?"

"Maybe you shouldn't."

"I think he needs it. I think I do, too."

"Then do it straight. Don't hem and haw. Say, 'Devon, this is what I saw,' then offer consolation, 'they did not suffer.' Don't say anything about the dog unless asked."

"No time like the present."

"Be kind, my husband."

Joe knocked on Devon's door.

"Yes?"

"Devon, may I come in?"

"Of course."

Devon's motel room was neat and clean. Devon was sitting at the small desk. He put down the Bible he was reading. It was opened to the Gospels. Thank God it was not Revelation.

"Devon," Joe started, "I have something to tell you."

"Would you like something to drink first? I have some excellent Northwest wine."

"I think I would, thank you."

Devon went to the dresser and came back with two glasses and a bottle of Willamette Valley pinot noir. He poured one for Joe and one for himself, sat, and said, "If you've come to apologize again, there is no need."

"That's not it, Devon. I said earlier I found no one alive in my search. But I did see something." Joe paused. Devon was silent, his head down. "I saw your family."

Devon began to shake.

"They were at peace, Devon. Nestled on the couch. They did not suffer starvation. They were together at the end." Joe stopped and waited. He was suddenly unsure of Devon's reaction. Would he be angry?

Devon straightened. Looked Joe in the eye. "Thank you," was all he said.

"I'm sorry for them, and for all the other family and friends of the Survivors."

"I am sorry for your family, also."

Joe could think of nothing more to say. They sat in silence, drinking wine. Then Devon said, "Joe? I already knew it. The first day," he said with a haunted look, "I saw. Beverly was on Skype . . . I saw . . . it happen. My wife, my children!" he choked. "I was not there! I couldn't . . ." He stifled a sob.

Joe remembered the laptop on the coffee table. That must have been harder than anything Joe could think of. "I am truly sorry."

Devon straightened again. "Thank you. I have made peace with it, but it still hurts." He looked at Joe. In his eyes was a sad, knowing look. "I saw it. But all here imagined it. And some may have starved."

Joe could not answer. What about his children, brothers, sisters? What about all the other Survivors' families? He stopped thinking about it.

Devon turned inward again, and Joe quietly left.

Joe returned to their room.

"Well?" asked Jan.

"He knew it. He saw it happen. He said, 'thank you' to me." Joe was shaking.

CHAPTER 19

Tsunami

Time passed. No more marauders. No aliens. The Survivors healed, became as comfortable as they could, yet remained armed and aware. They stayed in the motel despite being able to move anywhere they wanted. It was comforting to be with what felt like family in a home. It felt safe.

The Survivors were beginning to tell the date by the position of the sun. They had made and calibrated the crude gnomon-style sundial Bill and Sally envisioned. From the position of the shadow whenever the sun shone—which was sometimes rare—they could tell the time of day and the month without a clock or calendar. It was August. A hazy sun showed. A light breeze came from the south.

The Survivors had tomatoes, potatoes, and green beans growing. Now they had fresh vegetables as well as clams, crabs, fish, and beef.

A garden of ornamentals colored the sides of the motel. Azaleas and rhododendrons flourished in the coastal climate. Their blooms were large and fragrant but fading in the summer. Hydrangeas and roses still bloomed.

CHAPTER 20

Seaside

Joe and Jan were in the Ace Hardware store in Seaside. Their water heater had lost its heating element.

The Survivors had previously swapped out the gas heaters for electric, and they had upgraded the generator to an industrial-strength unit. With another for backup. They were becoming plumbers, along with emergency medical techs, mechanics, electricians, carpenters, farmers, hunters, and whatever skill was needed.

For the Jones, it was time either for a new tank or repair. Since this was their tank, the Jones got to make the choice. Repair. It was easiest. Hauling out the old one and replacing it would be a hassle. Jan wanted to get out more, so they took the ride to the store at Holladay and Broadway in Seaside rather than walking across the road to the Builder's First Choice. They parked the Humvee at the door. Then, they found the right component, and walked out, put it in the truck.

The morning was close to sixty-five degrees with a thin overcast. It was relatively calm. In the afternoon, the breeze would shift from the north. It would pick up, and the day would be bright. Right now, it was peaceful.

"Let's take a walk down memory lane," said Jan. They were getting used to the occasional bundle of bones and rags.

Joe thought. "Won't be the same. You sure?" In the post-Bug era, visiting historical sites without having to pay or move through crowds was fun. They could access anything at any time. But somehow, it was still sad. Something was always missing.

"Let's go. We can remember. The Shilo or Maggie's may be clear of bones. We can reminisce about good times."

"Why not?"

They walked up Broadway over Memorial Bridge. The insides of the shops were relatively untouched by time. They saw the beginning of the end, though—the cracks, peeling paint, sand blown up on the doors, grime on the windows, stains. Without constant maintenance, entropy took hold. Nevertheless, Jan remarked about the good times as they passed various shops and stores. "Remember this one? The Christmas Shop? We wandered around in there for a while."

"Yeah. Tipton's. You wanted to buy it all."

"Well, we have our pick now." The inside of the shop was remarkably intact.

They continued past the Times Theater, once a glittering monument to the past, now grimy and dull. They crossed and walked past the bumper car building. The doors were open, and the cars sat forlornly, waiting, never again to hear the laughter and joy of the drivers.

"Maybe this wasn't such a good idea." Jan was having second thoughts.

"Let's try the Shilo."

They walked up the steps to the east doors. Joe had to pry them open against the grit blown up against them. The went into the darkened entry, up the hall to the dining area where they ate on their previous weekend vacations. They stood looking out over the patio to the brightening sea. The light from the hazy sky made it sadder inside.

"Joe, let's go. This isn't right."

"Maybe we should take a walk on the beach. That has to be the same."

Before she could answer, they heard a slight bang. "What was that?"

Joe looked out the grimy window. The long stretch of sand between the Boardwalk and Pacific rippled. A low haze of dust rose. A sound like a massive train grew, coming with incredible speed. Then, it felt like a bomb went off under the building. The front windows cracked. The restaurant went up and down and rocked like a boat on a stormy sea. Jan fell, bouncing along the floor helplessly. Joe went over to her and fell as well. They managed to crawl over to one of the tables and hold on. The ground shook. The building shook. Walls swayed; glasses fell from shelves. Tables and benches juddered across the floor. A kitchen flue fell with a crash, pieces bouncing randomly like they were alive.

Jan and Joe were tossed around.

"Shit! This is the big one. We got to get out of here!" Joe cried. But the shaking went on. They could not stand, much less walk. The building groaned. They heard a sharp cracking sound. Something fell heavily above. This was a single-story building; what had hit the top? The ceiling rippled. Joe looked out the south windows at the Wyndham. The big eight-story luxury vacation condo looked like it was breathing. The balconies moved in shaky sync with the rolling, boiling sand. The shop's windows under the building buckled, and glass plates fell onto the rolling sidewalk.

Moe's side windows fell out, and the Promenade jumped and shuddered. The decorative concrete light posts vibrated. The power line to the streetlamps twanged with a sharp sound, heard even over the crashing, booming roar of the earthquake. The Jones clung to the table, which was alive in their hands, trying to escape their grip. It battered at them, hitting Jan's ankle. "Ow!" she said. The shaking continued for a long few minutes, then slowly diminished. Outside, seagulls were squawking, circling. A loud murder of crows blew past.

"We got to get out of here!" Joe yelled again. "The tsunami is coming!" They ran out the door. Jan was limping. They made it out onto the Promenade at the Lewis and Clark statue and looked down Broadway. Most of the shops had survived the shaking, but some had moved off their foundations. Debris and broken glass littered the sidewalk. They stared at the center of the shattered road. It was broken and torn, holding the shape of the last seismic wave that passed through. In places, the buckles were a foot high.

They started down. "Ow!" moaned Jan again. "My ankle. I can't stand on it."

"Sit for a minute," Joe said. He looked at her ankle. It was bruised, already swelling. "Hold on to me. We can still make it to the Humvee."

They limped toward their Humvee and saw the Broadway and Avenue A bridges through the dust of the crumbling older buildings. The bridges were sagging, their abutments gone, sloughed off into the restless Necanicum. The First Street bridge and abutments looked solid, but to get to it they would have to backtrack behind the Bridgetender Tavern and the Convention Center. The wooden deck and walkway had sunk. The tavern had tilted on sunken pilings toward the restless Necanicum. The banks of the river were flattened. And worse—the water level was rising even as they watched. The Humvee in the Ace parking lot waited for them in vain.

"Shit!" exclaimed Joe. "We can't make it across in time. Even if we did, the surge would catch us before we could get past Avenue U, or to the Lewis and Clark road. And those bridges will be out, anyway." He thought the Cove would magnify the tsunami effects. Tillamook Head would split the wave, forcing a higher volume into the Cove. It would roll down all the avenues like a flood. But Avenue U would be the worst, and the mouth of the Necanicum would be no better. Tsunamis loved funneling up coves and river valleys; that also magnified the effect. It was why the Japanese called them "harbor waves." The Lewis and Clark road was not reachable. The 101 Neawana Bridge at Twenty-Fourth would be toast. Farther down Broadway, the Neawana Bridge held, but a line of power poles lay across it like tossed Jenga sticks. If all they had to weather was rising water, it would be worth the chance, but he knew the flow would kill them. Even the Humvee would not save them. They left it.

"What are we going to do?" Jan was breathing hard, gritting her teeth against the pain.

"We go to the Wyndham. It's still standing. Let's go!" They made for the building, hobbling and tired, watching for the coming tsunami. Wood power poles were down everywhere, especially those encased in concrete at the base and holding transformers. They were snapped off at head height, and power lines snaked across the roads.

A transformer spilled its oil on a cross street at Dooger's. They continued up Broadway. A desultory neon sign, then another, fell across Broadway at Columbia in front of them. The Times and Funland signs had finally given in to the shaking and gravity, their corroded bolts not up to the task.

Joe and Jan broke through the Funland Arcade and out the back door across Columbia to Avenue A and headed for the Wyndham. They made it in a few long minutes.

Joe calculated the time. He remembered the experts gave them between five to ten minutes for an early small wave to hit. That must be what he saw in the Necanicum. The crest would build for fifteen to twenty minutes. Then the monster would hit. It would come as a possible fifty-five-foot surge. If it was going to take twenty minutes, it was close now. Up on the Prom, he checked the west guest doors. Locked.

"Shit!" exclaimed Joe. The word was appropriate now.

"Would you stop saying that!"

"Sure. When we are out of it."

"This is a damned tsunami, for God's sake."

"Tsunami!" he said, thinking fast. "I have to break this door somehow."

The Jones were no spring chickens. Time had dulled their abilities. They were tired, breathing hard. Jan was near the end of her strength, and Joe was close, too. Now they needed to get around or through the doors. Joe looked for a way. It was obvious; they were glass paned. Break it down!

"Wait here!" He ran a few feet south and grabbed one of the heavier, sharper rocks from the front garden. "Stand back!" he warned, in case these were laminated safety glass. They were. The rock bounced off. However, the aluminum frames were susceptible. He bashed at where he thought the lock was.

"Joe?" Jan held her Glock out.

"Right." He stepped back. Jan aimed and fired three shots through the lock plate. Joe wrenched the door open.

"C'mon. We got to move." They climbed through the damaged door and into the dark interior. They found the stairs in the weak light and started up. Jan hopped on one foot. Fortunately, most of the guests had left before they died; they met no clothed skeletons. The air was stagnant and dank but smelled only slightly of decay.

They made it to the fourth floor before Jan gave out. They found an open door to one of the penthouse suites on the southwest corner. Their view was to the west and south down the Boardwalk. Joe guessed they were about fifty feet up. Thank God there were no bones here. Some of the balcony doors were open, including this one. Occasional air and rain had blown through.

Panting and exhausted, they were in time to see the tsunami arrive. Seen from fifty feet above the Prom, it looked like light and shadow cast through a massive louvered blind. The ocean seemed to sigh. As the mass of seawater slowed when it reached the sand, then came together, the sigh became a loud muttering. The first surge rolled in, hit the Prom seawall, and recoiled. They watched in awe and fear as the ocean then rose up in a towering wave over 100 feet high, spanning the entire pale blue horizon. The Jones had to look up to see the top. "Tsunami," Joe muttered.

It crested at over a half-mile out and smashed into Tillamook Head, then was reflected and refracted. The surge crashed into the beach at the cove first, scouring out tons of sand and rock. It turned into a muddy howling mess and flowed to shore in a roaring rush. The sound of the wave was almost painful. The roar of the surf in winter was loud, but this thundering was unbelievable. They saw the surge smash into the foredunes up toward Avenue 1, blasting froth fifty feet up. It stalled, surged again, and crested the dunes, where it rolled to the Prom, smashed into the seawall and balustrade, and threw up another fifty feet of froth. It smashed into the three condos they could see to the south. The surge was partially reflected, and it roiled around the condos. But the ground floors were inundated.

It crested the Prom by ten feet and rolled down the avenues into the Necanicum valley, smashing anything that got in the way. Cars and houses that had lost their footing in the earthquake made way. Joe glimpsed the marauders' bus disappearing off the Prom, pushed by the unimaginable force of the tsunami.

"Are we safe here?" yelled Jan.

"We're about to find out," Joe yelled back.

Without a dune in front of the Windham, the surge blasted foam up from the Prom seawall sixty feet in the air, spraying the Jones with cold, salty water. The surge rose up and topped the Prom there by fifteen feet, smashing its violent frothing way into the ground level of the building. The Wyndham was a massive building, but they felt it shake like another small earthquake had hit. They watched as the surge raced down Avenue A in a ten-foot deep river, seeking to meet itself surging up the Necanicum riverbed. Joe ran out and down the hall. Jan heard him using their firearm "key" on a south-facing suite. The reports were loud in the confined space.

"What are you doing?"

"I want to see this. The suite here has a good view east."

Jan hobbled in to find him out on the balcony, looking over the houses. They watched the wave fill the valley. Over the tops of lower waterlogged houses, they saw the turbulent, vengeful mass wreaking havoc—rolling, pushing the rivers back, rushing up the valleys and creeks. Swirling chunks of driftwood banged into the building three stories below as the tsunami rose even higher. The Prom lights disappeared.

The Neawana, Neacoxie, and Necanicum surged backward under the onslaught, and the wave carried debris from houses down the lettered avenues. The houses they could see on the cross streets were flooded but not carried away, but those in the main path of the surge were gone. Most higher houses in sight on the south Prom were flooded on the ground floors. The 40-feet high and 200-yard wide foredunes dampened the initial speed of the flow.

At first, it seemed the Pacific had risen permanently. The water rose to just a story below their floor, flowing down Avenue A. The decorative poled lights on the Prom were barely showing. The valley looked like a boiling lake, with only the top floors of the hotels on the Necanicum showing. Then, the level over the Prom lowered. The rush eased. Leveled. The decorative lights and the balustrade showed, then the walkway itself.

They felt safe seeing the first surge abate. For a while, following waves advanced and retreated, covering and uncovering the Prom. Waves rebounded off the bigger buildings and east hills and battered what was left of the town. Chop, cross-chop, and whirlpools formed as the wave and rivers collided and threw debris at anything standing.

Gradually, the surge stabilized, and the ocean ebbed and returned to normal levels. Whitecaps danced restlessly.

The river valleys were now experiencing massive flood events for miles upstream. Pent-up river water periodically followed the retreating tides and flowed in rushes through what was left of the town, washing much of the destruction out to sea. But much remained, clogging the streets—broken pieces of houses, cars, couches, beds, the personal property of the original inhabitants being tossed carelessly around. The debris created dams against the pilings of both the standing and collapsed bridges. Gas and oil sheened the flow. Joe figured that most of the seaborn debris would find its way back to the beaches in later storms. This was going to be a mess. The seaside beach would be contaminated for a long time.

They waited. The water level swirled, waned. Natural tide waves came. They were coming close to the turnaround. They could see the big condos on the Prom, survived but waterlogged. Big sheets of laminated glass lay on the soggy sand.

The north brick façade on the Sand and Sea Condo had failed. Its ground floors and those of the neighboring condos were hollowed out by the crashing surge. The dunes were cut through in spots by the rushing water. Most of the foredunes were moved to the prom by the unrelenting current, carrying ocean water, sand, and debris as the surge pressed forward. What had not stopped against the Prom and buildings was dragged into the valley. Some were carried across the shallow valley and thrown against the hills.

Jan saw a massive piece of driftwood stuck against the balustrade in front of the Sand and Sea. She recognized it as one that had been partially buried just off the path through the beach grass. It had a large bolt in it. She often wondered how it came to be there. Jan could not help but wonder what would have been the toll if the city were inhabited. On an August day like today, it would have been thousands. She envisioned people running for their lives, the collapsed bridges stopping them. Live wires sparking. The wave catching them. She quit thinking. Not now. Not ever.

The Jones did not know it, but the cause of the earthquake was a catastrophic drop in the deep seabed where the thick Continental plate rode up over the Juan de Fuca plate along its 600-mile fault. Massive forces sought to correct over 330 years of compression. In just a few minutes, the Continental plate moved fifty relative feet west at the fracture line, releasing unimaginable amounts of energy. This was caused by the eastward drift of the Juan de Fuca plate and by the viscous drag of the crust by the asthenosphere at depth. A tsunami wave formed as the Pacific sought to level itself after being subject to the seabed drop. At over 500 miles per hour, the rolling wave raced toward Seaside's 3-mile front. It was followed by secondary waves, like ripples when a rock is tossed into a calm pond. When the waves reached the shallow water fronting Seaside, they merged, slowed, and rose up, carrying over two-hundredths of a cubic mile per mile of disturbed seawater. Enough to temporarily fill the Necanicum valley with rushing water twenty feet deep.

Most of Seaside was built on a sand dune spit created over the previous 4,000 years. The spit rerouted the Necanicum from its original outlet at the cove toward the north and, in another 1,700 years, had moved the Necanicum even farther north. Now the confluence of the Necanicum, Neawana, and Neacoxie creeks was two miles north of its original inlet.

Subsequent ebbs and surges rolled in and out over several hours. As the tsunamis ran in and retreated, the backed-up water followed each out in a massive flood. The river and two creeks combined to scour out the bay. The river was now a 200-yard wide linear channel 10 feet deep. The sand once there was now a mile out into the Pacific.

The Seaside dune was deep. The water table was twenty-five feet down. The seismic waves traveled at hundreds of miles per hour through the sandstone and mudstone over 120 feet below. The surface waves were somewhat attenuated by the sand.

The several-minute shaking and liquefaction had not reached the foundation levels of the Prom buildings. The sand remained packed under them. But the foredunes were moved, flattened, and cut through by the tsunami in places, and the Prom was under several feet of sand and beach grass in places. The slurry was banked against the lower floors of the condos. Some decorative light poles stood in soggy dunes. It had taken several hours for the surges to abate.

As the Jones waited, they thought about their Humvee and their truck back at the Survivors Motel, the thing that saved them from the Bugs. The thing that saved Wanda. The Jones waited out the onslaught. It would be a long walk back without the Humvee. What about the other Survivors?

CHAPTER 21

Survivors Motel

At the motel, the Midders were relaxing on the back deck. Devon had taught the girls how to play chess. In the ages before electronic games, board games like chess were prevalent. As time became less important, chess became interesting again. It was originally a strategic game simulating war. Checkmate! The king is dead. The kingdom is yours.

Teressa pushed her pawn forward. "Here I come," she said triumphantly.

"Not so fast, sister. Knight takes pawn."

From across the plowed and planted field, in the trees, a flight of sparrows burst out, flying randomly. The Necanicum shuddered, like in a heavy downpour. The girls looked at each other. More birds took flight. Crows called noisily. Then, a bang emanated from the ground. They stood. John and Mary came over.

Then the shaking began. The ground rippled. The highway cracked. The Necanicum rose and fell, sloshing around like a washing machine. The Midders fell to the deck, which bounced as if trying to throw them off. They held on to the deck rails. The initial hit was the worst. After a long time, the shaking subsided. The ground returned to its stable self. The river flowed like before. The motel held its place, although it was now sloped a little toward the river. The Midders stood. "That was the Cascadia earthquake," said John. "A tsunami is coming. We need to get out of here. This is an inundation zone."

"Where will we go? How much time do we have?" asked Mary.

"Up to the Head. From what I remember, we have maybe a half-hour," said John.

"The Lakes are in their upstairs apartment with Alima. We need to get them. The Jones are in Seaside, God help them. That's going to be a mess," said Mary.

"Where is everybody else?" John asked.

"Devon is in his room, reading," said Teressa.

"Terry and Wanda are in Cannon Beach. That one is going to be bad, too," said Vanessa.

"What about Bob, Dennis, and the Morris'?" asked Mary.

"I don't know. We need to move now. They're tough. They'll survive. Let's get the Lakes, Alima, and Devon, and go." John was adamant.

Devon came out. "What was that?"

"Earthquake, the big one. A tsunami is coming. We need to get to high ground." John stayed adamant.

"We're well back from the beach. Are we not safe here?" wondered Devon.

"No." Across the channel came Dennis and Bob. With them was the dog. It immediately went inside to its den and looked out at the Survivors like she thought they should find shelter, too. Dennis and Bob were cutting firewood. They stowed the tools and came up to the deck. They looked worried.

"It will be coming now! We have just ten or fifteen more minutes. A little longer, as it will take another few minutes to get up the riverbed," insisted John. They looked at their vehicles resting on the broken asphalt. They had survived.

Teressa came down from the apartment with Alima. "The Lakes are staying. They are not going. We could not convince them."

"We can't leave them," said Mary.

"We can't force them, either," said Devon.

"They may be right. The force of the water here will be less than at the coast. You remember the tsunami videos. Inland there was less damage." John was rethinking his original thought. "The surge will push debris from Seaside up the channel. Still, it may be something Survivors Motel can stand."

"You're damn right it can stand!" Stan stood like a rock at the door. "I am staying!" Behind him, Joan nodded her head.

"Quick vote. Live or die here, or run for it?" John asked.

The Tillamook Head was less than a mile away. The interchange held up. The cars were ready.

Stan suddenly said, "Where are the Morris'?"

"I think making baby Morris in their suite," offered Teressa.

"How do you know that?" asked Mary, but she had heard them, too. Sally was loud. "Never mind. They will come here. We will talk about this later after . . ."

The Survivors turned to a growing cacophony.

Alima was scared. First, the shayatan. Then the cyclone, then wrecked on the shore. When she came with Dennis to this place, it had just been attacked by bad men. Now, an earthquake and tsunami. She was familiar with this phenomenon. It petrified her. This place was unlike her home in Manila, though. There looked to be a lot of land between them and the ocean. Yet she looked up the valley in fear.

Devon stepped up to her. Mary watched. In a surprising display of affection, he took Alima's hand and said, "We will be safe here. God will protect us. He will protect us all." There was something about this woman. She did not pull back. *She is somehow reverent*, Mary thought. She had heard her previously, quietly praying in a language she thought was Tagalog. She knew Manila was predominately Catholic. Yet she also had a feeling that Alima was not Catholic. Her name was Arabic. It did not matter. They were Survivors. Alima was a Survivor.

Alima felt at ease with the Lakes, and even Devon. They were easy to be around and had knowledge she did not. They seemed to understand and care for her. What would these people think when she revealed her religion? She was beginning to think it would not matter to them. Would it matter to her? Would Allah understand? Then, the massive sound of the approaching tsunami interrupted her thoughts.

There was no vote. They stood on the deck and watched the river fill back up and breach its banks, spreading over their crops, rising even as the tsunami rushed toward them. They heard the muted roar of surf moving up the river, pushing the remnants of Seaside toward them, growing louder and louder.

CHAPTER 22

Honeymoon Suite

Bill and Sally felt the shaking from their honeymoon hideaway house just 100 feet away from Survivors Motel. The house was abandoned. No bodies were found. They had claimed it as their honeymoon suite. It had taken a little effort to make it into a livable love nest, not the least of which was getting over the feeling of trespassing. Now they were comfortable. Having sex in the motel was problematic. Sally was a screamer. Now they lay spent. Life was good.

Then, a bang made the bed bounce. "What the hell?" yelled Bill.

"Earthquake!" Then the rolling and shaking hit. The bed, with them in it, rocked across the floor and banged into the wall. The house cracked, and plaster fell from the ceiling. Furniture bounced and fell. It seemed to go on a long time. The house held together. When it stopped, Bill said, "Let's get dressed and head to the motel. We need to worry about a tsunami."

CHAPTER 23

Cannon Beach

Terry and Wanda stood together in the warm sand and hazy sun, looking out at the sparkling Pacific from near Haystack Rock. The massive 235-foot sea stack was a remnant of lava flows millions of years ago, caused by the same geological volcanic events that created Tillamook Head. The Humvee was parked up at the top of E. Gower Ave. They were sightseeing, starting at the First Street park, taking some time for themselves. It was peaceful. They were getting used to the silence. Even the contented muttering of the ocean was muted.

Then, a bang. The ground shook. The sand rippled; dust blew up. They held on to each other, staggering around, trying to keep from falling. The shaking continued, and the ocean shook and sprayed. The sand became like quicksand. They fell and crawled up to higher ground. The earthquake went on for a seemingly long while as they held on. Haystack Rock shuddered and spalled off loose rocks. Then, the shaking slowly eased. The tide began to rise.

"There will be a tsunami soon. Maybe fifteen minutes."

"Where is the high ground here?"

"South. We got to run for the Humvee." Terry had saved her from the Bugs; he had saved her from the lions; he had saved the girls from the marauders. Now an earthquake and tsunami. Could he save her from this? Wanda was at the last of her ability to rebound. She stood spell-bound.

"Let's go." He pulled her, running, splashing through the remnants of an underground creek that was not flowing now but backing up. The ground was depressed, forming a "V" that ran up to Hemlock. The concrete outlet was gone. They made it up the ramp to the Humvee.

The Humvee was upright, but the road was a mess. They climbed in and bounced over the broken asphalt, trying for the Haystack Scenic Hill Viewpoint. As he turned at Hemlock, Terry saw a problem through the dust of fallen houses. The road was gone; a twenty-foot deep chasm had swallowed Hemlock Road just short of the hill holding the Hall-mark Resort. The underground creek had collapsed into a cavern. Now they had to do something else. The Tillamook Head or south on 101 was higher; they were the only ways now. To get to the Head or south, they had to go down into the Ecola Creek bed. Would the bridges be passable? Terry guessed that the Highway 101 bridge was their best chance if they had to go north. It was newer, better built, and relatively short. They were closer to the Fir Street bridge, but he guessed it would be gone, and it was ground zero for the coming tsunami.

He headed south on Hemlock and took a left on Dawes and a right on Spruce just before the rift. He drove as fast as he could, the tires close to the chasm, and hit the throttle. They cut through a yard and a fence and plowed between and over some thin alder and through some salal. They bounced through and over the culvert onto 101. Maybe south would be clear. Nope, the overpass and highway had crumbled into the collapsed cave across the road following the underground creek bed. Most of Sunset Street was slipping into the chasm, which was now fill-ing up with trapped creek water.

Terry turned north. They sped toward the Ecola Creek bridge. The Humvee bounced over the broken asphalt like a big, cumbersome dancer. Wanda was thrown around inside her seat belt.

That bridge held, barely. The abutment had sloughed away from the deck, but there was enough left for the Humvee to span. The southbound lane was broken, a gap showing the pilings poking up through the deck. Some of the northbound lane remained. Terry aimed the speeding Humvee toward it, and they hit it with a bone-jarring bang. The Humvee bounced on all fours. Above the howling of the Humvee's engine, Terry heard a massive roar. He risked a look as they passed over the creek, the right side tires scraping the bridge barrier.

The creek's water was rising rapidly. A wall of dirty, frothy seawater rose up not 100 yards away, roaring like a thing alive, carrying pieces of houses and restaurants. Cars and a tumbling tourist bus rolled ahead of it, crushing, pushing the copse of thin alder trees aside. The Humvee was moving as fast as it could go, but Terry pressed harder on the pedal. Highway 101 started to rise. The leading edge of the tumult slapped at its wheels.

Up the 101, the Fir Street overpass was gone, covered by a massive landslide. Half the hill had sloughed off, 100-foot tall trees across the road like broken chopsticks. They lay atop thousands of cubic yards of scree. Broken mudstone piled high in front of them.

Terry and Wanda stopped on Highway 101 and watched helplessly as the rising cauldron flowed up the hill behind them. Terry looked for a path, but the overpass was hopelessly blocked by the massive slide. Rocks and trees covered the road. There was no way to get over or around, even with the Humvee. They were trapped.

"We got to get out of here!" Wanda was panicking. "We can climb up there." She pointed.

"No. We're safe here." Terry checked his own panic. "We passed the tsunami sign back there. See, the wave is slowing. When it retreats, we can drive back and up the off-ramp." He looked back. The bus was not in sight, now under several feet of ocean.

Wanda watched fearfully but trusted Terry. Just another thing to be saved from. Then, as she sat, something shifted in her. Yes, Terry had saved her, but she was the one who survived. She was the one who persevered alone in the dispatch room. She was the one who backed away from the lions. She had help, she knew. But it was she who did it. She was strong. She was part of Oregon State law enforcement. And most of all, she was a Survivor. She thrust her shoulders back and straightened. There was only so much adversity that could be tolerated meekly. Needing, trusting others to survive was not the way. She would survive or not, with or without their help, but she would not be frozen again.

Terry noticed the change in the set of her body, noticed the pursed lips, noticed the clear eyes, noticed the look of fear leave her face, replaced by a look of determination. He smiled.

The surge slowed, stopped, and abated just feet from the Humvee. They sat and watched the flow surge and ebb. The trees near the creek began to show. The bridge uncovered. It was completely collapsed now. A bus lay at its pilings.

Hours later, the lower road uncovered. In places, the off-ramp was washed out or covered by sallow landslides. Pieces of houses and logs from the beach cluttered it, but it was passable. They started down and then up to the highway, skirted the edge of the slide, and continued up to the Head. At the Cannon Historical Wayside, Terry had to skirt around close to the hill on the east side of the road; the west side of the road had slid off down toward the ocean. Trees lay randomly pointed down the slide. The Humvee clawed perilously close to the drop-off. Wanda watched with stoic gaze at the now-visible white-capped ocean as Terry fought the wheel.

"Want me to drive?" she smiled. "Looks like you're having a problem."

"Hah! Ain't nothing. Nice to have you back."

"Nice to be here, alive anyway."

Then the way was clear.

"Your turn," Terry said.

Wanda laughed and grunted as she maneuvered the Humvee around washouts and slides, around fallen trees, and back to the motel. Terry was proud, something he hadn't felt in a long time.

CHAPTER 24

Seaside

Joe and Jan watched the waves subside. The floods abated. Aside from the destruction, all was as it had been a few hours ago. Yeah, aside from that, thought Joe. "All right, now we have to make it back."

"How? The bridges will be out. I'm pretty sure the headland between us and the Survivors has collapsed over the highway. We got a problem."

"Yeah. I have an idea. Let's see about the Humvee."

"It is toast. Soggy toast. The seawater drowned it. And I cannot make it down there now." Jan's ankle looked like a burned loaf of bread.

"Maybe not. If I get to it fast enough, I can take out the glow plugs, crank any water out. Replace them and start it up."

"You actually think so?"

"I have to try. Remember, there were a lot of cars salvaged after Katrina. Even after being underwater for a long time. I think if we get it going, I can drive up to the Prom. That looked like it survived. The light poles are standing. The inland roads we can see from here are covered with wrack and power poles. I pick you up, then we go over the golf course. Plow around the river to the north and west and then up to the

Survivors on the flood plain. The Humvee is made for stuff like this. The diesel tank is sealed. The engine is watertight. The only thing will be crossing the river sometime before Survivors Motel."

"Tsunami!" Jan exclaimed, copying Joe's remark. "What have we got to lose? If it doesn't work, we can always walk." She caught herself. "Maybe not right now, though. Yeah. We need the Humvee." They hopped down the stairs. Jan brushed the sand and water off a wet bench, sat, and waited.

Joe walked down the broken Avenue A and cut over toward the First Street bridge, through the parking lot and past the Convention Center, which had held up well, even with a mass of debris and driftwood piled against it.

He crossed the bridge to Holladay, which was clogged with the remains of several houses. The river was backing up from the partial dams at the Twelfth Street and First Street bridges. The center span of the Broadway Bridge was now just a pile of broken concrete in the river. This was going to be harder than he first thought. The Holiday Inn and Rivertide survived, but the 1914 Gilbert and Kerwen Buildings were crumbling into the roadway.

He got to the Humvee. It was pushed into the hardware store but was upright. Joe popped the hood. "You know what? I think it will start without checking the glow plugs. This thing looks sealed tighter than . . . well, it's sealed." He talked himself through what he knew about the engine configuration. The air intake was angled down, so water would not have flowed in. There was no way he was going to service this beast right now, anyway. It would either start or not. He sat on the wet seat and found the start switches and took a breath. The plugs heated up. The engine cranked. It started. After a little sputtering, the noisy, smoky, diesel-fueled monster came to life, blowing water out the exhaust. He backed out and rumbled the steaming beast over the First Street bridge, over wires, and around poles. Over to Avenue A and up to the Prom. He found Jan waiting, looking out at the suddenly higher but sunny, calm sea. Just another day for Mother Nature.

"This is bad. I was beginning to talk to myself," Joe admitted. "Somebody knew what they were doing when they designed this critter."

"You talk to yourself all the time. Usually, nobody's listening but you," laughed Jan. "Let's see if it can get us home." Relief filled her voice.

"Maybe I do, but you're listening now. Let's think about this," said Joe, in imitation of Bill's mantra. "The bridge at Avenue U will probably not be serviceable. Even if it were, the next bridge will probably also be down. And the headland, as you noted, will probably have slid over the highway and into the river there."

"What were you saying?" Jan laughed again. "Oh, I get it. You think we can skirt the river through the golf course. There's going to be a lot of debris there."

"Hah. Actually, I think we can go farther up the cove. There are houses and roads there past the bend in the river. The elevation is higher there. Maybe we can get around it."

"Well, we'll know when we get there."

They got in and started out, drove up onto the Prom and turned south.

The Prom was remarkably intact. The balustrade held. Lots of sand covered the walk, but the Humvee handled it OK. Driftwood banked against the balustrade and what was left of the dunes. The Humvee was sometimes a tight fit, but there was enough room. They passed the big condos. The ground floors were gutted. Sand and grass-covered up to five feet of the bases. The Prom benches held, but the garbage cans were washed down the avenues. Past Avenue G, the forgotten marauders' bus was washed down and impaled on the bridge barriers. The killing house was gutted, folded down on itself. "You know," shouted Joe over the noise of the Humvee, "I'd forgotten about that."

"That's good. Forget it again."

Further south, the expensive houses still stood. What was left of the dunes resided in their front yards, filling up their ground floors.

They got to Avenue U and continued up Beach Drive toward the Cove. There, the tsunami had blown massive old driftwood logs up onto the road. There was no way to get through.

"Tsunami! We have to backtrack. I have another idea," said Joe.

"You sure we shouldn't think about this?"

"Ha, ha! No more thinking. Just doing."

Joe drove the Humvee down Avenue U. As he expected, the bridge was down. Some flood wrack pushed up against the rubble, making it into a small leaky dam. The Necanicum was backing up behind it. "OK. We follow the golf course, scoot alongside the river here until we see a way to cross. Somewhere after the headland slide."

Jan looked out at the waterlogged sod and said, "You sure we don't want to think about this?"

"Nope." Joe drove through the fence and over the putting green and down onto the sodden grass. He artfully dodged around or sometimes over the scattered debris. The flood had carved clear paths here and there. As he said, the Humvee was made for this. However, the stands of beach pine and hardwoods survived. This was a problem; the Humvee was formidable but could not knock down trees that even the tsunami hadn't. After a few aborted tries, Joe managed to get around the slowly backing up Necanicum. In a few hours, the river would fill this area. He saw it on the news several times when winter rains flooded the plains here.

Racing the flood in slow motion, they made it onto the flat near the Circle Creek Campground, which was beginning to fill up. The Humvee was churning through the muck admirably. The Muddy and Shangrila creek banks were almost flat. The Humvee waded through them without getting the Jones' feet wet. They went alongside the rising Circle Creek. Ahead of the backing water by a few yards, they found the old highway. Then came the massive wall of debris that had been pushed up from Seaside. It was deposited at the headland slide, diverting the Necanicum into Circle Creek. The wrack ran all the way across to Rippet Mountain. With backwater sloshing around the wheels, Joe searched for a path.

"There!" pointed Jan. A break in the wall showed. Joe backed up, aimed for the break, and floored the Humvee.

"Tsunami!" they yelled as the vehicle smashed into the area between the broken roof of a house and an uprooted tree. They banged over the mess, got high centered for a second on a chunk of driftwood, and then burst through and stopped. They sat stunned. The way was suddenly clear. They found the old 101 and crossed to Rippet Road. The road was cratered but provided better travel than the marshy lea.

"Time to think," said Jan. "It would be better to cut over to the highway here."

"Good thinking. It looks a lot drier over there. And we're past the bridge. We don't have the river to cross here." He powered the Humvee up onto the highway. It was remarkably clear. They were on their way home.

CHAPTER 25

Survivors Motel

As Joe and Jan started from the Wyndham and Terry and Wanda started from the landslide, the Survivors stood on the motel's deck and watched the river. The Necanicum, which had been flowing out, now began to back up again, spilling over its eroded banks and snaking across the field. Then, the crashing roar lessened. After a while, it was silent. The Survivors waited.

Dennis said, "I'm going to take a look." He started for the Humvee that survived the bouncing.

"I wanna go, too," said Teressa.

"Me, too," said Vanessa.

Mary looked at Dennis. He saw their mother's concern. "We'll stick to the road. The Humvee can handle this. I'll return quickly if the tide is approaching. I think it's stopped." Mary nodded, but the sisters didn't see it. They were off and running across the road to the Humvee.

Dennis started north. After just a mile, he got stopped by a landslide past the bridge and the Knife River Quarry. He got out and looked through the brush and trees to the soggy expanse. He was close enough to see what had happened. A mass of debris was stacked up at the bluff landslide just before the Circle Creek Campground. The wrack continued across the flat all the way to the high ground that rose up to Rippet Mountain on Tillamook Head. Driftwood, pieces of houses, and uprooted trees cluttered the landscape. The tide had retreated, but now the river was rising. He guessed the Avenue U bridge had a debris dam. *How deep will it get at Survivors?* he wondered.

As he watched the water rise, he saw movement in the wrack. "Look! There!" exclaimed Teressa. Dennis followed her pointed finger. Blasting through the mess was a muddy Humvee, churning violently. Inside were the Jones, bouncing around inside their safety belts. The Humvee stopped and sat for a minute, then climbed up to the road. They heard Jan say, "Well, look here."

When they got back, another Humvee cruised down the highway. Inside were Wanda and Terry. They were all home.

But the river continued to rise.

The Survivors stood on the deck and watched the river creep closer. "We need to move the Humvees up to the overpass," declared John.

"No, we don't," asserted Stan. "During previous winter storms, the bridges were dammed up with fallen trees. It was raining hard, and the river was running high. It did not reach here."

They watched. The water flooded the field and reached its max, the flow overtopping the debris dams. The backup did not reach the motel. Stan smiled. "Told ya!" he gloated.

On the coast, nature seemed in a hurry to erase mankind's creations. Seaside, Gearhart, and Cannon Beach were largely destroyed. The buildings that had survived the force of the earthquake and tsunami were subject to seawater inundation. Molds and mildew were now at work in the breached houses, buildings, and businesses.

The violence of nature tilted Survivors Motel and partially submerged their crops. They assessed the damage. They thought the water was mostly fresh, from the Necanicum. Only time would tell if the veggies survived. The motel could be straightened; it was stiff enough to stay whole.

But that was for later. In the evening, the Survivors listened to each other tell their scary, colorful adventures. As Wanda told of the monster tsunami chasing them up the road, an aftershock hit. The deck rolled with an easy motion.

"What the hell?" mumbled Jan.

"Aftershock," said Bill. "There will be more. But I think the worst is over. No more tsunamis. We just have to wait it out." The aftershock did not last long, and nobody was knocked down.

"These will happen for a while," added Bill. "It will be nothing like the first one and will not produce any waves. They will be less and less until we can't feel them. It's just the land adjusting to its new shape."

The Survivors sat together in thought. Each was silently thankful for their safety.

Then Devon spoke. "I've been thinking. How can I—we—thank God without preaching or begging?" He screwed up his courage and offered, "I would like to say something here. I do not want to offend anyone, but I feel the need." He looked around at the Survivors gathered on the slanting deck.

Jan started before Joe or Terry could ask any questions. "Go ahead. We all know where we stand here. No judgment, no conflict."

"Right," Joan added. "Keep it together folks . . . Survivors."

"I just want to thank God for keeping us safe. No begging. Just . . . being grateful."

"All right, that's good enough for me," said Terry. "I had the same thought as the wave was chasing us up the road." The Survivors laughed.

"You know, I didn't use to think much about how or why things happen," Devon continued. "I always left it to God. Until the Bugs, the marauders, and this catastrophe. Now I think God has a hand in it, but not in the causation. We can't see His Hand ourselves. I have a habit of prayer, asking God for guidance. I don't look at it as begging, like, 'Save me Lord!' Yet I have always asked for something—strength, courage, some sort of ability. I see it is maybe better to have a conversation. Not an argument. Not to say, 'You know, I think you screwed that up.' Not to cry about our lot in life.

"But . . . there's nothing wrong with asking, 'What were You thinking, God? What were You thinking when billions of people were being killed, murdered by these godless . . . Bugs? Why did you let that happen? Why did You let the marauders survive? Why did You let the earth move under our feet? What have we done to deserve this?' I have asked these questions, and at the risk of sounding vain, I get this answer: 'I did not cause those things. They are the work of free will and physical forces. You survive on your own strength.'" Devon stopped and looked around. "But I heard inside my heart and without volition, 'Sometimes My hand is lightly on the scale.'"

He stopped, his head down as if in deep thought. Joe thought of his decision to take the gun out on the first day. The happenstance survival of the group at Survivors Motel. Yeah, there was something there all right. But it required their action. The Survivors needed to act to make it to the "scale" in the first place. He remembered two quotes from somewhere in his past: "God helps those who help themselves," and "Fortune favors the brave."

"Maybe so," Devon glanced up at Joe with a smile, like he actually heard what Joe had been thinking.

Alima observed Devon. She knew instinctively that he was a holy man. He did not seek to rule, merely to guide. Somehow it felt natural. Unlike Islam, which required Jihad and the struggle to gain Allah's blessing. These people who accepted her so readily seemed natural. Was this really the way Allah wanted it? Were Allah and Devon's God the same entity? Could she already be blessed? Could a person actually converse with God? She knew you did not converse with Allah. You simply obeyed His commands or suffered His punishment. She had heard this kind of god discussed before, in the Old Testament—a jealous, vengeful god. But the Bible and the Koran were written by men. She felt herself becoming enlightened, reaching for some elusive truth. Was this a good thing, or a trick? She awaited an answer.

Devon noted Alima's confusion. He was sure now that she was a Muslim. Yet she seemed sincere in her seeking. As the others accepted him, he knew they would accept her and allow her to have her own beliefs. Devon thought he knew more about the Mohammedan beliefs than she did. Muslim women were mostly excluded from the Koran. It would be interesting to discuss this with her at another time—the right time.

CHAPTER 26

Year Three

Enemy

It was October. Over two years had passed since the day of the Bugs. No aliens had appeared. No more marauders. No more earthquakes. No more tsunamis. No other survivors. The Survivors were healthy again. They had some leftover aches and pains, but everyone was functional. No toothaches or heart attacks. The garden survived and was above the river now.

They breached the dams at the Dooley and Avenue U bridges and opened the road to Warrenton. This was a monumental engineering feat for the Survivors. They salvaged backhoes and a timber claw, which remarkably survived the tsunami at high ground, and managed to break up the debris formed behind the bridges. The Necanicum ran freely in its new channel, at least until the Broadway rubble. The banks had sloughed to almost level but were now being cut again by seasonal flows.

The Humvees were able to ford where the roads were washed out. As the rains increased, and the river rose, the Survivors brought gravel from the Knife River storage and created riffles so the Humvees could cross the rivers. The Survivors became expert heavy equipment salvagers and operators. That they didn't need to watch for other vehicles or obey any laws was a bonus.

Then, the diesel in the underground tanks began to go bad, and the fuel began to gel. No amount of biocide worked. So they salvaged the next best thing: gas-powered Hummers and Jeeps. They really liked the armored Humvees, so they kept them anyway. The Jones kept the Ford.

Eventually, the Survivors had a collection of top-of-the-line four-wheel-drive vehicles. The gas in the underground tanks was slowly going bad, but it was still serviceable. The vehicles ran rough, but they did run. *At some point*, Joe thought, *we will have to salvage older cars*. They would run on stale gas.

The big box stores at Warrenton had survived and held supplies for the time being. They had their pick of anything, no cash needed. But the Survivors were learning to get along without them.

Things were back to another new normal. The Survivors adjusted and remained in the motel. These were comparatively good times. The Survivors were relaxed but always somewhat on guard.

And there were pregnancies. Wanda was at six months; Sally was showing. Life was good. But not for long.

Dennis and Bill had gone into Warrenton to look for more winter clothes. Stan remembered how to shoot an M16, and Devon could now shoot with accuracy. In fact, he was the best shot with a long gun around. He had a steady hand. Even Bob had to give him his due.

Joe, Bob and Terry were hunting along the upper Williamson Creek. Since the tsunami, they were leery of clams and the slowly repopulating crabs. Fish was nice, but a juicy steak was good,

There was slushy snow at the head of the old logging road where Joe was waiting. Bob would call him to bring the truck and its 10,000-pound-rated winch to the kill. They had just bagged one of the feral cattle that roamed the forest. The meat would see the Survivors through another month. Canned Spam and tuna will only take you so far.

Rendering the kill was done in the field so the sensibilities of some of the Survivors were not offended. And they needed the break from the motel. Too much closeness.

Bob had taken a stand with his 7mm mag, about 100 yards off the road. Terry had driven the cattle into the killing zone, and Bob had dropped one cleanly. Terry was slogging over the ice-laden spruce and Douglas fir needles, through ferns and salmonberry scrub toward the body. Bob lost sight of Terry for a minute as he dipped into one of the rills feeding the creek and a salmonberry bush got between them.

When Bob saw him again, something wasn't right. Terry was staring at a point on the face of a cliff on the mountain about eighty yards away. Bob could not see what it was. Trees and brush were between Bob and the cliff. All Bob could see was Terry's back, but he sure wasn't on track for the kill.

Then, Terry fell. Just collapsed. Bob could see no reason.

Bob started down the slight slope toward Terry. When he got close, he looked to see what Terry had seen. As he did, a violet, almost black light shone from the face of the mountain, and Bob saw the most amazing thing.

Two beautiful people appeared. No, not just beautiful—angelic! Perfect physiques, golden skin, calm demeanors, smiling with beautiful intent. Dressed in fine silver threads. These had to be God's angels. He had a sudden and surprising urge to worship them, to sit at their feet and learn, to discover the secrets of the universe. He started toward the angels but stumbled in the thick underbrush and fell into the creek. It was shallow, but it was cold and stunned him into awareness. What the hell was he doing?

One of the figures pointed to a long tubular mechanism toward him. It was similar in shape to a rifle but had a small globe where the ammunition magazine should be. A small flower of violet light flared. The fir tree in front of him suddenly developed a hole. There was no sound, no smoke. The hole simply appeared. The matter was eliminated without any consequence.

Bob put his head down under the bank. A movement in the air sounded like a sigh. He instinctively knew he had to remain hidden and avoid looking at the angels. He and Terry needed help. Joe was up on the road with the truck and an AR15 gun from the shop. After the marauder incident, they did not go anywhere without protecting each other. He could call Joe on the walkie-talkies they had for communications now. But what could Joe do?

Another hole appeared in the bank above him. The angels—or demons, he now thought—could just keep shooting whatever it was they used until he was hit. A hole in him was something he did not want to think about. He mentally slapped himself. He needed to start thinking of these beings as enemies. He looked behind him. The rocks in the creek had holes in them. This "gun" they used was pretty damned powerful. He slid to his left. A hole appeared where he had been two seconds later. For a second, the water in the creek was disturbed. No splash; it looked like it imploded a little, like a drain had opened and closed.

He had to do something quick, or there was going to be a hole imploded in him. Again, not something he wanted. Bob grabbed the walkie-talkie. The range was advertised on the boxes as up to five miles. He was a lot closer than that. They worked for what he needed. He called Joe's channel.

Joe was with the Hummer, waiting for Terry's signal. He would then drive to the location of the kill, if possible. If not, he would get close enough to use the winch. It had several hundred feet of aircraft cable rated at 1,500 pounds.

The walkie-talkie made a noise. He picked it up. "What? Where are you guys?" Joe heard Bob's voice. It was not the confident voice of the man he knew.

"Joe, Joe! We're under fire. Terry's down. Something I've never seen before. Makes no sound. Goes through rocks and trees like they were nothing. We need help. I'm pinned down. God, there was another shot, close. I haven't much time left. Hurry!"

What the hell had happened to Bob? This was not like him. Joe could hear no shooting. But he did not question the Survivor's sanity. "Where are you? Where's the shooter?"

"I'm in the creek. Cold. The shooter is up on the slope of the mountain, about halfway up. I'm running out of room here." Then, as an afterthought, even while under fire, Bob retained some awareness. "The rate of fire seems to be about one every few seconds. They seem to know where I am, even out of the line of sight. They could get me any time now."

Joe sighted through the scope, scanning the mountain face over the old logged area. He found Bob cowering in the creek bed. Why was he not shooting back? He could not see Terry. But nothing was out of place. No sharp reports hit his ears. He saw Bob flinch, but there was no evidence of an impact or report. He scanned farther up. Nothing. Just rocks and scrub.

There! He saw the shooter's weapon aiming. Only that—just the point of the gun showing through a break in the tree line. It was steady, lined up with where Bob lay. "Bob, backtrack, backtrack! I see it now."

Bob skidded back as a hole opened where he had been seconds ago. How did they do that? There was no line of sight.

Joe saw the dim black flash. All he could see was the barrel of the weapon, a speck 200 yards away behind a rock outcrop. It was a long shot for him, but the AR15 was very accurate at that range, and there was nothing else to do. There was no time. He settled his arm across the hood of the Hummer and sighted through the scope. The crosshairs found the strange black rod. He adjusted for the range and drop.

Joe could not count on a single shot to make them pull back; he was going to have to pull the full clip. The rifle could shoot 800 rounds a minute. A 30-round clip of 223 Remington bullets would exit the muzzle at 3,200 feet per second in a mere 2.3 seconds. Once he started shooting, the sights would not be accurate. He took the safety off, switched to the modified full auto, lined up on the rod, and pulled the trigger.

Joe had never fired a full clip. It was a waste of ammunition. But he knew the basics. He held the barrel down against the continuous recoil. Thirty rounds exited the gun so fast he didn't have time to breathe. The hood vibrated in tune with the hammering gun and ejected brass. Heat built up under the grip. In the following silence, Joe re-loaded and sighted on the target. The area where the black rod stuck out was hidden in the dust raised by jacketed bullets' impacting the rock in front of the rod.

Then, the air around the area moved with a hissing swirl. Joe blinked. It was there, but now it was not. There was nothing in his sights. No dust, no trees, no rock outcrop, no rod, no nothing. He scanned around and had to pull the magnification back to see the size of the event. A giant hole had opened in the mountain where the rod had been. First something, then nothing. No massive sound. No explosion. Just swirling wind, filling the void left by the disappearing matter.

Bob heard the AR15 spitting rounds at the maximum rate. He heard a rush of air, like a big whirlwind. Then nothing. No new holes opened for several seconds. He took a chance and looked up. At first, he could not believe what he saw. Then he saw Joe up on the road, also gaping at the sight.

Where the beautiful, strange people had stood, a 100-foot hole—or rather, a cave—had opened. One hundred feet of trees and rock had vanished; 100 spherical feet of solid matter was lost. The edges were discrete and even. Nothing in the surrounding basalt was disturbed. No explosion. It had been a silent event.

He looked again. No, not quite all was gone. He saw a black form of some type resting in the center of the void. It looked like a submarine's nose cone resting on the solid rock of the mountain. Like it was floating. It was matte black. There were no discernable features.

For several moments, the two men stared, unable to understand what had happened. Joe started down the slope to Terry. The man was trying to stand now but looked stunned. He was not moving well. Bob got to Terry first. He was trying to talk to him. Joe could not hear the words, but he could understand that Terry was not responding.

Terry rose and stood unsteadily. Bob yelled at him, "Terry, get a grip! Let's get the hell out of here!"

"What happened?" Terry mumbled. "I was doing something . . . What . . . The steer . . . Where is it?"

"Terry, we got to go. Come on!"

"No, the steer . . ."

Joe went over to him. Terry's eyes were glassy. He did not appear to be injured, but Joe thought he looked like he had shell shock. Bob tried to pull him away. But Terry was big and strong and planted himself. "No! I got to know what happened."

Joe was shocked at Terry's attitude. "What the hell?"

"Terry looks like he's stunned. He won't move. He wants to know what happened. I haven't a clue. Except I saw the most beautiful woman I have ever seen. I can't even describe her. An angel. God, she had me. I would have walked right up to her; except I fell into the creek. When I hit the water, some kind of spell broke. Someone up there started shooting."

"I heard your call, but I heard no shooting. I saw the black rod, though."

"Yeah. There was no sound. Look here at this tree. See the hole? It just appeared. No sound, no warning. Whatever they are using, it blasts right through trees, rocks, whatever." Bob stopped. "What the hell did you do that caused the mountainside to disappear?"

"If I had to guess, it would seem I got lucky."

"What?"

"I hit a bullet with a bullet. I'm guessing one of the jacketed rounds hit exactly when the . . . gun, if that's what it was, fired. It would be like putting a round into the barrel of a rifle just as the trigger was pulled. At an angle, no less. The odds against that are astronomical."

"But the woman and man are gone. Along with a bunch of the mountain."

"You say the weapon they used just opened holes in a solid tree with no sound. Well, what if the weapon exploded silently using the same technology, causing an area to cease to exist?"

"What in God's name . . . ?"

"I don't know, but we best retreat. Terry! Wake up! We got to go."

A slit of light appeared on the black monolith. It opened silently.

A white flag poked out.

She had no name. She was part of the Community. She was, nonetheless, an individual. She shared her public thoughts with the Community. She had private thoughts she shared with specific individuals. She knew what happened to the individuals who first tried to eliminate the savages that had somehow escaped the exterminators. In prefatory meetings, she was assured by the Keepers, along with the Community, that the exterminators would eliminate the savages, the odds statistically approaching certainty. She also knew that there was no such thing as certainty. Even with the end percentage of survival of the savages calculated as approaching zero, she knew there would be some left alive.

The Keeper's engineering of the triple helix XNA in a nano-spore was relatively difficult. Manufacturing the bio-automatons that had delivered of the spores had taken precious time. The world of the Community was now being affected by the singularity at the galaxy's core. The event horizon was imminent. The Community had to abandon the world sooner than expected. The manufacture of enough spores to cover this planet had also taken much of the Community's food supply, forcing an extended period of rationing as they traveled in the Mother Vessel.

The Community had run probability studies and concluded that the planet would be cleansed by this time. The Mother Vessel had arrived just weeks ago and dispatched several attendant vessels to survey the planet. This vessel was part of such a survey crew looking for likely places to inhabit and, peripherally, for survivors. Among several others, this small group of savages was discovered. The Community had camouflaged the vessel until an assessment was made. Somehow, these had escaped the primary weapon of the Community, and then the attempt to shoot them conventionally. But they would not escape her.

Here they were in front of her. Three ugly savages with primitive but deadly weapons. The Community was not startled. They knew the possi-

bility of such an anomaly. The Community now needed to exterminate these savages using more direct methods. By force of arms. One by one. The exterminators were gone, and no other method of exterminating these savages was acceptable.

How these pathetic creatures survived was unknown, nor was it relevant. The vessel was hidden so it would not cause the savages to flee before they could be exterminated. The Community could do that through dint of arms if the savages could be sedated. It was her duty to get their minds open enough for the Community to stun them.

The savages had learned little from the first encounter. The Community was so far advanced from these primitive beings that communicating with them was difficult. Their method of communication was oral, a clumsy language without depth. She learned it in just a few minutes after the weapon malfunction that destroyed the first attempt at extermination and made another attempt necessary. It was time-consuming and challenging to actually speak. But it was necessary to open their minds. She felt the Community within herself, calm and focused. Ready to strike.

The Community had not fought a war for over a millennium. After the null gun technology was invented, it became imperative to forge a lasting peace on their planet. Any further advancement in weaponry would, with high probability, destroy them all. They had managed to live in peace after the agreements and before the planet was threatened by the galaxy's core singularity. They needed this planet.

Individuals in the Community lived for as long as they wished in their temporal bodies. They had perfected the ability to regenerate tissue at will. She enjoyed the physical existence. The feel of another in close physical contact was exhilarating beyond the mental effects. She wanted to spend a few more centuries in this body.

An individual could also advance to the next level at will. Several had done so rather than look for another world. But it was an individual choice, not to be made by another, especially a savage. She was not ready to move on. Nor were the two lost in the null field implosion. What she saw in this world was the possibility of paradise. It would be theirs.

The Community had done everything in their power to exterminate the savages humanely without altering the natural world. The exterminators were not alive. They were designed to self-destruct on command. All had gone according to plan except . . . the first individual entrusted with the null field gun was unskilled. It cost them two lives. Their loss was still felt.

The savages would be exterminated! She stepped out.

"Humans. Let us talk together," she said in her best imitation of the emotion love.

"Don't believe your eyes!" warned Bob. "And don't believe your . . . anything that happens. These things can cast a spell. They are deadly. I think the closer they are, the more powerful the spell. That's why Terry is still stunned."

Together, Bob and Joe pulled Terry down behind a boulder. Terry was at last getting his bearings and let himself be moved. They poked their heads around the rock carefully, rifles first. The figure holding the flag came forward. Like Bob said, she was beautiful. Joe felt the pull. It was reassurance, safety, protection, hope, faith—a bundle of warm emotions. It was hard to hold on to reality. Joe started to move around the rock when Bob punched him. "Stop it!" Bob said. "I feel it, too. It's not real."

Then they heard it again. The most beautiful, melodic voice. They heard it both with their ears and in their minds. Warm, reassuring, trustworthy. In perfect English. She stood on a ledge beside the nose of the ship, looking small in comparison.

Terry's mind was working again. His commanding presence was rebooting. "Hell yes, it's real! Nearly killed me. Joe, you skedaddle back to the truck, out of range of the effects. Both of you sight on the lady and shoot if I fall again."

"What are you planning?"

"This human is going to talk to that thing and see what's what."

Joe said, "Just so you know, I did not feel the effect where I was. But I will be on guard."

"Cover me!" said Terry. He stepped out. Joe hustled back to the truck. Bob put the front sight of his 7mm on her chest. She did not move.

Terry walked out about ten yards and stopped. "What do you want?" he asked. He was fifty yards away, but she heard.

"To live," she replied. Terry heard it easily despite the distance.

"You're alive. What else?"

"This planet." Clear, beautiful, warm, musical, and chilling.

"You caused the Bug infestation?"

"The extermination. Yes."

"Why?" Terry was incredulous.

She almost sighed. "I will tell you a story. Perhaps you will then understand. We, the people of Athra, have lived in peace for the last millions of your years. We have evolved far beyond your ability to understand. Our planet is remarkably similar to this. But our planet is much older and near the center of the galaxy. It is within a few years of being consumed by what you call a black hole. We cannot stop it from happening. The effects have already caused our world to become uninhabitable. We have searched the galaxy for thousands of years looking for a home. This is it! One of a kind! You have no idea how precious this is."

"Get their minds open," the Community spoke to her. "Target the one on the hill also," she sent back.

"Before you react, I will pose this question. What if this planet was about to be destroyed by forces you could not stop? Suppose the next planet out,

the one you call Mars, was habitable. Indeed, the same as Earth. Suppose the planet was inhabited by billions of warlike baboons." The one in front of her was susceptible, but the one behind the rock was skeptical. And the one on the hill was closed. She felt the nearest one begin to open up. Waiting.

"I see where you're going with this. How many are you?"

"No, you do not," she thought. The Community shared her laughter.

"One hundred twenty-five thousand have survived the time of searching."

"If we were only the size of a city, like you, we would seek to occupy enough land to live."

"No. You would not. Think about this. Had we landed and asked your government for land to live on, what would happen?"

"There would have been a lot of talk and argument. But in the end, there would have been an arrangement."

"Now, when you found out that we can affect your minds, that what you do with electromagnetic radiation and senders/receivers we do with our minds—a form of what you call ESP—that our abilities and technologies were a million years in advance from yours. What then?"

Terry was thoughtful. "There would be trouble."

"More than trouble. You would seek our secrets. You would be fearful and then violent. We are very capable, but you would eventually destroy us."

"So you destroy us first."

"Yes." The same musically disarming tone. "It was not difficult to come to this decision. What we found on this world is abhorrent to us. A perversion of nature. You are worse than the warlike baboons I postulated. You kill animals for food. You murder and torture each other. You hate each other in the name of various nonexistent gods. You have created a miasma of revulsion in this world. You have added nothing. Indeed, less than nothing. You have abused this world. You were destroying it. You were covering this world like a plague. You were causing your own extinction. You were transient. You have no redeeming value." She slowed her condemnation before it alarmed them. It had the desired effect, though. "We do not know how you alone survived, nor how you managed to murder us. But this situation will be rectified."

Bob was now wondering what was happening. The Alien had not included him in the conversation. Joe was also curious. Terry was beginning to see her point. It was logical, after all. He felt the pull. Yet, somewhere in the back of his mind, his lizard brain stirred. The tone had become less musical in the last sentence. He felt like something was coming. A storm? No, but something . . . something.

"They are ready," came the thought. "Now!" She ordered the attack.

As if doused by a powerful anesthetic, Terry blacked out. Bob fell at the same time, a black haze covering, obscuring, erasing his thoughts.

Two figures exited the ship. Each carried a black rod. Blacklight flared. A sharp report followed; a single shot followed by a three-round burst from an AR15. Then another burst.

Joe could not hear or feel the words being spoken. That was a good thing. His mind was not completely open. Nevertheless, he felt the shock of the psychic blast as it felled Terry and Bob. He wavered. Blinked. A hole appeared in the window to his right. They were shooting at him! Instinctively, he pulled the trigger. The shot went wide. The report seemed to clear his mind somewhat.

Still, the mental blast had hit like a solid left jab. It felt like when he once fought in a Golden Gloves tournament in the old Portland Armory. He was hit with a nice combination by a much better fighter in the second round. The lights had dimmed, his vision telescoped, his knees buckled, and the canvas had leaped up at his face. All sound went away. He started hearing again at the five count. Someone was yelling, *"You can't quit now!"* He struggled up at the eight count, but the fight was stopped.

He felt the same shock now—just mentally. There was no referee to stop this fight. It was deadly earnest. He was up at the eight count. Small motes of light swam in his eyes. *"You can't quit now!"* something said. And he could not. The lives of his friends, of Survivors, were at stake.

He sighted on the figures standing in front of what he now recognized as a ship. The crosshairs danced with his unsteadiness. Hoping for the best, Joe squeezed the trigger on a triple. One of the figures stumbled, and both retreated into the door. The report and kick of the weapon helped to bring him farther back. The rod poked out of the door and blossomed again. A hole appeared in the hood right in front of him. They were getting better. He sighted on the door and squeezed the trigger in another burst of three. Maybe he could get lucky again.

He missed. Jacketed bullets sparked off the black hull to no effect. The rod pulled back. The door closed, and there was no indication of it ever having been. Joe looked down toward Terry and Bob. For a long minute, there was nothing. Then Bob stood, shaking his head. He looked around like he was lost and then walked unsteadily in a circle. Finally, he moved toward where Terry fell. Joe did not approach. Instead, he held his sights on the black ship.

After what seemed like a long time, Bob and Terry started back toward the Hummer. When they arrived, Joe was ready to go. They piled in, and Joe powered the truck away from the ship and mountain, spraying gravel and dirt as he held it to the road. A few minutes later, they arrived at Survivors Motel.

After the savages left, the vessel glowed with a violet light. The 150-foot by 24-foot vessel carrying 65 individuals slid out of the berth it had made on the mountain and rose silently. Then, it oriented itself and sped west, seeming to accelerate faster than possible. All the Community scout vessels were recalled to the Command Center on the large continent for consultation. The vessels were without arms, save for the null field guns. An extended scan of the world showed several more groups of savages. Their weapons were crude but effective. And they were accomplished warriors. Another strategy for extermination was necessary.

CHAPTER 27

Analysis

All at the motel had heard the far-off shooting. They knew it was not normal. What had happened? The hunters returned, and Terry quickly called a meeting. The Survivors sat around the main table, and Terry, Bob, and Joe recounted the event, each from his own perspective. There was silence at first as each wrestled with the account. Was it accurate? The result of a hallucination brought on by an air-born mold? A joke? Eventually, each concluded that this was real. The weight of the reality was crushing. Terry watched as the Survivors began to understand; then he stood and opened the meeting to discussion.

"Hey! You're bleeding!" exclaimed Wanda. There was blood on his pants. He looked down at the oozing flow. There was a hole on his right hip. He had felt the wetness but attributed it to laying on the slushy ground.

"Devon, we need your help," Wanda cried. "Lay down, you big lug. I need to take a look."

Terry reluctantly laid on his side on the table. Wanda loosened his belt and pulled his pants down far enough to expose the wound. Terry started to say something but wisely held his comments to himself.

"From the angle, it looks like it happened while you were on the ground. It nicked the hip bone, and there's a lot of flesh missing from your kidney to hip. What happened?" Devon packed the wound and started to bandage it. There was no way to close it. At least from their descriptions, there would be no foreign material in it to worry about.

"I didn't feel a thing," mused Terry. "That's what Bob was saying. This is a result of the aliens' shooting."

"You guys have to explain that," said Jan. "Are there any more hits, Joe?"

Bob and Joe were checked out. No wounds. Terry was remarkably healthy. He had no shock like he would have if hit with a bullet. The aliens' weapon was at least painless. He got up, pulled up his pants, and said, "OK, let's get to work. We need to know what the hell happened and what the hell we are going to do about it. It looked like the ship was buried; maybe it crashed. I don't think it is going anywhere soon."

Bill Morris then offered his time-tested thoughts. "Well, let's think about this. We know three years ago there was the UFO scare and what was called the XNA find. We can assume the XNA produced the things we called 'Bugs.' Now, we can assume with assurance that the cause of the Bugs was—is—the entities you met."

Bob added, "They . . . she said there were perhaps over 100,000 of them. If they get together, we are doomed." He was still shaking from the effects of the stun.

Dennis thought and said, "That may be a lie. Let's get to the physics. You say they tried to shoot you with some sort of ray gun. Bob noted the rate of fire was about once every few seconds. And they were not especially accurate, even though they seemed to know where he was. Even without a line of sight. That would seem to say they were not expecting resistance. They have advanced targeting ability but poor manual aim. And their ability to make war is limited."

"That's right. She said we were unexpected; they must have expected a near 100 percent kill rate. Their weapon of choice was the Bugs. They may try again."

Wanda paled and said, "I can't do that again." Then she straightened, remembering who she was. "Whatever happens, we will survive. Like Dennis said, that may be a lie. These things apparently . . . lie!" she said with assurance.

"Nothing has happened yet, Wanda." Terry stood and consoled her, forgetting his wound. "You are right; we will survive."

"How?" Devon asked. It was the thought on everyone's mind.

More silence. Then Dennis asked, "How did you manage to destroy the ray gun?"

"I let fly with a full clip on auto. My guess is one of the rounds hit the ray gun just as it fired. The backfire blew the ray gun's 'clip.'"

Devon offered, "An impossible shot, or was there was a hand on the scale?"

Silence as the Survivors processed the thought.

"Maybe it was God's hand," Joe said as he looked at Devon, "but it was my bullet, my gun."

"How many of these ray guns did you see?" Dennis asked.

"Three."

"It seems they do not have many of them. Or people to shoot them. If they did, they would simply have overwhelmed us without the mind trick. And they need stationary targets. Maybe they are afraid to use them."

"No, I think they just can't use them well. It is their weakness. They need the mind trick to allow the guns to be used without resistance," said Joe.

"Great. All we have to do is lure them out of their ships and into a firefight and cut them to ribbons. Shall we issue an invitation?" John half-joked.

"I don't think we have to. They will be hunting us soon enough," noted Bill.

"All right!" Terry said. "I have some combat training. One thing I remember is that you plan for what the enemy can do, not for what he might do. We are going to have to guess what they can do. Any thoughts?"

Once again, Bill offered, "Well, let's think about this. They can plant their Bugs again, but that takes another year. And they cannot be out when the Bugs are because the Bugs would probably attack them, too. They won't do that. They can fly their ship, but I'm guessing from your descriptions that they cannot shoot while flying. The doors have to be open. My guess is they will fly in, hover or land, blast us with the mind trick, and shoot from the ship through their open doors. I don't think they will risk shooting from outside the ship unless we are stunned."

"They are not good shots. I mean, they probably can't shoot accurately on the fly. They need stunned targets," Joe said. "Unless they practice."

"If they bring all their ships, we are doomed," said Mary.

"Remember when the UFO sightings were reported in the tabloids?" Bill said. "It was world-wide and reported as night traveled around the world. One of the conspiracy blogs opined that there were few actual UFOs. That they traveled silently and swiftly, avoiding all detection except occasional visual sightings. And those were just because the UFOs passed between a viewer and some light source. They were like a shadow. Anyway, it was guessed there were actually between ten and twenty. Government sources declined to comment, making the statement seem true."

"That does not agree with what the lady said. She said over a hundred thousand were here. A lie?"

"How big was the ship you saw?" asked Jan.

Joe answered, "We only saw what was sticking out of the mountain. It looked like a nuclear submarine nose. I'd guess it was fifteen, twenty feet in diameter. What do you think?" he asked Terry and Bob.

Terry answered. "Yeah. About that. I had the feeling it was bigger. Maybe a hundred feet long."

"If these are ships of a sort, they could carry a lot of people," said Bill. "Their technology, if their propulsion and power systems are so far ahead of us, could account for big numbers in a few ships. We are only now beginning to understand the nature of matter, time, and gravity. The theory Hawking had, that all matter came from an infinitely small dot and all matter needs to be 'observed' to exist, would argue we don't know shit. Pardon my French."

Terry laughed. "Well, let's sleep on it. Tomorrow, Dennis and I will go to the Astoria National Guard Armory and Camp Rilea Military Reservation and see if we can bring back some heavy artillery. Then, we go see what the black ship can handle." Something gleamed in his eye. His wound was forgotten. He would be a formidable enemy. The aliens had made him one. And the Survivors needed a warrior. "Meanwhile, we will set up sentries. We can't have these things sneaking up on us."

Alima listened but was confused. Aliens? Yet the Survivors believed the men. Was this something Allah had done? She would wait for direction.

They retired for the night. Tomorrow would be a new day.

That night, Joe and Jan talked. There was no moon, but the stars were bright, glittering behind slow-moving clouds. It was cold and getting colder. They snuggled under heavy blankets.

"Well, ain't this a bitch?" said Joe. "We just can't seem to get out of trouble."

"Makes you wish for the old days, huh?"

"Not so much. But we were just beginning to adjust to a major reality shift. I kind of liked the way we are now. No clocks, no traffic. No bosses, wars, crime . . ." He stopped at that one. "Well, anyway, it was peaceful until the marauders and these crites came along. But we should have suspected it, I guess."

"Yeah, twenty-twenty, right? What could we have done, anyway?"

"Not much. It probably happened the best way, anyway."

"Yeah. Something is going on we can't see."

"Let's hope it continues to be in our favor."

"Should we be thinking about foil hats?"

"Maybe. There were some people who swore by them. But radio waves pass through metal, and brain waves probably would, too."

"We could do an experiment. We could make foil hats."

"Or a Faraday cage. But my memory of radio waves is that the lower frequencies pass through matter more easily than ionizing radiation."

"There's something else, too. Remember our talk about the marauders? The cockroach theory? Well, to these aliens, we are the cockroach."

"There's just one big difference. We did not invade them. They invaded us. I don't think we are cockroaches, either," Joe said, laughing. "We ain't gonna figure out these aliens anyway."

"Well, we could sleep on it."

"Amen, let's sleep."

The next morning, after much more thinking on the part of the Survivors, they sat at the table in the early light. According to Devon, they had to resolve an issue.

"Respectfully, what if this is God's will? Should we be doing something to help or hinder that? The aliens said we were causing the sixth extinction. That we were destroying the Earth. Could this be God's way of 'fixing' that?"

Sally interrupted, "That thought goes against God's hand on the scale. Doesn't it, Devon? And we cannot trust that the aliens told the truth. Number one, they have their own agenda. And number two, they are definitely wrong about us destroying the earth. There have been five major extinctions on this earth in the last many hundred million years, according to present-day knowledge. These were caused by catastrophic events from which the evolved life could not adapt. Events such as meteorites caused landmarks like Hudson's Bay, the Gulf of Mexico, the Mediterranean Sea, and the Aral Sea. And even the smaller craters noted today. These caused severe climatic changes very quickly, and climatic changes last thousands of years. These extinctions were probably helped by mass infections. A virus has been found in Antarctica that no animal, even sharks—and they have remarkable immune systems—is immune to, including us. It has been there since Pangea was the dominant land-mass. We are mere pinpricks compared to those events. The earth itself survived. Changed, for sure, but here we are."

"I read a while back about how some scientists were worried global warming was about to melt some Arctic ice that held even more green-house gas," added Bill. "Well, how did that gas form, and how did it get frozen in the first place? Sure wasn't us."

Teressa chimed in. "But we have been taught in school that what we are doing is altering, if not destroying, the Earth's ecosystem."

Mary answered her daughter, "Maybe. There were close to eight bil-lion people living on this planet, eating, breathing, heating, and cooling themselves. Clothing and housing themselves. It had to have some im-pact. But the earth itself recovered from all previous catastrophic events. Did they teach about the five known past extinctions? What about ice ages, comet and meteorite impacts, the tilt of the Earth's axis (10,000 years ago it was 90 degrees from the sun, or zero declination; now it is around 22 degrees off), core spin variation, polarity reversals, and a whole lot more? The orbit's variation, apogee and perigee changes? Sunspot activity? These are energies the size of which are unimaginable. All without man's doing. Remember, this world was once a mass of molten rock some billions of years ago. Look at it now. In another bil-lion years or so, it will be incinerated by the expanding, dying sun."

"Number three," Sally continued. "It's true some believe like the aliens, that we are . . . were . . . living in the sixth extinction, using up resources faster than they could be replaced. The population becoming unsustainable and eventually starving. But neither they nor the aliens know the future. We might have pulled it out in the end. No chance now to find out."

John said, "Mary and Sally are right. But the past is gone, and the fu-ture is made by our decisions now. Back to God's will. If He wants to destroy us, it shouldn't be too hard for Him. But I don't think that's it, and I don't think we should allow ourselves to be . . . murdered by these . . . godless things." His voice trailed off. He struggled to control the re-vulsion he felt. "Remember, Devon, they denied God's existence."

"Point taken," said Devon. "I think God put us here for a reason. Let's see what it is."

"All right," said Terry. "Let's get back on task. Let's go around the table. Say your piece, and let's get moving."

The unanimous consensus was to fight for survival. There was no doubt; even Devon agreed they should not let the aliens have the Earth. They had beaten the Bugs and the marauders and the tsunami. They would beat this.

But how?

Alima listened to the exchange. She saw some sort of extraordinary strength in the Survivors. Allah did not bring the aliens. They professed no god. There were no shayatan. And what Devon said hit her hard. If Allah wanted to destroy her, she would be dead. Mentally, she started making her own way. If Allah disapproved, He could easily destroy her. And He had not destroyed the infidel Survivors. Why?

"Let's talk about what happened to Terry and Bob. How the hell did the aliens do that?" Mary asked. "You know, they said they were advanced by a millennium over us. That we were mere savages compared to them."

"Yeah, so?"

"It has been argued that although most of our brains are used, we humans consciously control about five to ten percent at any one time. Suppose they control a lot more, say eighty percent. We know our neurons and synapses put out about ten to fifteen watts of power. Electro-chemical actions produce a measurable magnetic field and low-frequency electromagnetic radiation. If the aliens are advanced by some exponential degree and can combine their power, well, that is a lot of power."

"We actually produce twenty to twenty-five watts," said Devon. "I had to take some classes on brain function . . . before. The cerebellum, or upper brain, has about seventy billion neurons. The latest I read said that although our bodies use almost all of our brain to function, only ten percent is under voluntary control. The brain operates at 10 to 100

cycles per second, very slow compared to a radio station, which operates at thousands of cycles per second. There have also been some actual
brain-to-brain interfaces documented." Devon had their attention now.
This was something he knew could be of help.

"I saw some of the work on BBI," continued Mary. "There was also
something about the possible exponential ability of the brain, or artificial enhancement from machines."

"Right. It was thought that if we used all the theoretical interactions,
it would be more than the atoms on the earth. So if these aliens have
progressed as far as they say, and they can work together to amplify and
project thoughts, they have a terrific advantage," Devon said. "To spec-
ulate, these things can then project emotion into our brains."

"So, how does that work?" asked Terry.

"Well, speculating again, they could project conflicting emotions.
Like love and hate. Safety and danger. All at the same time. My guess is it
would paralyze our brains, effectively causing some circuit breaker-like
shutdown to protect from madness."

"So, they use that to knock us out?" guessed Jan.

Sally said, "Remember, they first used a sort of love spell to lure
Terry and Bob in. It would seem they have a wide capability and a lot
of power. Suppose they could focus energy to swamp our senses. Ten or
fifteen of them would produce a lot of power." She thought for a moment. "No, not our senses. Like you said, our emotions. Remember the
feel-good spell before the knock-out punch."

"Yeah," Joe said. "I felt it just like that, even over a couple of hundred
yards away. I nearly passed out, too."

"That means they have a limit based on distance. Like a light close
up can blind but is only a speck at a distance. We need to stay away from
them," said Devon.

"Easier said than done. They also have an ability to track us, even
sight unseen," said Bob.

"My guess," offered Devon again, "is that they see into the infrared
and ultraviolet spectrum better than us. They need no special electronic
amplification like we do."

Terry went to the bottom line. "They are declared enemies. We have to fight them. We have to defeat them. There is no other choice."

"But how?" Devon asked again.

CHAPTER 28

Preparing

Terry and Dennis went to Camp Rilea first. Dennis drove, and Terry sat at an awkward angle, his wound was hurting now. They had passed by the camp before without a question. Dennis was sure it was just a training facility with no major arms. They had to try, though. What they were looking for, they didn't know. Something that could challenge the alien ship, something as powerful as they could find. They drove past the guard post, parked, and entered the red-roofed armory through an unlocked door. Bones and the scraps of uniforms of servicemen and women were strewn about the door. Brass casings winked in the weak sunlight. Inside, it was dark. Using flashlights, they found the ordinance room. It held plenty of M4s, M17s, and lots of ammo.

They went out the side door. As their eyes adjusted to the daylight, Terry let out a startled grunt. "Huh! What the hell is that?"

Dennis could not believe it. On the parade ground, amid the countless open Bug pits in the hard-packed earth, was a monster under a tattered camouflage net. "That's a goddam Abrams battle tank! How the hell does this backwater training camp rate a battle tank? Maybe it's a training prop?"

They searched the base for anything else they could use. In another camouflaged area outside the PX, there were six more tanks. They were not decommissioned.

"What was this all about? Did the Army decide to get ahead of a possible invasion? Was this something to do with the UFO sightings? Is that why there were so many uniformed personnel here? Did someone in the government actually think ahead, and much more, actually do something?" Dennis wondered.

Dennis remembered the history of the camp. It was sometimes used for combat training. It fronted the Pacific Ocean for live-fire exercises. The tanks must have been brought in by the sea at night, not to have been noticed.

"It doesn't matter how," Terry said, as if reading his thoughts. "Can this thing be used?"

"I don't know. But I heard of these beasts in action in Desert Storm. They had a kill rate of about four hundred to nothing against the Iraqis who had top-of-the-line Russian tanks. More were hit with friendly fire than were hit by the Iraqis, and even those were not disabled. Let's see what's in this thing."

During their search for instruction manuals, they discovered records of crews of tankmen stationed at the camp. None had survived, but it became apparent that someone was ahead of the curve in this. However, they had not foreseen the enemy's Bug capability.

It took hours of manual reading and jerry-rigging with stabilized fuel, recharged batteries, and help from Bill on booting up and reading the software from a disk found in the Commander's office, but the Abram's tank finally rumbled and clattered into Survivors Motel, howling like a fire-breathing dragon.

It was early afternoon. The cloud cover was low, and the Twin Peaks were fogged in. The Survivors got a chance to see one of the premier fighting machines of the era. It was a true monster, 63 lethal tons of

1,500 HP rolling armored firepower. The Survivors stood around the beast in awe. Dennis explained the firepower as well as he knew it. There were three machine guns for repelling infantry, two 7.65s and one .50. It could shoot conventional explosive warheads and newer kinetic warheads. They were fired from the 120mm cannon. The kinetics, called long rod penetrators (LRPs), had rocket assist and were used in the Gulf War to overwhelming advantage. The LRPs were without a warhead and did not explode. They actually penetrated armor with such energy that they vaporized the interior of enemy tanks even miles distant. The Survivors decided they would try this on the ship.

Bill was thinking about the technical knowledge of the enemy. "We know that when the ray gun was destroyed, a massive amount of matter ceased to exist in a local way. Like an explosion without noise. Or an implosion. The gun itself, when used properly, seemingly caused matter to cease to exist—in a focused way. Like a rifle. The ship itself was not affected by whatever caused the matter to disappear. My guess is that the ship operates within a completely different set of technologies. It may be vulnerable to kinetic energy. But more likely . . . will not."

"Well, we are going to find out," said Terry. "We can't wait for them to come at us. That's another combat tenet. Always attack when possible. Dennis and I will go. Now, if we are not back by nightfall, my advice would be to move a long way away . . . quickly."

The Survivors sat in stunned silence as they took in the meaning.

"Terry. You got to say more than that. If you don't return, what about us? What about me?" Wanda stood. There was no panic there, but there was a need.

Awkward silence.

Then Joan spoke up. "Terry, we will not move. There is no place to go. You are either successful or . . . we are the Survivors!"

For the first time since the day of the Bugs, Terry was confused. He felt a wash of emotion. Like most warriors, he suppressed emotion. Do the mission. Do it now. He fumbled for a thought. "I . . . I . . . don't know . . . what to say."

"Good God, Terry," Jan butt in. "You're worse than Joe. Tell Wanda you love her. Tell her you will return. Comfort her . . . and us."

"At last, someone worse than me," Joe mumbled.

The feeling of dread eased. The mood marginally lightened.

Vanessa stood, "Remember Terry, we are Survivors, and we will survive!"

"All right," started Terry, getting his bearings. "You all know me. I'm not going to lie. I don't know what's going to happen. But . . . I do . . . love you, Wanda. And in a way, all us Survivors. Dennis and I will do our damnedest to make the aliens go away, one way or another. Can't guarantee anything . . . " He stood there uncertainly, not knowing what else to do or say.

Wanda ran to him. They embraced. Tears flowed. A dam of stoicism broke. Teressa and Vanessa ran to Dennis. Then, the Survivors came together in a common hug.

The comfort could not last.

"All right," Terry broke the huddle. "Dennis and I will see what's what. We will return, even if the gates of Hell open up."

"Hey, that's my line," complained Joe.

"Yeah. A damned good one, too." Terry and Dennis went to the tank and disappeared inside. The beast awoke and headed to its first alien battle. Live or die.

The Survivors watched the tank cross the river on the old train bridge and disappear into the woods. Stan took charge. "Now, we need to prepare. If any of those things escape the tank, they will meet their doom here. Let's check out what they brought back. There's lots of firepower and ammo. And watch the tank's path."

It was not long before the Survivors heard a tremendous double boom from up the Twin Peaks. The concussion shook the motel. Then silence. They gripped their weapons and waited.

Dennis drove the beast. He was getting the hang of it. They rumbled up the logging road to the ship's position. Terry armed it. The ordinance procedures were clear enough. The long-range aiming procedures were not necessary. That required GPS and forward observers anyway. This firing would essentially be at point-blank, at a big stationary target. Terry seemed able to operate the mechanism well enough.

The enemy was not there. After maneuvering the massive tank a mile up to the peaks, they found that the ship was gone. Were the aliens afraid or getting reinforcements? Where it had been, only a massive void remained. The ship had inserted itself into solid rock without disturbing anything.

"Damn!" said Terry. "I really wanted to try this baby out."

"You know; we should test fire it anyway. We need to see what it can do. And we need the practice. We should have done this before."

"You're right. Let's see what happens if we aim at that boulder a ways up from the hole the ship made."

"Yes, sir. We are loaded and hot."

They were stopped at the spot where Joe had fired at the ship. Terry looked at the monitor. Manipulated the controls. The servo motors engaged, the turret swiveled, and the barrel lowered until the boulder was in the crosshairs. The sighting mechanism showed that it was 412 meters to the boulder. All went silent save for the engine, which idled with a deep rumble. The sight stayed steady on target. Terry flipped up the cap over the firing button. "Let's see what this baby can do." He punched the red button.

There was a tremendous blast and whoosh, and the tank rocked on its treads. The round covered the 400 yards in a little over a second. It was not as silent as the enemy's weapon, and it was a lot messier. But very effective. The twenty-foot boulder disappeared in a massive blast. The shock wave rocked the tank like a parked car rocks when a semi blasts pass. It was impressive. When the dust cleared, the boulder and another ten feet of the cliff behind it were gone. Just a pile of rubble and swirling dust remained.

"Hoo-ah! What a weapon! If this doesn't do the job, I can't think of what would. How many of the rounds do we have, anyway?"

"The ammo box has a bunch."

"Let's get back and make a new plan."

"I'm beginning to like this beast. But it does not get many miles per gallon. We need to hunt up some more stabilizer and refuel."

Back at the motel, after a collective sigh of relief, the Survivors held another meeting. They sat around the table in the gathering dusk, and a lantern suspended off an old light pole softly hissed above. Moths flew around it, confused by the glow, unable to navigate.

The effects of the LRP were told with many adjectives. The Survivors believed Terry and Dennis. They had heard and felt the blasts from over a mile away. But the bottom line was that they were back to square one.

"Two things," offered Bill. "The aliens have not returned. If their intent as stated was to exterminate us, they should have been back quickly. They either have their hands full somewhere else, or they are uncertain of how to proceed."

"If what they said was true, they have enough ships to swamp us. They are working on something else. A better weapon? Firing ports in their ships?" said Dennis.

Joe had been thinking. "Probably both. There had to be some survivors in the military. Perhaps there is a war happening we don't know about. But in any case, we need to be able to defend ourselves. Now!"

"If that's true, they are not very smart. One of the things I remember from training is 'Bring the greater force on the lesser.' If I were running their campaign, I would simply swamp any resistance one site at a time, bringing all my weight to bear each time," suggested Dennis. Then he rethought, "Maybe that's what they are doing."

"She did mention they were at peace for a millennium. Maybe they have forgotten how to wage war. Or, there are several groups of survivors," thought Bill.

"More likely, they do not see this as a war," opined Joe.

"Doesn't matter. We still have to do something now," said Terry, pragmatic as always.

"I've been thinking more about the ray gun," continued Bill. "It has to have an effective range. It can't just eliminate matter forever. If that were so, every time they used it, there would be holes through the earth. It has to be limited somehow. We can we measure the holes where they shot at Bob at about 100 yards and the hole made in the truck at 400 yards. Perhaps there is a spread or tightening of the size. It could indicate the range. Maybe we can see a depth in some rocks."

"What will that prove?" asked Devon. "If they come with force, it won't matter much if we get holes punched through us at a distance or point-blank."

"From what Dennis says, the tank can be accurate at a mile within our ability. It's one of the things about battle. Can we see the enemy before he sees us? Can we shoot the enemy before he shoots us? If we see and shoot before they can see and shoot . . ." said Terry. Then he shrugged.

"The Abrams was not made to shoot like an anti-aircraft weapon. But if what we thought earlier is true, that the ship has to be stationary to be a shooting platform, then we have a shot at it—as good as theirs. Even if their weapon is effective at a long-range, they are not very accurate," said Dennis.

"Maybe an anti-tank weapon," offered Sally.

"Wait a minute. You said in order to shoot this ray gun, they had to open the door," said Jan.

"That's right. So what?"

"They are vulnerable when the door is open, are they not?" she continued.

"Right! Theoretically, they must be stopped or hovering as well. Unless they adopt firing ports," said Bill.

"I think the hull is capable of being altered. They have done it already. The door opened without a seam. They should be able to open ports at will. Still, if we can put an RPG through the door or a port, it will do some kind of damage inside," said Terry.

"RPG?" questioned Devon.

"Rocket-propelled grenade. Fired like a bazooka."

"Yeah? But who can shoot one?" They all looked at Dennis.

"Hell, anyone can. In Iraq and Afghanistan, the natives learned in about two minutes how to arm and target one accurately."

"Well, let's get some and learn how."

Terry and Dennis went back to Camp Rilea. The back dock filled up with weaponry. Bob and Bill went out to the site of the alien ship and the implosion.

That night, Terry and Wanda lay together in their room. It was cold, and they snuggled together for warmth. "Terry?" Wanda whispered.

"I'm here."

"Promise me you won't do that again."

Terry felt Wanda's need. "I promise."

"Thank you. But if you can't, know I will survive. I like what we have, but I won't die without it. I don't want you worrying about me."

"I know that. And I will keep that promise. I won't go running off without . . ."

"Good enough. But for sure you have to be around for the birth of your son."

"Son?"

"We'll see," she smiled in the darkness. Terry felt her smile.

"Yes, we will," Terry said with conviction. A son would be good, but so would a daughter. He meant what he said, and he would try. But he knew so much was out of his hands. There was so much he did not know. And he never before had such a load. Always, he had been his own man. He knew it caused his divorce. He couldn't change who he was. Or could he? Could he be changed by another's need?

Again, he mentally slapped himself. He had to be the warrior here. He could not flinch. Yet he felt he was different from before, laying here with this woman. This woman who loved him enough to let him be himself. As he drifted off to sleep, he felt a warmth he never knew wash over him. He shuddered. Wanda stirred and nestled closer. Terry struggled to contain this newfound joy. *Just in time to die?* he wondered.

It was raining the next day. The Survivors met again in the common room.

"OK. The Survivor think tank has been busy while you guys have been playing around," said Bill, aiming the comment at Terry and Dennis. "We have an answer to the question we posed earlier. Bob and I have been out to the site. We took a laser penlight. We found the holes made in the trees when the aliens shot at Bob. It looks like the beam went for about 500 yards. Then it just ended. It went into a fir tree and just stopped. Dead ended."

"So what does this do to help?" asked Terry.

"Well, their weapon has a range limit. We think it has to do with the rate of fire. We thought the rate of fire of their weapon would change how far it reached. Bear with me now. Assuming Einstein was right, and there is nothing faster, the weapon could operate at the speed of light. So the pulse to penetrate 500 yards would be about 3 billionths of a second. At that power, it seems to take about six seconds to recharge. Now, if they set the range at say, 100 yards, the rate of fire could possibly be 6 times faster. Say once per second. At close range, they could shoot like an automatic machine gun. They would not have to be great shots."

The Survivors absorbed the possibility silently.

"Their rate of fire may be due to something else entirely. The triggering may be set. Maybe firing too fast would overheat the gun. We have no clue. We just have to shoot before they do, at a long-range," continued Bill.

"One other thing. Assuming Newtonian laws apply to these beings, they will not be able to just zip in and stop without turning to jelly. Unlike science fiction. Assuming they are of our abilities, they will need to withstand less than five or six Gs. That means we will see them coming."

"Unless it is night," said Devon.

"Right, they probably do better than we do at night. But we will be on blackout mode."

"That's a lot of 'probably,' isn't it?"

"It's what we have. If they come with ten ships and night vision, well—it won't matter what we do."

"One last thing. Maybe the most important thing. They stunned us with their mind weapon. They will use it again. We have to hit them before they can use it," said Bill.

"Well, we have more weaponry we can use. And we will fire the first shot," stated Terry.

"Our turn," said Dennis. "Back at Camp Rilea, Terry and I found a stash of RPG 7 launchers and warheads along with M4s and ammo. We found the training instructions, also." Why the armory had such old but reliable weapons was still a mystery. Dennis still guessed something was suspected because of the UFOs. Spreading out the assets was just a precaution.

They would need to test fire to see if time had degraded the weapons. They left the Stinger anti-aircraft rockets alone. They believed that the UFOs would have no heat signature they could lock onto, or the ships would have been detected when the aliens spread their seeds. And the Survivors were after a big target.

The rain eased into a mist.

"Let's see what these things can do," said Dennis.

Alima stayed at the motel with Joan and Stan. The rest of the Survivors drove up 101 and turned at Rippet Road, went up to the old quarry, and gathered around Dennis. He set up an old door against the rocky hillside in an abandoned gravel pit to prevent the explosions from setting any fires. Then, he moved back about 100 yards. Dennis lifted the weapon.

"This is called a shoulder-launched man-portable light antitank weapon. This is the shaped charge and rocket," he said, putting the tubular tail into the launcher with a click. "It is an explosive charge shaped to focus the effect of the explosive's energy. It can penetrate steel armor to a depth of seven or more times the diameter of the charge—six to eight inches of steel. What it can do against the aliens' ship is anyone's guess. Its effect is purely thermal and explosive in nature.

"An RPG 7 comprises two main parts: the launcher and a rocket equipped with a warhead. This is a high-explosive anti-tank round.

These warheads are affixed to a rocket motor and stabilized in flight with fins. The launcher is designed so the rocket exits the launcher without discharging an exhaust that would be dangerous to the operator. In the case of the RPG 7, the rocket is launched by a booster charge, and the rocket motor ignites after only ten yards, so there is little danger to the shooter from the exhaust. However, it needs to be well-aimed. Nobody stands behind it. Questions so far?"

The Survivors stood silently in a semicircle. No one knew what to ask. Even Terry and Joe, who had some experience, stood mute. The lesson continued. "This is the launcher. The warhead and propulsion unit is armed like this." He pushed and twisted; there was an audible click. "It is now armed. It is essentially, for our purpose, a point-and-shoot weapon. Use the sights, like the M4. Like this. Stand back and to the side." Everybody moved, watching closely. Dennis held the weapon over his shoulder with his hand on the trigger. He carefully aimed at the door some 100 yards away. The weather was now cloudy, and no shadows formed. He pulled the trigger.

The effect was startling. There was a whoosh as the projectile left the launcher. Then another hiss as the rocket motor ignited. With astonishing swiftness, the rocket homed in on the door with a little exhaust plume. Dennis's aim was true. The warhead hit just to the left of the center. The piezoelectric nose sent a shock to the igniter, and the shaped charge blew with a shattering blast. The concussion was felt almost instantly, carrying the horrendous sound.

"Good God!" exclaimed Devon. "If that can't do it, nothing can!"

"Maybe. But we need to plan for what the enemy can do. I think everybody needs to be able to shoot the M4s, M17s, and this weapon. It is reloadable. We have over a hundred rockets. And in addition, we need to keep the Abrams ready too. Let's get to it!" said Terry. Explosions and small arms fire echoed over the land for most of the day.

Wanda and Sally stood back and watched but did not shoot. They were concerned about their pregnancies. They learned, though.

When they were back at the motel, Joan spoke up. "Now we need to think of something else," she said. "We have pregnant women here. They can't be part of a firefight. I suggest keeping them back at the honeymoon suite when and if the shooting starts."

"Alone?" asked Sally.

"I suggest Stan accompany you for protection."

"Not without you, Joan!" Stan interrupted. Imperative. No argument was to be entertained.

The Survivors set to making battle plans—a new and frightening thing. Devon thought, *These Survivors are random people thrust together by circumstances beyond their or anyone's control. Now they are tasked to kill other sentient beings.* Malevolent as they may be, the aliens were still human-like. Yet he saw the necessity. This was like the marauders. *Surely, God will condone our actions.*

They went to work.

That night, Joe and Jan sat outside in the cold mist and talked.

"I think keeping Wanda and Sally back is a good idea," said Joe.

"Oh yeah. Why?"

"Well, they're pregnant. Wanda is showing."

"What about me?"

Joe wondered what this was about. Jan was not afraid. She was not asking to be kept back. "What's going on here?" Jan smiled in the dark; Joe felt it. "You . . . you're . . ."

"Maybe, you stud. There have been no pills for a while now."

Joe was stunned. "Wow!" he began to stutter.

"All right, Joe. I don't know for sure yet. You can relax."

"We have an alien invasion. You drop this bomb, and you want me to relax!"

"Sorry. Yes, relax. We are together, no matter what."

Joe took a deep breath. "OK. But you better not do anything stupid."

"I promise. You, too."

CHAPTER 29

Attack

There was trouble. It was not something those who remained in the Community had ever experienced. Mistakes. Failure. The Community found these earthlings had a higher survival rate than expected. The projected kill probability was in error. Several pockets of resistance were discovered. The savages must not be allowed to repopulate. The Community did not have the will or the ability to compete in a population race. They did, however, have the ability to destroy the savages with superior intellect and weaponry. That one of the savages had somehow managed to propel a projectile into a null gun at exactly the moment of activation, physically damaging the return gate, was a statistical anomaly so far removed from probability the Community did not have a number that could be assigned. But assuredly, it would never be repeated.

Of the eight world sectors, the ones called Greenland, Africa, Australia, and South America were considered cleansed. The one they called Antarctica was barren. Another force was working on Europe and Asia. This force would cleanse the sector called North America, which was perceived as the most difficult. Populations subjected to tyranny were easier to sedate. The continent was large, and groups of savages had survived in several areas. The main groups of survivors were in the temperate zone. These savages were an anomaly, somewhat resistant to sedation. Surviving against overwhelming odds. Like insects, they thought. But far deadlier. An anomaly for a reason.

So far, there were thirteen known pockets of savage survivors in the NA sector—the most of any sector on this world. The strategy devised by the Planners was to use one vessel per pocket. The vessels were retrofitted with firing ports for the null guns. During combat with the savages in the large island Australia, which was also somewhat resistant, they found that the weaponry the savages used was ineffective against the hull of the vessels. Even the rapid-fire brass-coated explosive projectiles could not penetrate it. The hulls were designed to assimilate space debris using null field effects, something that was necessary while sailing the gravitational winds.

While the null technology could not function when the gun ports were open, the meter-thick carbon/tungsten/deuterium hull did prevent penetration of all but the most potent thermal projectile weapons. The savages did have greater weapons, but none were known to be functional at this time.

The ability of the Community to stun the inferior brains of the savages proved to be the best weapon they had. It had worked for most encounters, except for the savages in this place called Oregon and another called Texas. Some of those in Europe, Australia, and Asia were also difficult to stun, requiring the concerted effort of several Community members.

The pocket of savages the farthest west was near the greater sea at the forty-fifth parallel. These were the savages who had murdered three of the Community in their initial confrontation, the only casualties they had suffered so far. This force was sent back to exact revenge. They set the scanners for the savages' signatures. The null guns had to be fired manually. Their best marksmen were chosen.

They had practiced for several weeks. Firing from a moving platform was difficult, but they were ready. The range was limited to 100 meters. They would sweep in at ground level plus ten meters. One vessel in line with the other, the second one ready to clean up if the first vessel missed any of the infestation. They would rake the site, seeking the savage signatures.

They would move at thirty kilometers per hour. Pivot 180 degrees and re-sweep if necessary.

Using the gravity drives, it only took an hour to travel from the main staging area on the east coast. They came at night over the basalt promontory from the ocean, skimming the treetops at low speed. The scanners activated as they moved over the top. Several stationary targets were immediately located. The first vessel with ten firing ports dropped down to the attack. They readied the psychic weapon. The savages were asleep, susceptible to an overload of concentrated theta and delta waves.

CHAPTER 30

War

Bob and Joe were on the watch that night, with a commanding view of the valley below. They were able to see any approach of the UFOs. Weeks had passed since the initial encounter with the aliens, and it was cold. Daylight was short, and temperatures were in the forties during the day. Rains and winds passed through periodically. The nights were close to freezing.

Early guard duty is the worst and hardest job. When dark and silence are pervasive, it is difficult to maintain alertness. In the case of the Survivors, though, they could talk without worrying about detection. Nobody was coming on foot. They worked in pairs to help ease boredom.

The Survivors' thoughts were all the same. When would the aliens come? Hell, would they even come? Of course, if they were like humans, they would want revenge. But were they? Would they?

The plan had been set. Several trips to Rilea and local hardware stores had been made. Weapons had been assigned. Firing areas had been assigned. Flares had been assigned. The killing field had been set. Communications had been established using old-style handheld walkie-talkies. Now was the waiting time. They were cold and bored, and worse, they were not even sure the aliens would return. Or from which direction. The observation point up the old Tillamook Head Road was in a good position to watch the entire valley. But the aliens could come from anywhere.

Watching for a black, silently moving UFO on a black night was not easy. Hidden in the trees, covered by waterproof thermal ponchos, the sentinels watched the sky for a sign. Would they come over the Head, up the valley, or down from the Coastal Range? Or some other way? Straight down?

Bob and Joe were tired. Nonetheless, they stayed aware. The life of the Survivors was in their hands. They could afford no losses. None! If they were to become a viable community, there could be no life lost. Especially the women.

It happened just after midnight. The calm air was crisp with winter dew. The crescent moon was low in the sky. Bob grunted and stepped away to relieve himself. That would not happen for the next few desperate minutes. A black shape passed overhead. So silently that it was just luck it passed within a few hundred feet of the pickets. It was not fast, but it would be on the Survivors in minutes.

The attack had begun. Bob hit the emergency beacon and grabbed and shouldered the launcher as Joe was doing the same. There was no talk now. Only action. Their plan and training would be enough, the weaponry would be enough, or the end of the Survivors was at hand. If more ships arrived, there wasn't a prayer.

They aimed and fired. Rockets sped toward the ship.

In the motel and tank, the emergency beacons screamed. And the plan went into effect. Fourteen bodies reacted. Four split off and went to the safe house: Wanda, Sally, and the Lakes. Stan carried his M16.

Flares were loaded. Launchers were armed. Places were assumed. As with those up on the lookout, there was no talk. Fear and anger prevailed.

Like silent birds of prey, the first vessel homed in on the savages' sig-natures. The null field over the hull collapsed. The ports opened. The stun projection sequence activated. And for the first time in the recent mem-ory of the Community, they were ambushed. As the vessel dropped down to within stunning and firing range, before they could use the psychic weapon, there was a terrible blast in the aft section near the fusion power source. Then another. The hull was not substantially damaged, but the sonic wave stunned the gunners, and the gravity engine controller was affected. The vessel shuddered and dipped. The gunners were thrown off balance. More projectiles impacted the hull, dangerously close to the open ports.

From his vantage on port seven, the gunner watched as several bright flares lit up the landscape. He searched the collective memory for an ana-log. In an instant, he knew these were explosive armed rockets. And they were homing in on him. He was helpless to fire back. They were too fast. He scanned for signatures. When he did, he felt the emotions below. In their first encounter, he had felt the emotions of the savages, as had the rest of the crew. The savages then were confused and open to suggestion. How the lone one was unaffected and actually returned fire was unknown. But now, now the emotions were anger and fear. The blast of feelings washed over him like a wave from the sea. He shielded himself from it. But it was as strong as the Community's defenses. Normal mind-to-mind commu-nication between Community members was almost unlimited, depending on ion concentrations in the atmosphere. These emotions were so close as to be almost painful.

The explosions that rocked the vessel seemed to have affected it. The crew had shut down the gravity drive and were using the emergency re-pulsion drive. He surmised these incoming rockets would do no good for his vessel. All this he knew almost instantly. It happened within seconds. The Team shared this information almost immediately. They were am-bushed. Two hits in the aft sections of Vessel One. Several more mid-vessel. An immediate breakoff was ordered. The vessel stabilized and veered away.

Without the gravity drive to protect them, the repulsion drive could ac-celerate the vessel at rates that would turn the crew to jelly. For that reason, it was mechanically limited to three G acceleration. And this vessel did that. It was not enough. The rockets were now supersonic. The port seven gunners ducked down and watched the port light up. Another flare? Then more rockets hit. The concussive shock, heat, and light washed through the port and temporarily blinded him. He felt the vessel drop, felt the impact as it hit trees and rocks below.

The hull held, but one of the rockets had passed through port two. The blast had killed several gunners and affected the others. Another hit through an aft section port, and the repulsion engine stalled. It was solid state and would need to be rebooted. There was a protocol for that, but the engineers and technicians were also temporarily stunned by the blast. The interior of the vessel was not made to withstand this method of attack. It was not designed to be in a shooting war at all. There were no reinforced partitions or bulkheads.

He told himself he was safe. He reminded himself the hull itself was impenetrable. Even without the null field, it would distribute any thermal or kinetic force over the entire hull. The rockets' warheads were mere pinpricks, but inside they wreaked havoc. The controllers were not designed to withstand the compressive wave emanating from internal hull vibration. And the Team itself was stunned by the blast and concussion.

Up on the side of the Twin Peaks, Terry and Dennis watched through the tank's monitor as the first ship veered off, lit up by the flares fired by Alima, Teressa, and Vanessa. They watched as the RPGs launched by John, Bill, Devon, Jan, and Mary struck the ship. All of them! Good shooting! Although it was hard to miss a thing that large.

The ship wobbled and sank onto a copse of alder close to the field, near the river and less than a half-mile away. Dennis ground the gears of the Abrams and engaged the 1,500 HP motor. They started the sixty-three-ton tank for a shot at the downed ship and ripped through an old clear-cut, crushing anything in the way. Brush, small trees—it didn't matter; they need to finish off the wounded ship. They needed a clear shot. One not blocked by brush or trees. Terry watched the bouncing monitor, looking for the image of the ship. Another flare went up. And there it was, a massive black shape with small black rods protruding at various angles. He yelled at Dennis to stop.

The tank slid a few yards as the treads locked up, then settled. One of the rods turned toward him. He had only a second to spare. Now to see what would happen when the LRP round struck the ship. He did not want a glancing hit; it had to be dead on. He held the fire button like it was a bomb. The screen showed an open port. Maybe he could hit it. The crosshairs pinned to the soft light coming from the interior. He punched the fire button. The tank rocked back on its treads.

Through bleary eyes, the number seven gunner saw the machine coming through the local brush, looking like an angry metal animal. It stopped 400 meters away, within his range. The turret turned toward the vessel. Again, he searched the collective memory for an analog of the machine. In an instant, he had the answer. From archives of the wars millennia ago, a picture of a metal alloy machine that ran on a hydrocarbon distillate. It was slow and clumsy. It utilized a gas-propelled explosive projectile ejected from a barrel at sub-hypersonic speeds. Slow compared to the null gun, but dangerous, nonetheless.

The null field guns could easily incapacitate it. The vessel null field shield could easily negate the kinetic weapon. But the field was down to allow the ports to be open. The null field guns were set at100meters. His was the only port gun functional. He reset his gun for 500meters. He felt the Team move with him. It steadied him. He needed to fire before the savages. He aimed from the rest on the port. One shot at full spread should incapacitate the machine. He fed the hydrogen atom into the firing chamber. He triggered the gun. He felt the almost imperceptible disruption of the space-time continuum as a tickle on the back of his neck. The void held in stasis was allowed for a specific number of spins of the electron in the hydrogen atom to open the stasis field, creating a conical null field at light speed. The scientists knew the matter in the weapon's path went into the void. After that, it was just a theory. The consensus was that it went into another dimension. A moot question.

Now the field was down. As he fired, he saw the metal machine launch a projectile at the vessel. This would not be good. However, the engineers managed to close the ports and activate the repulsion engine before it hit. The port slid shut as he pulled the gun back. The projectile was deflected. Yet, it caused the collapse of several more null field components. The hull rang like a bell. And the repulsion engine failed again. They were vulnerable. A stun sequence would not penetrate the anger and hatred of the savages. The null field was reactivated. All other systems were deactivated. The savages must think the vessel was dead. The second vessel was approaching. That one could not let the null field down. An alternate plan was made instantaneously.

In the weak glare of the flares, Bob and Joe saw the tank start for the first ship's wreck. From over a half-mile away they could not see the port or the rod extend from the hull of the second ship. After the RPGs had impacted the ship with sharp concussive blasts, the night went silent. Then, the night erupted again, first with the dull flash and then with the roar of the cannon. A shooting starburst from the ship. At first, there seemed to be no other effect. Then, the ship seemed to glow. The glow ran the spectrum from infrared to ultraviolet. Then, nothing! No movement, no sign of life. The ship simply remained inert. It was now downed and shrouded in darkness. The smell of rocket exhaust, cordite, and molten metal wafted up to them on the night air.

The night went still, except for switching for fresh weapons and reloading the cannon. All eyes searched the sky for another ship. Would there be more?

Bob and Joe watched the scene below. Their rockets and tank seemed to have downed it.

"We got to get down there and help," said Bob.

However, the saying "no plan survives the first shot" was proven again. Another ship passed overhead. "Yeah. Right after this," yelled Joe. They sounded the warning again. Shouldered their rockets.

The plan basics continued as more flares lit up the second black ship. Their rockets were not effective this time. They simply disappeared on the hull. It continued to the river valley and Survivors Motel.

The leader of the Team of Vessel Two issued orders. The Team responded instantly. The null field was activated in time. The savages had learned. These were dangerous enemies. The thought of savages was replaced by the more applicable word. Enemies, but still decidedly weaker than the Team. The problem was the null guns. They could not be used with the null field in effect. Nor could the psychic weapon be used when the null field was active; that tactic left them vulnerable to the kinetic weapons. The answer was to use the null field itself as a weapon.

This decision was made within a few seconds of the encounter. It was a last-ditch effort. The negative voids powering the null field were not inexhaustible. They could not be replaced with the technology available on this world—something that was not thought to be a problem at the outset. They could retrofit one of the nuclear plants the savages had shut down to make more negative voids, but that would take months.

They needed to move now.

The sister vessel was disabled, but repairs were being made under the cover of feigned inability. They could still communicate between Teams. There was power operable in the vessel. It could be regenerated, but not while the enemy was attacking.

They decided that the surviving vessel, with power to the null field, would simply roll over the encampment. The enemy's weapons could not penetrate the field; it would send the entire camp into the ether. They started back under reduced power. The engineers had determined that the rockets would not be a problem if the field were on.

They started an attack run.

The Survivors continued in warrior mode. The ship rose over the highway at a slow pace, almost invisible in the dark. A flare went up. Then another. The ship loomed like a shark, effortlessly skimming along the treetops. Bill noticed the difference first. There were no open ports to aim at. And what was worse, the trees in the path of the monster simply disappeared.

Bill yelled through the intercom, "It's going to roll over us! The technology that snuffed out our rockets will be used to . . . hell, I don't know . . . vaporize us, I guess. We need to get the hell out of here."

There was nowhere to go. The ship was coming closer and closer, eating the scenery. It moved unerringly toward the Survivors. "We can't hide," chimed in Devon. "Let's at least let them know we're not going down without a fight." In his mind, he saw Alima's face. He felt her trust in him. He thought himself a child of God. But right now, he wanted to kill the ship and whoever was inside. He became a protective warrior. A feral look crossed his face. He aimed the RPG and pressed the trigger. The rocket sped on target. And disappeared. No explosion. No effect at all.

Mary felt the same protective need for her daughters. She fired her RPG. Same result. Almost. The Survivors did not see it, but there was a brief black-light flash on the center of the ship's nose at the exact spot Devon had hit. "Time to run!" she yelled and took off toward her daughters.

"No!" yelled Bill. "Head for the tank. It's our only hope. We have to turn the ship toward the tank!" He started for the beast on a dead run. It was a wild hope. That the LRP could penetrate the shield through the nose of the ship. Maybe, like a submarine, it had its sensors there. Or maybe the shield was weaker where it bent around the nose.

They started off in the dying light of the flare, stumbling across the plowed earth, helping each other, running out of breath, pulling each other toward salvation or death.

Inside the vessel, the scanners noted the movement of the majority of the enemy. They had bunched up nicely. It altered its course accordingly. There were only eight savages running. A wider scan showed two more up on the promontory from the initial attack. Two in the metal machine. And four in the house behind the motel. The outliers would have to wait. The primary targets were to be eliminated first. Time was of the essence.

The last kinetic weapon had caused a breach in one of the outer forward section void containments. One square millimeter. The secondary containment held. The null field was now at 75.345% and dropping. They could not keep ingesting scenery at this rate. They must act quickly.

Inside the tank, Dennis slid the LRP into the breach and closed and locked it. Terry lined up the sights on the ship. It was headed straight for them. He could not see the running figures, but he could hear the progress over the com. There was no time left. The ship was closing fast. If Terry waited any longer, he risked the possibility that the LRP would cause a blast that would finish the runners, too. At the same distance they fired at the rock, he punched the fire button. The night was split by the blast.

Bob and Joe helplessly watched through field glasses in the light of the dying flares as the ship bore down on the running figures. They saw the tank fire. It looked like nothing happened. The ship continued. The runners were doomed. No more ships had appeared, and even if they did, there was nothing Bob or Joe could do now. They started down. Live or die with the rest of the Survivors.

Inside the hunting vessel, the unneeded Team members waited inside the common room. The video feed showed the savages running away. The sensor array made the ship's hull appear transparent, and they could watch the action like a 3D movie, like looking out a spherical window. It showed the progress of the vessel, easily gaining on the targets. The savages would be neutralized within a moment. A thrill passed through the team. Then, the video shifted. It focused on what information was shared before for what was known as a battle machine, as described by the computer. From the last communication, they knew the effect it had on Vessel One. But Vessel One had the null field down. This vessel was functional, as noted by the trees disappearing when touched. They sped on.

Then, the machine fired. The instant analysis showed a rocket-propelled tungsten rod. Tungsten! It was supersonic almost immediately. The point of impact was the weakest point on the vessel, where the hull was without its primary null field for one square millimeter. They felt the bump as the projectile hit. The impact was dampened by the secondary field, but the field around the nose collapsed.

The Team was not without decision-making power. An instant decision was made to crush the savages' machine mechanically, before the rocket firing machine could reload. The vessel had the power to do that. But trees were now being smashed out of the way, impeding progress. Nevertheless, the massive black oblate bore down on the savages' machine like the wrath of one of the savages' nonexistent gods.

Bill saw the ship's intent and yelled into the com, "Scatter!" Some needed to survive. The Survivors did just that. They were exhausted but managed to stumble left and right out of the ship's path. It was up to Dennis and Terry now. The massive ship bore down.

John pulled Mary to the side. He set down his empty RPG and pulled his M4 from its sling, firing as the ship slid past. He noticed that the rounds sparked off the prow and disappeared midship. He relayed it to Dennis. The tank had fired with the same result as the RPGs. Maybe now . . .

John yelled into the com, "The magic field is down now at the nose. Shoot again!"

Then the Midders needed to escape. They followed the trail in the dark to the safe house and their daughters. They would make a stand there, for better or worse.

Inside the tank, Dennis and Terry worked to reload. They were not tank men, but speed was necessary. Both operated like they had trained in the military. By the numbers. And there was hope. The nose field was down. The ship had not stopped but appeared to have been slowed. From the looks of it and from John's message, some of the magic shield was not functioning. Trees were being knocked out of the way now, only disappearing when they touched the sides. They need to shoot again and fast. The LRP was loaded. The breach closed and locked. The ship was a mere 200 yards away. Would the rocket even engage before it hit?

Terry punched the fire button. The tank rocked on its tracks.

Inside the vessel, the Team was encased in twilight. Emergency protocols were enacted. The field was partially down, but the video feed was active. They saw the machine fire, the flash and the contrail. There was stunned silence. Then, this one hit with a bang that reverberated along the ship's hull. The lights went out, and the rest of the field went down. The forward compartment with the electronics and engineers was bathed in tungsten/carbon/deuterium plasma. Everything from the bow to the Team's quarters was instantly vaporized. Over a quarter of the vessel was a boiling mass of superheated gas. The remaining Team felt the lives exiting the torn bodies, bound for the next level. The vessel yawed and sank to the earth. One of the forward null guns was compromised and sucked in all it could. The forward part of the vessel interior disappeared. Nothing but the hull remained. All went silent.

The Survivors watched as the behemoth sank down, crushing a copse near the river within 100 yards of the first ship. Within 300 yards of the motel. It must have weighed thousands of tons to do that. They shuddered to think what would have happened to them or the tank if the ship had continued. There was no color spectrum with this ship. But it went still. No signs of life. The air stunk of scorched metal. Bill opened his mic and spoke.

"Retreat to the motel! Now!"

"No!" yelled Terry through the com. "Not everyone. Dennis and I'll watch a ship for sally ports. Shoot any survivors who carry arms. Detain any who surrender. We need Bob and Joe to watch the other one. We need some light here."

As if on cue, Bob and Joe drove up in the ATV they had used for the trip to the lookout point, lights blazing. Dennis and Terry clattered up in the Abrams, splashing through the shallow Necanicum, blowing smoke. The machine's combat lights stabbed the darkness, lighting up the dark bulk of the ships. The Survivors watched the seemingly dead oblates, carrying M4s and M17s at the ready.

Nothing moved out of the ships. No more ships came. Daylight was hours away. What were they to do now?

"Terry, this isn't a war like we know it. There are no Rules of Engagement, no Geneva Convention for them. These things will stun us if they can. I say kill any and all without warning," urged Bill.

"You're right. Any we see, light them up."

The Survivors, minus the Lakes, Sally, and Wanda, who were in the honeymoon house, gathered in the field between the downed ships. They waited for Terry to speak.

Joe, Jan, Bill, John, Mary, Vanessa, Teressa, Bob, Devon, Alima. Dennis and me, Terry thought. *What the hell do we have here? Twelve unremarkable people. These people just brought down a far superior force in two massive vessels that moved without noise and sported ray guns, for God's sake—in open combat. What the hell! Are we really that good? There must be a reason.* But the obvious one eluded him.

Live or die.

"OK! We seem to have beaten back this attack. I don't see any trying to get out of the ships. But I've got no idea about the status of the downed ships. There could be survivors. They could be working to repair whatever damage we caused. Now, we must assume that the ships are still deadly. Any ideas?"

"Well, let's think about this," Bill said. The rest of the Survivors echoed him. "Yeah, yeah. Let's do like an after-action summary. From what I saw, the ship the Abrams hit second with two rounds was holed. It went dark immediately. The other, I think, was hit with RPGs inside. It turned a rainbow of colors and went dark. This needs to be the first priority to ensure that they are out of commission and the ray guns are neutralized."

Bob said, "It looked like the RPGs had an effect when the force field was down. When they opened the ports to fire their ray guns, there was no magic shield. When the shield was on, the RPGs had no effect."

"Why didn't the second ship stun us?" asked Mary.

"Maybe because they can't with their magic shield up," suggested Bill.

"So, they are at a disadvantage when they are operating behind the shield. They can't shoot and they can't stun," said John. "And it looks like they couldn't stun us before we fired, even with the shield down. It must take some time to activate the stun."

"But we can't shoot when it's up, either. Stalemate, except they can still use the shield to vaporize us. And when that doesn't work, they tried to squash us with their weight. Still, we somehow managed to penetrate the shield with the tank," said Dennis.

"I think it was a combination. And again, the odds were out of sight. We seemed to have hit it exactly at the same spot with rockets and the tank, multiple times." Bill shook his head. "Hand on the scale again?"

"But our strategy, our shooting! We have to do it ourselves," Joe added.

"Well, we have to use this to our advantage," said Terry. "Right now, both ships seem to have their shield down now. Someone needs to do a little recon." Eyes turned to Dennis.

"I'll take a look." He brought the M4 to port.

"Not so fast, Dennis," said Terry. "Let's think about this." Light laughter. "Yeah, you're the one to lead. Now we need backup. But we cannot afford to have two of our best assets at risk."

"Assets?" wondered Jan warily.

"OK. People who know warfare. That leaves Joe out. If something happens to us, he will be the best military mind here."

"Nice try, Terry. You are needed far more than me. Looks like nothing is going to happen right now, anyway. They have not tried to stun us. We need more light. With that black-on-black stuff, we could walk right into an ambush. If we use light, we will just be a target. These ships are big. The two side by side could fill up half a football field.

God knows how many are inside. And remember, they can still affect our minds. If we go, we need a chain." There were a bunch of strange looks shot back, including Jan. "A chain of us at fifty-yard intervals. So if one or more falls, the others start shooting. The stun effect has a range limit."

"Good idea. But we need to watch tonight for any sorties from the ships. And especially if they manage to repair them. Any ideas? The night vision scopes were not very good at seeing the ships. We needed the flares to target them. Besides, the batteries are low."

"How about using the tank to just blow them up?" said Vanessa.

"We may have to try if the ships begin to move, but only as a last resort. It is always possible the ships may explode or implode and take us with them. We just don't know enough to risk anyone now. Let's set a watch and start again in the morning light. Best we keep the Tillamook Road lookout active, too," said Terry.

Alima watched these people as she listened to their discussion. Before the shayatan had appeared, she had been a ship's steward's assistant and server for the Ocean Pride cruise line for three years. She met and knew many people from various walks of life. She liked most of them. She was friends with some, but it was nothing like this. These people were thrown together in the worst possible way. From what she had gathered, the Survivors were similar in background, but here there were old people, young people, and some in between. They were black, brown, tan, white, and now Asian. They were business people, merchants, technical people, hunters, soldiers, and what else? Somehow, this was just what was needed to survive. Yet they, like she, should be terrified. And still, they seemed almost calm, task-oriented. They had lived through the shayatan, they had lived through a band of evil men, they had lived through the tsunami, and now they were contending with a far superior alien invasion. They should be reduced to . . . what? She reminded herself that she too had survived the shayatan and the tsunami. Now she would help them survive the aliens. If this was what Allah put her here for.

"I will help. I survived the . . . 'Bugs.'" She had picked up the word from the people here. "Shayatan" did not now apply. "I survived for a reason. There must be a purpose for it. Let me approach the ship right now. I need to help." She sighed. "I am the least skilled of the group . . ." she tailed off.

"Not a chance!" said Terry. "No one is expendable here. You did your part well. But you have one thing right. We need to go now. Ideas?"

Alima breathed out. Allah did not want her to sacrifice herself. There must be another mission for her. Devon smiled at her. It was interesting that she would volunteer. She did not notice his smile; her eyes were downcast.

"One thing at a time," said Dennis. "The ship was holed, so we can access it. It looks to have sunk into the ground enough so the breach is reachable. The other is still sealed. It appears to be floating. The shield is probably on. If we light the holed one up, not with firepower, but with the ATV lights, we can approach it on foot from the side and take a look inside."

"Let's try this," said Joe. "Bring the other two ATVs down and set Bill and Sally up on the head to lookout. John and Mary with the sisters off to the hillside, with flares ready. Devon, Wanda, and Jan with RPGs at a right angle over there. Dennis and I will move the tank to the point and get it set to shoot. Dennis will stay to fire if necessary. Bob and I will go in with the M4s."

"Sounds like a plan."

"Except for one thing," said Jan. "I go with Joe. Alima can't shoot. I can." There was to be no discussion.

"Agreed. Everyone rest for a minute and get locked and loaded. We move in ten minutes."

"Wait a minute," said Joe. "If we are to do this, Jan will be the 'anchor.' Stay back at least 100 feet. If these things knock us out before we get them, it will be up to you to save our asses."

Bob chimed in. "I will go first. I shoot pretty good. Joe can back me up with Jan behind him." They all knew what he meant. He was a lone ranger here. All the others had aligned into couples. They stood in the lantern light and felt the camaraderie that troops since Roman times have felt. We who are about to die salute each other. It was a powerful stimulant that put tears in some eyes.

"Agreed again. Ten minutes. Hoo-ah."

"No! No! No!" yelled Dennis. "We can't have all our firepower aimed at a ship some of us are entering. We have to allocate. We have to watch the other ship, and this one. Wait for the best light conditions to recon. A light poked into the black hole will just be a target."

"You know, he's right," said Terry. "Let's make another plan. Again."

There was a sigh of relief. No one really wanted to beard the lion in his den, so to speak. Especially at night.

They spent some time hashing out a makeshift battle plan, without a clue as to the enemy's remaining capability.

True democracy is a messy thing, Jan suddenly thought. *Coming to a consensus is difficult, but it can also save your life.*

That night, Joe and Jan talked in low tones from the lookout, eyes on the sky, and rocket launchers ready.

"What do you think of our chances now?" Jan was calm yet worried. She needed reassurance. Joe was unsure of how to answer.

"Well, I left my crystal ball at home. But we beat them pretty bad here. If they are meeting resistance in other places, we may beat them all together." A sudden thought came to him. "You know, Bill or Stan should have thought of this already. We use walkie-talkies, don't we? These are only one way to communicate. What about CB? Citizens Band radio. If there are others, maybe they will also think of this."

"Sure. There have to be some stores around that have it. And I re-member seeing a lot of antennas around here. If there are others, a coor-dinated effort would be best. But do you know how it works?"

"Generally. It has a limited range, except for very powerful stations. We need Bill and Sally, the young techies, to do research. Maybe Stan would know. It is an old technology, after all."

"We'll bring it up tomorrow after dealing with the downed ships. And I think the Lakes and girls have already been playing with it."

"Yeah, we need to reach out. Any help we can get. Plus, we may be able to help others. After all, we have survived. So far."

"Yeah, so far. Let's do it."

That night in the common room, Devon and Alima sat across from each other in the dark. No candles this night. "Alima," Devon started, "I have asked you here to discuss . . . religion."

Alima tensed. "What do you mean?"

"I believe you think you're a Muslim. Before you say more, let me explain as best I can the situation here. We may die here. I want to make peace before that," he sighed. "When the Survivors first came together, I thought I was a Catholic. I believed I was to lead these people in the way of righteousness. You saw how that worked with the abortion question." Devon smiled to himself. "Now, I see myself not as a Catholic, but as a man of God. A man with beliefs. I hold to those beliefs. I council, but I do not force my beliefs onto the others."

"But I am a Muslim. I cannot change that. What will these Survivors think of that? I've heard the antipathy for Islam spoken here."

"I saw how you felt when you volunteered to do that dangerous thing for us. It was a brave and foolish thing. You were relieved when it was rejected. I think you were testing Allah. It should not be that way. Do not define yourself as a Muslim. You are a woman with beliefs. You have a right to those beliefs, and all here will accept that. Provided you do not do what I did and seek to force them on anyone. I know a little about Islam. I will be happy to discuss it with you; I will not proselytize. I know the history of Christianity and Islam. It is filled with animosity and hatred. Let it not be that way here."

"If I don't obey the laws of Sharia, I will be punished."

"By who? Not anyone here. If God . . . Allah, wanted to punish you, wouldn't it have happened by now? Wouldn't He have sent you into the ship?"

"There is an afterlife. Allah will be there." Alima trembled; she was scared.

"What does the Koran say about women and the afterlife?" Alima gave him a blank look. She did not know. "Among other books, I have a copy of it. Let's go through it together. Maybe you will allow yourself to read the New Testament also."

Alima looked hard at Devon, for all that she could barely see him in the gloom. "Are you seeking to convert or trick me?"

"No. I have stated my position; I am a man with beliefs. No one can take them from me. No one can force me to change. I answer to God. You are a woman with beliefs. No one can take them from you. No one can force you to change. You answer to Allah. Let's see if God and Allah are the same."

It was a radical idea. "I will discuss what I know with you," she said.

"Good. Also, open your heart to Allah. Ask Him what is best. Do not let me or any other tell you what to do. Let Allah guide you, but do not just take orders."

"How am I to know what's best without . . . orders? The Koran?"

"Let's consult the Koran."

Was this another infidel trick? Would he show her the true Koran?

As if reading her mind, Devon answered, "When this is over, we will go to a mosque. There is one in Beaverton, not far from my old home. You can read for yourself."

Alima went silent.

"Ask Allah directly. He will answer or not. Just like God."

She silently prayed for guidance. Then asked, "What do you want of me?"

"Be yourself, Alima. Just be yourself."

CHAPTER 31

Captive

The ship appeared monstrous in the early morning daylight. Bob, Joe, and Jan looked like ants approaching a hotdog. Stan and Joan were reactivating the short wave radio. Stan also kept an eye on the downed ships. He had a clear line of sight from upstairs in case anything went wrong. *Out of range of the mind trick*, he thought.

The hole the LRP made was a perfect circle about five feet in diameter. It was about three feet off the ground, since the ship had sunk into the lea. The daylight did not penetrate the stygian darkness inside. As they approached, Joe turned to Jan. "If we get in trouble, make sure you don't hit us, huh."

"You better drop fast, then, because I will be letting the aliens know we are here, and we mean business."

"You hear that, Bob?"

"Got it. Cover me." He peeked around the edge of the hole, scanned with his light, and saw nothing. Then, he turned the light out and climbed up and in. He stepped quickly to the side to avoid being silhouetted by the light from the hole. Rifle ready. Disappearing into the gloom.

Inside, the ship was pitch black. Bob waited for his eyes to adjust. He could sense no movement. Then he turned on the LED light taped to his M4 and continued to scan the interior.

The fusion engineer awoke to the smell of burnt metal and the knowledge he and a lone female repulsion engine technician were the only ones alive in this vessel. Most of the Community who survived the blast had moved on to the next level voluntarily. He did not. He was consumed by a rage, a hatred—emotions he did not know he had. He felt a similar need in the female for revenge. He knew the vessel was now inoperable and would be salvaged only with great effort.

His lungs burned; his head hurt. He needed fresh air. The discomfort was new to him. His long association with the Community was peaceful. Each member was encouraged to excel in any way they chose. He studied quantum entanglement physics. He understood the nature of the null field. How it was discovered that a negative void could be created between the states of matter. It was thought to be a true void without even a passing single neutrino. Without even dark matter and energy. Almost a true void.

The science of the void was developed to counteract the effects of the singularity threatening their world. But it was not enough. He learned how it could be manufactured and controlled. Its power and limitations. Nothing was perfect. There was no absolute. He knew the negative voids the Community brought with them were not inexhaustible. It was proposed during earlier meetings that the vessels should simply use the null fields to eradicate the savages. This would be done simply by using the vessels as weapons. The idea was originally discarded because the remaining voids would be exhausted quickly by chasing savages through rough terrain. The vessels would then be susceptible to kinetic weaponry. Here, in this case, the use of handheld weapons was authorized.

Reports from other action on this continent showed the use of some of the heavier kinetic weaponry was effective against the vessels when the null field was deactivated. This action was not the only one losing vessels. In the mountains of Texas, several vessels were damaged. The savages there had access to battle tanks, mobile cannons, and rapid-fire weaponry. Of the original flotilla of thirty-seven vessels, only thirty-four were now operable.

His studies did not prepare him for this. His thoughts were shared. The female was one of the Community and thus a part of him. He could still feel the sadness in the departure of the rest of this Team, and now he felt the Team in the other vessel. Though the drives were inoperable at this point, repairs were underway.

The ways of war and subterfuge were coming back to him. It was interesting to him that he could devolve so quickly into a warrior. It was, in a way, exhilarating. He shared the feeling with the Community in the next vessel. A warning came back. Do not attempt individual action.

Then the thought came to him from the Elders. He and the female were now to act under orders. They would yet exterminate these savages. He allowed the entire Team into his thoughts. A plan was made in just a few seconds. When the time was right, they would strike. The female knew her part in the plan. One or 100, the savages were vulnerable when within range with open minds. It was used before with success. He must see to it that it worked again. The team in the other vessel was at full strength. Ready.

Bob found the first half of the ship empty. Surprisingly, nothing survived the tank round. Like the ship in the mountain, the hull was intact, except where the LRP entered. But there was no residue of anything inside. Had one of the ray guns imploded? He did not know and quit wondering. He continued farther, passing under a giant silvery torus at the center of the ship. A panel of some sort escaped the blast or implosion. He moved past it. Farther inside, the ship smelled vaguely of vegetable rot. He carefully kept his mind as closed as he could make it.

Bob came upon the male alien first. He did not ask questions. Kept his mind closed and on task. There would be no chance for mind control.

The male was spared the worst effects of the LRP by being behind a massive gray machine of some sort that was partitioned off from the rest of the ship. However, several bodies were scattered around. Bob could see no obvious wounds. It looked like they just lay down and died. The rotting smell was worse here. The wall was warped but had held. A door was open near the center. He came upon the female next. She was cowering in the back of the ship with more bodies around. There were no more live aliens. Both were injured but did not complain and obeyed when he ordered them out.

In the daylight of a soft sun leaking through a low haze, the aliens looked more human than before. They were beautiful still, but somehow more vulnerable and less angelic.

Bob had them at the point of his rifle. "They're all yours, Terry," he said. It was a statement per the discussion about what to do with any prisoners.

Dennis was in the tank 500 yards away up Highway 101. Earlier, he noticed a hole in the turret about two inches in diameter. It was a hit from the previous night. If it had been three feet lower, the tank would have been disabled. And maybe himself.

He now had a direct line of fire broadside to the apparently dead ship. Joe and Terry waited at the holed ship's nose. The others were split into two forces: one across the river from the dead ship with RPGs primed and ready, the other up away from the holed ship. They were protected by heavy undergrowth at right angles to the ships in order not to be at conflict with the tank's and Bob's lines of fire. The non-combatants—Teressa, Vanessa, Wanda, and Sally—were up on the 101 overpass road in a Humvee, watching through powerful binoculars. Ready to warn of any problems. All were warned of the possibility that the aliens would retain some mind control power. To be on guard. No open minds. No questioning.

Terry's face took on a look of fierce determination. What happened to him in the first meeting had scarred him. "I will interrogate them. We need to know what we got here." They stood outside the massive black ship in the sharpening sunlight. "Set here!" he ordered. Both aliens sat on the ground.

Bob left for his sniper's post 300 yards away, carrying his 7mm. He was calibrated in. Joe stepped back. Jan went to the motel with her RPG armed and ready. Terry loomed over the two aliens. They sat passively. "Here's what is going to happen. You will answer my questions without delay. If there is any attempt to use your mind weapon, there will be an all-out attack on your downed ship. We know what you can do. You have seen what we can do. So let's see what's what. I will be the only one asking questions. My mind will be the only one vulnerable. If I fall or otherwise act strangely, there will be a bloodbath. Do you understand?"

The male was assigned the lead role. "We understand." *This would be a little more complicated than foreseen. But he could feel several of the other savages' uncertainty. He targeted all near, although three of them were at the limit of his range. Quickly, the Community also targeted the ones in range. This would be like a game of three-dimensional chess. He could play against up to three opponents in the twenty-by-twenty cube. He was sure the savages had not even mastered their two-dimensional game. He could operate in four dimensions if necessary.*

"How many are in the other ship?"

"There is no one alive in that vessel."

"How far does your mental shockwave go?" This was a test question that Terry thought he had the answer to.

"I, myself, can project up to a kilometer. A full Team together can project several kilometers. My vessel's Team, perhaps five kilometers." This was a lie. Although the Community could communicate over hundreds of kilometers, the effect of mental shock was considerably less.

Terry's lizard brain stirred. All this was a lie. He was being toyed with. The alien was seeking to delay and confuse him. Terry moved over to the female. "What is your name?"

She moved into her role. "I have no name. I am who I am." Her voice became taunting. "You ask inane questions. You have no idea of the reality of this situation. Your pathetic voice communications are without depth. Your emotions are chaotic. You are not fit to be on the same planet with such as we. When the Community learns of this, it will squash you trash like the cockroaches you are." She had pulled the image from Joe, who was standing back and thinking the image exactly as she said it.

Did she project it, or did she pull it from me? Joe wondered. He suddenly knew she got it from him; she could not have thought it by herself. Unnoticed, the downed ship glowed with a subtle brief spectrum of light. Ultraviolet to infrared.

It was progressing as planned. The engineer felt Joe's alarm. He felt the confusion of some of the other savages. Any confusion would work. A confused mind was an open mind.

"Terry!" Joe yelled. "This is a setup! She just read my mind." But Terry was lost in a terrible rage. He reached out and slapped the female. It was a heavy blow, and her head snapped back. Confusion blew through the Survivors. What was Terry doing?

Not yet. Came from the male. We need them all.

The female rocked back up, then straightened and looked at Terry with disgust. "Is that all you savages know how to do?" Her voice was musical, taunting. Terry raised his hand again.

"Terry! Back away! We can't compete like this with these things. I feel them ready to do what they did before. He lied! There are more in the other ship!"

Now!

Joe fell, and Terry staggered. On both sides of the ships, the RPG holders fell. Stan and Joan fell in their apartment. Jan fell on the motel deck. Bob was far enough away that he could pull the trigger before his eyes dimmed. The report brought him partially back, as it did for Joe before. Dennis was also far enough away not to pass out immediately. He punched the fire button.

On the overpass, they felt the shock. They staggered but did not fall, they were not completely stunned. They were out of effective range.

Inside the vessel, they were within minutes of finishing repairs. The order to stun the savages was premature because of the violent reaction of the one called Terry and the attempt of the one called Joe to disengage. The rage and pull-back affected the strength of the projected stun. The savages at the outer range were able to fire their weapons.

And the shield was down to employ the sedation.

The unthinkable happened. It was the end of the Team.

The tungsten projectile ruptured the hull and spalled into the interior. All efforts to repair the vessel ceased. They were trapped in a choking hell, feeling the coming death blow. They did not wait for it. All exited their bodies for the next level.

To the two alien survivors, it was a bad blow, but they recovered quickly. They felt the rest of the Team leave for the next level, but the nearby savages were stunned. It was merely a setback. The male and female now saw their chance. All was not lost. If they could access the savages' weapons, then the killing would be easy. They had learned how to use the gas-propelled projectile weapons. Holding the mind force, the engineer started for the one called Terry first.

But Terry was not completely out. As in the haze of a dream, he saw the alien reach for him. A rage washed over him, and the alien staggered back, apparently affected by it. Terry stumbled in a circle, like a punch-drunk boxer fighting to stay upright. He saw the woman reach for Joe, who was slumped over, head hanging like he was asleep. He tried to yell, but no sound came from him. The alien reached for him again. Terry realized he was reaching for his gun. Terry found his voice. A sound escaped the torpor, a primal roar of anger. Again, the man stepped back. Terry grabbed the sidearm and tried to draw. His hands felt like they were stiff and numb with cold. He could not do it. The alien leaned toward him. Terry hit a brick wall. He blacked out and fell.

The engineer heard the two weapons fire, but the far savages were still partially stunned. The near ones were down. He had to use considerable effort to subdue the one called Terry. He was a big, strong savage with a strong rage. But no match for the engineer's mental power. He noted the female used a comforting emotion to subdue the one called Joe. She was successful. This could end here after all. He sent a message to the command center for another vessel to retrieve him and the female.

All this he did within a few seconds, his mind working flawlessly toward the goal. As he gripped the firearm, he detected another emotion. Very close and closing quickly. A primitive emotion. A danger! He wrenched the pistol out and was knocked down. A terrible, crushing pain erupted from his wrist, and he dropped the gun. Another first for him. He screamed at the sight of a four-legged furry carnivore chewing on his hand.

And he heard the sound of the savages' weapons firing again.

She was still trying to see where she fit in with her new pack. The dog had mostly healed from the bite wounds. Her leg was functional. She was now at a good weight and fitness.

The man who saved her from the coyotes was not the pack alpha. The female who tended to her was not the alpha. She was not concerned about competition for or with the alpha. She knew she was barren and no threat to the fertile females.

There just seemed to be no alpha for this pack at first.

She enjoyed the attention and praise from the pack. As she got to know them, she smelled the sickness growing inside the old male. She smelled the pup growing inside the tan female and the new one growing inside the fair-haired one. She knew the pack would protect and feed them and her. And she would protect them. She brought them one of the rodents she caught once. But they did not seem interested. She was well-fed, and the rodents here were a lot harder to catch than the ones she lived off of in the place of big buildings. She did not need to hunt. But she needed to be needed.

In her way, she knew them all. She smelled and licked them all. They all petted and acknowledged her. She could tell them apart without being able to see them. No one seemed to pay her more attention than any other. In her mind, that made all, except the young females, above her in the pack. It slowly seemed that the big one was more alpha than the others. But the roles seemed to change with situations she did not understand. She decided she would protect all of them against all others.

In the previous strange night, she was fearful of the loud noises and pack commotion. She did not know what to do. There was no enemy she could sense, yet the pack went into fight mode. She smelled their fear and aggression. It was confusing. Now, after the noises and foul smells died down, she felt a different danger. When the noises and commotion of the night before startled and confused her, she hid in her den. She was now determined to fight alongside the pack. She eased out of the den and saw the big one being attacked by a strange-smelling two-paw. Not human and not an animal, but real at last.

A protective rage filled her. She knew her place in this fight. She was needed. She charged at the thing without concern for her safety. All sound left her. A total concentration on the thing was all there was. Powering towards the enemy. Her weak leg forgotten. Then she was on it, and a battle growl came from deep in her chest. She leaped at its throat. The thing raised a paw at her, holding a metallic thing she recognized as a noisemaker. She locked on to the two-paw with a fury. She was filled with joy at the taste of blood, the crunching of bone. The noisemaker fell away. She continued to savage the thing.

Joe felt the woman's hands on him. They were soft and comforting. They reached for his sidearm. He could not stop her. A great despair washed away the warm feeling. He failed. The Survivors would die because he could not fight his way out of the comforting fog.

There was a whip-crack sound. Then he felt the rush of air as something blew by. He did not know what it was until he heard the growling and screaming. The dog! By God, the dog!

Then there was another whip-crack sound. At the same time, there was the sound of a hammer hitting a wet board. Something splashed over his arm. Then another whip-crack. And as if a light turned on in a dark room, he saw clearly what had happened.

The alien grabbed at Terry. Was overpowering him. He was losing. Then, a hurtling ball of fur latched on to the alien's arm and began shaking him like a terrier with a rat. Terry heard the first whip-crack as a distant sound. The second whip-crack was louder, with a dull splat. There were screaming and growling and the sound of someone yelling. As he came to, he realized it was him yelling. Terry shrugged the stupor off, rose up, and finally managed to get his gun back. As he did, the light turned on for him as well. The alien writhed on the ground with the dog latched on tight. A third whip-crack echoed past. Terry called off the dog, who sat back like nothing happened, panting and watching Terry like a loving servant. Terry lined up the M17 on the alien and started to pull the trigger.

"Terry! No! Bob! Stop shooting!" cried Joe, yelling into the walkie-talkie as well as at Terry. "We need this guy! STOP!" Terry managed to twist away as the hammer fell. The round dug a hole next to the fallen alien. One last whip-crack sang past. Then silence. The female alien lay next to him. She was without much of her head, though, and definitely not a threat now.

In the tank, Dennis loaded another LRP. He was in a fog and did not know what effect the first round had, but he did not wait. He aimed and fired again, purely from rote training. The blast helped clear his head. The light in the room clicked on.

The sound of the cannon brought the rest of the Survivors back, waking as from a deep sleep to the morning alarm clock and to the morning sun. They were lying on the moist ground. They found the

RPGs at their feet, unfired. Their walkie-talkies crackled with Joe's call. Then all went silent. The normal sounds of the forest and lea were muted. Nothing moved. Nothing made a sound. Something bad had happened; all nature knew it and respected it. Or shunned it.

Slowly, the Survivors made their way back to the meeting ground. No one talked. No one wanted to break the silence. It was as if the silence were protection from further hurt.

In his sniper's blind, Bob vaguely remembered shooting with no target and then the image of the woman's face in the crosshairs as he shot again. He worked the bolt and pulled the trigger again out of reflex. The sound of Joe's yelling into the intercom caused him to stop before he could pull yet again. But he was without a will of his own for a moment. He sat and cried out in pain, rocking himself until he could stand. He put down the 7mm and let out a big sigh. He started to get up from the blind. Then the shakes started. For several minutes, he could not control them or himself. He could not stand. He could not think. The reality of what he had done was lost to him in a misty haze. It was something he did not want to find right now. But it was coming, like an avalanche he could not stop.

Slowly, his senses came back, and a light shone on what he had done. He saw what he had done! He had killed the marauder without any thought, except the feeling of satisfaction of a good shot and regret he could not stop the RV. But this shook him to the core. The spell she wove over Joe flashed back at him when he shot. There was an immediate, intense feeling of love followed by overwhelming, debilitating sorrow and sadness.

He killed one who loved him.

CHAPTER 32

Strategy

The silence did not last long. "What the hell happened?" demanded Terry. "What the hell!" He was shaking like a leaf in the wind, still stumbling but upright. Talking to no one and everyone. The Survivors watched numbly until Terry managed to get himself under control. The women came down from the overpass in the Hummer.

Bill recovered first. "I'd say the dog just saved our bacon." He looked at the cowering alien and his bloody hand. "I'd also say we are not out of the woods yet. I bet this one can communicate with the others. If he can, he has. But we don't know for sure. And we need to know what they are capable of. He can tell us. Joe was smart to save him. But I think Terry is the wrong guy to try to open him up. No offense, Terry, but I think you would kill him. My guess is Joe is best suited to try."

"What about you?" asked Joe. "You are probably the smartest one here. No offense to anyone. We need the 'well, let's think on this' guy now." Then a feeling of dread hit him, and he got serious. "I am scared. She nearly killed me and us. I could not stop it. It is the most insidious thing. God damn! We need to figure this out. I can't do that again."

"Yeah, you can. You can do it. Remember, you're the one who has felt the power and actually fought it off once," said Bill.

"Yeah, but I was a long way away then, and this time, a lone alien nearly killed me at close range. Let's look at this a different way. Who here has the least interaction . . . the least effect of the blackout shot? The strongest minds, I think. Jan, Sally, or maybe Mary would be better, or Wanda."

Jan shook her head. "No," was all she said.

"Not me," said Mary. "I think I would kill him, too. He is a danger to my children."

"I want to kill him right now! And I will not be sent away in hiding again. I can help load," asserted Wanda.

Joe looked around. Bob was still in a semi-dream state, standing apart out in the field. Dennis looked like he was dazed but held the M4 steady on the alien. Finger on the trigger. The alien was dead if he even twitched. Terry stood, unsteady, a man ready to kill. These would not be good questioners. And he himself was at sea. Lost, afraid. He knew instinctively that the women were their best bet. Joe needed to get this straight. "How about it, Sally? You have escaped to worst of the mind thing. I think you are as smart as Bill, too."

"She is," said Bill, rebooting. Trying to make light. He looked at her and amended the statement. "No. She is smarter, of course. She has an MBA in industrial motivation, too."

Sally was not amused and looked ready to bolt. But she didn't. "I have felt the stun just like the rest of us. Like Wanda, if there are more, I will be here to load. It is an all or nothing situation. If you are killed, we are next."

She composed herself. The Survivors saw a strong, determined woman making an impossible decision. "It is not a strength issue. But I have thought about the blackout spell. It requires us to have an open mind. Or a questioning mind or a confused mind. Or simply to be paying attention. Anyway, for the aliens to access us, they have to have an open door, so to speak. Just to be thinking about them. The cause of the blackout is probably sensory overload. Like we surmised, but in this case, emotional overload. They can project a massive amount of emotion—love, hate, and everything in between. Like Devon said, all the wavelengths—alpha, beta, theta, and delta—in some sort of directed synaptic transmission. The effect is to stun. To override our brain circuits. We have to shield ourselves against them. I will try. But I am afraid. I want someone close for the protection of me and my child."

"Anybody close can be affected," said Joe. "None of our weapons can be close. He did get Terry's gun. She almost had mine. We were dead if not for the dog."

"Hah!" said Terry, getting his mind back from the fog. "The dog! It can be our bodyguard. See how the alien watches it. He is afraid."

While the Survivors talked, Teressa saw Bob hanging back, looking lost. He was not participating. There was something wrong. She walked the hundred yards to him.

"What's wrong, Bob?"

"I can't . . . I don't . . ." He began to cry again. "I killed her . . . she was sending me . . . love. She loved me!"

"Come here," she said. "Come here."

Bob looked up and saw her as if for the first time. A young woman, one who weathered the worst. He walked to her.

"Sit here." He sat on a log, his face in his hands. She sat next to him, put her arms around his neck, and held him close. She crooned and cooed to him. "It's all right. It's all right. We love you. We all love you."

Mary noticed the pair. Vanessa was now walking toward them. Mary started forward. Teressa saw her and raised her hand in a stop motion. Vanessa continued. Mary stopped and watched. Now the rest of the Survivors saw. Talk stopped. Intuitively, they knew, felt the problem, the need. Vanessa reached Bob and Teressa and held Bob like Teressa did. They watched the two young women comfort the man.

After a few minutes, Bob stood, looked at the two women, and smiled. "Thank you." He could think of nothing else to say. Vanessa brought him his rifle. He looked at it as if it were a foreign thing. Then took it. "Thank you," he said again.

"You're welcome. Let's go home."

As they walked the distance to the group, Bob steadied. But something had changed in him. In all his life, he had not felt the unconditional love from another human that he felt from these remarkable women. He thought he loved his wife; he thought she loved him. And he did, and it was good. But this—this was a taste of heaven. For a brief moment, he saw into a beautiful truth. It faded as he got near the Survivors. But some remained. The alien's trick was exposed and discarded in the light of true love.

"Are you all right?" Joe asked when Bob arrived.

"I will be. When I pulled the trigger, I felt . . ."

"It's all right," said Teressa.

Joe was startled. "Love, you felt love! That's what nearly killed me. These aliens have such power, and they use it to destroy." He shook his head. "If they used that love power, we would all be dead now. God, they are stupid for all their knowledge."

Reality came crashing back. "We just gave the alien a weapon," said Terry.

"No," Bob said. "It was phony, fake. It was like the difference between an electric heater and a fire. Both put out heat—one artificial, manufactured, one real. I can't explain it, but what we have here is better than anything the aliens have."

"He can't stun us all. He hasn't even tried," opined Mary. "And I think he doesn't know the love spell. Their power is in the combined sending. Some use love, and others hate. It's the combination that is deadly."

"We have to assume he can let the others know. We need a plan. Move all weapons away from him. Tie him up! We got to plan!" Terry was still shaking but had regained some command. "We need to move him away." They moved the alien out into the field. "Sally, will you watch while we discuss this?"

"Why me?"

"Please?"

Sally looked around at the Survivors. They did not know what was happening, but they trusted Terry. "OK."

Terry looked at the dog and said, "Watch him!" The dog sat and fixed the alien with a laser stare. Sally sat well away from the alien, behind the dog.

The Survivors moved away, set a plan. It did not take long.

Then they came back.

"Thank you, Sally. I needed to know how he would react to being alone. I think he's done. Now we will make plans."

They set up a protocol as a group. They did not worry about talking in front of the alien. They said he would know if they were lying to him, anyway. He maybe could not read their minds, they said, but he could pick up images from nearby people. They needed to be sure to let slip only what he already knew.

The alien was tied tightly. The dog watched intently, almost eagerly. It was plain that should he stun any of them, he would face the dog while unable to run or fight.

Now it was time to act. To put the plan in motion.

Sally brought a chair and sat in front of the alien. The dog was at her right, her eyes locked onto the alien's. His wound was healing at an astounding rate. *These things are something else*, Sally thought. *What a waste*. She started her interrogation.

"I will not match wits with you. So let's get some things straight. You and your Community are alive or dead at my discretion. Any tricks will end with the dog on your throat. I know you think of us as savages. Too bad. I know you want to exterminate us. That will not happen. We are Survivors. You are at the end of your existence. That goes for all of you who want to kill us. So, here is the deal. There are two ways this can go for you right now. One: We kill you and all who attack us. Two: We live in peace. Now, we have surmised that you probably have called for reinforcements. You should know we have more of the LRP machines and RPGs. You know what they are and what they can do, even to a ship with the 'shield' on. You will call them off or die with them. You will give me an answer now. Peace or death?"

"Peace," *he lied. He knew there was only one rocket firing machine.* "I will set up a meeting. We can work this out. You are of a higher evolution than we first assessed." *He opened his mind to the Community. A secondary vessel that had been dispatched was temporarily held in place over a mountain in the Continental Divide. He did not know where the other savages went while the woman talked. He only knew they were afraid and not near. There was just a narrow increment of time and range when the stun was effective. It was necessary to use subterfuge.*

"Very well," she continued. "This is how it'll be. You will contact your Community and call for a truce. No ships are to be flown near or over us. You will land one ship on the field to the north. Your negotiation team will exit the ship and await our contact. We do not trust you to sheathe your emotional weapon. Therefore, I will do all negotiations. The rest of us savages will be hidden."

The alien came to a sudden respect. The female savage was using words he had not thought they would use: "Community" and "savages." A plan formed instantly. The detained vessel was dispatched. They would land and negotiate. When the savages were wondering how the negotiation was proceeding, they would strike and use conventional weapons to finish the job. This tactic was the death of some of the European resistance. The woman stated her demands. He agreed.

"I have let the Community know your intentions. We have agreed to negotiate as required. A negotiation team will arrive this afternoon." *You will be dead shortly thereafter.*

"Do not try to ambush us. That will not go well for you," Sally said.

We will not need to, gloated the alien.

Out of the range of the alien's perception, the Survivors talked in the motel while Sally kept him occupied.

"We are in a tough spot," said Terry. "We have planned an ambush. We can bet he knows this and has already or will let the next ship know. We know they will try to kill us. The problem is that damned mind trick. They will try to knock us out and then finish us at their leisure. We have no viable defense. We can't shield our thoughts or our minds. The second we falter, it's over."

Dennis was thinking. "I remember something about this problem during basic training. It was part of a history lesson about the Cold War. The Soviets had a plan code-named 'Dead Hand.' It was basically a doomsday weapon. It supposedly assured a counterstrike would be made, even if the leaders were killed in a preemptive strike. It was automated. We need something like that."

"Yes, like the ones terrorists use to activate vest bombs if they are killed. It's a handheld button that blows up when released," offered Joe.

Bill said, "That's what we need, all right. We need to MacGyver the hell out of this. Let's get to work. How will the aliens do this? What will be their plan?"

"They know we can kill them if their force field is not up. We know they have to shut it down to open ports or doors. So they will come in and locate each of us, land, and turn off the magic shield. Use their blackout power. Then come out hunting."

"Won't be much of a hunt if we are taking a snooze. The rockets have to be within a hundred yards to be effective. That's inside their range to stun. Even the tank has to have a line of sight."

"We could scatter using the ATVs. Hide until they leave," said Teressa, ever hopeful.

Terry was blunt. "No, they would just hunt us down from the air one by one. We need to stand and fight here. OK. If we know where they will be, over the field, then we get stands for the RPGs in the trees to the east. Secure and aim them. All on the same side, broadside. All equipped with dead hands. We put Sally in front . . ."

"No, we don't!" Bill jumped in. An icy chill filled the room.

"Yeah. You're right. That wasn't good. She stays with us. With you. Anyway, the ship will open the doors facing the tree line to the captive.

Every time we saw the doors or ports, they were on the sides, not nose. So they will be situated broadside to us."

"You can bet they will know we are waiting for them. What they won't know is our firing ability. When they black us all out and open the doors, boom! The noise will wake us up," said John.

"There will be some delay between the blackout and the door opening. The dead hand has to be delayed, say thirty seconds. How the hell are we going to do that? The aliens will probably not move too quickly. They will scan first. We need to wait for them to exit the ship with the door opened," said Terry.

There was momentary silence. "A weight and pulley system. A line tied to the trigger, wrapped around a pulley attached to the trees. A weight or lever is held by us. If we pass out, the weight or lever falls. The trigger is pulled," offered Joan.

"Good idea. But how to delay it?"

Silence. Then Bob exclaimed, "Fishing!"

"What?"

"Fishing gear. Deep sea stuff. Reels with drag capability. Weights. There is a store in Warrenton."

Stan said, "Hell, we have some reels and line here. In the back. Left over from when the salmon runs were a big deal. And we don't have time to run around searching."

"Yeah. All we need now is to collect the materials, set up, and perform a test run for timing," said Joe.

"Let's go!" said Terry.

They met again at the motel. Time was getting short. They worked out the necessary details. Lots of duct tape was used. Joe remembered an old saying his father used: "If you can't fix it with duct tape, you're not using enough."

There would be no negotiations with the aliens. Up to now Sally did not know the plan for fear the alien would detect it. She was startled at first. "What! You mean to say we will ambush these people without warning? I did not negotiate in good faith? What does that make me? A liar? A murderer?"

Bill was the only one who could answer her. He told the truth. "Yes, we deliberately let you believe there would be negotiations."

"You lied to me!" She was incredulous.

"Yes. It had to be done. Listen for a moment. These are not people. They are aliens, the enemy. Yes, I know it is barbaric. Yes, it is abhorrent. But it is necessary for our survival. This enemy has deceived us continuously. I believe even now they plan to destroy us. This one lied about a negotiation."

"You don't know that!"

"Sure, I do. And so do you. They have murdered our world, for God's sake! Killed billions. They won't stop now. But look at it this way. If they don't use the mind thing, then there will be no dead hand. Like the saying, 'Hope for the best, plan for the worst.'"

"I was negotiating a truce, not an ambush." Sally was softening.

"I believe the safety of this group, the Survivors, is worth more than the word of a proven liar."

"Like me."

"No! Him! You didn't lie. You believed what you said. It's on me, us. But you need to understand. It's them or us."

"You didn't trust me."

"Yes, we did. But not one of us could've deceived the alien. You had to believe what you said. You did what we asked, and you did it well. I am proud of you. I ask forgiveness for me and us."

A deep sigh, almost a sob, escaped Sally. She slumped in her chair. "They murdered billions! And I would have . . ."

Several Survivors chimed in with comfort and praise. "Remember, these things can affect our emotions. He was probably projecting sincerity," Joan said. Teressa and Vanessa went to her and held her. Sally suddenly felt what Bob felt, and she cried out with the sudden knowledge. As with Bob, it faded, but Sally was changed. Her love for Bill was enhanced. Her love for the Survivors was enhanced. And her respect for these remarkable sisters was beyond all understanding. The meeting evolved into a group hug.

"The alien will know something is up if we are near when he meets the ship," said Mary.

"We need to somehow shield our plans from him," said Terry.

"Yeah. Now Sally knows, she will not be able to hide it from the alien," noted Bill.

"Well, we know his range of spy ESP is limited. Right now, he is tied where we want to set the ambush. We just stay away from him while we work," offered Sally. "He may be uncomfortable for a while but . . ." she stopped, shrugged.

"Let's get to it. Stay away from the alien. When they land, the door will hopefully open to him," said Terry.

Devon offered to pray for success. Joe held his response.

"Well, God. Here we are again. Soon we fight for our lives. Some of us may fall. We commend our souls to your care."

This was the way Alima hoped Allah would bless. She wanted to live. She wanted to be a Survivor. She knew what Devon knew. There would be death for some Survivors. She felt the pain in Devon even now.

They readied to go to their posts. The time was at hand.

But first, Stan shared a few thoughts. He was a man of few words, but he felt something. Something that required him to speak. He did not know how exactly, but he stood. The Survivors looked at him expectantly. All felt something extraordinary. Something needed to be put into words. They waited.

Stan began, "I don't know how to put this. There is something happening here that defies words. So I will deal in feelings. I've never dealt with feelings much. When I got back from Nam, I separated that part of my life from stateside life. Feeling was part of it. Joan held me together for a while. She has been a blessing." The Survivors looked at Joan, whose weathered face blushed. "I want to say what I feel here. We are possibly the last of humanity. We are pretty damned lucky at that. But

I think it is more than luck. Devon thinks it is the hand of God. And that may well be. But I think it is more than that, too. I, my grandson, Joe, and Terry know the feeling of killing another human being. But like the marauders, these things are not human. I have no guilt—and I think neither does anybody here—for ambushing and killing these bunch of. . . whatevers.

"If all goes as we think, soon we will be in the fight of our lives. I think we will prevail. But there are no guarantees. I said before I read the Bible sometime back. Some things stuck in my mind. One was that we were created in the image of God. If that is so, we are making our own future." He paused.

"Now, we have something the aliens do not. Even in this world they described as being destroyed, there were redeeming qualities—love and compassion. For the aliens, they are a weapon only. We here, the Survivors, have a personal moral code that prevents us from murdering or killing for expediency. The closest thing to what they described are religions and dictatorships that have no tolerance.

"Soon, we live or die. It is in our hands and God's will. For what it's worth, there is not another place I would be at this time."

Alima recoiled at the mention of religion. Devon noticed. He took her aside. "He has seen death and destruction at the hands of radical believers. *You* will not be harmed by this."

CHAPTER 33

End Game

The dog was excited. Action loomed. She prepared herself for the loud noises and flashes. She would fight any dangers to the pack she could find. A long time ago, when the round things burrowed up and attacked her old pack, she had tried to fight them. Her alpha had also attacked them with a smooth piece of wood. But they sprayed him, and he died. His mate had tried to hit them, but she died, too. The cubs were killed. She could do nothing. The dog had knocked one down and tried to savage it. But there was nothing alive to kill. After a while, there were no other two-paws left. Instinctively, the dog sought another pack. She found a pack of her kind, others that had lost their two-paws. They had learned how to hunt the small scurrying things. But the smaller members of the pack were taken by larger packs. Then others were taken, and she was alone. At the end, she herself was about to be taken when the two-paw saved her. Now her new pack was threatened. These enemies were at least alive. Live things she could kill.

The vessel cruised in the afternoon. It moved slowly, almost sedately, as with pomp and gravitas. Inside, it was filled with activity. The sensors picked out the savages one by one. The community targeted them one by one. No one was missing. The null field was functional at 65.231%. All was as planned. As described by their member. He detected no subterfuge. He knew they would stand ready by their weapons. They did not trust the Community. But it was no matter. They would be stunned and then exterminated preemptively.

The stun even worked on the flying machines the savages used. By using the gravity drives, they could move alongside the machines, lower the shield, and stun the pilots. Or brush the machines with the null fields. The machines would then crash. Lowering the shield to stun when under fire was ill-advised.

Only one vessel had been sent to deal with this group of savages. The others were sent to Texas. The savages there used multiple cannons and were well spaced out. They were very accurate, even on maneuvering vessels. Plus, they were less susceptible to sensory overload. They seemed not to care. Most were men from a military base who had lost their families and now just wanted to kill or be killed. They were adept at war. The Community had already lost two vessels there. It would take several now to defeat the savages. The art of warfare maneuvering was rekindled in the Community. One ship would have to be enough here.

The vessel was set down, and the sedation sequence was completed. The null field was deactivated. The order was given. Stun the savages! Sixty-five minds combined; the savages dropped as if dead before they could fire. Their life signs were consistent with a partial coma. The door opened, and twenty-eight elite warriors exited and formed up, ready to move out. The savages were dispersed and over 100 meters away. Two were in the building across the way over 200 meters away. The warriors knew where they were. Two of their best shots targeted the building. One savage was in the rocket-firing machine. Two more were to target the machine. The order was given. They moved out toward their targets. The engineer was freed.

The Survivors quickly said their thoughts, then moved to their stations. Stan Lake rested his familiar M16 on the sill of the dormer off the bedroom he shared with his wife. She was by his side, ready to help reload. He would not hide this time. Like Sally said, it was all or nothing. He knew that death hunted the Survivors. They knew it, too. He saw it before in Nam. Before a patrol went out, the men had been like the people here, afraid yet determined, hanging on to their friends and battle buddies. The difference was that in Nam, the fate of the world had not been at stake. Not that the hawks safely back home would tell them. Here, now, it was actually live or die. The fate of the Survivors and maybe mankind rested on the wisp of a plan cooked up in a hasty few minutes. He knew the odds. He knew that a battle plan lasted until the first shot was fired. And that shot belonged to the aliens. So many things could go wrong. The aliens could do so many things differently than guessed. *Yes, guessed*, he thought. But there was nothing to be done about it now. He sighted again. The M16 seemed heavier than he remembered. And if he woke up, he would be shooting into a killing field. Shooting to kill. Again.

Stan saw the ship arrive. It hovered and landed. A light spectrum glowed. Then, the lights went out, and he slumped over the rifle, just as planned. But the coma was different his time. In the previous blackout, there was no awareness, no dreams. This time he dreamt. Stan was not religious. He did not attend church. He was of Pascal's opinion, but not exactly. He thought it was a nice thought that there was an afterlife and forgiveness. Lord, he needed forgiveness for the things he had done. If there was, great. If not, then nothing lost.

Wow! This dream was very real.

He was standing in a beautiful green field. The sun was warm, the air fresh. A gentle breeze moved the leafy branches of nearby trees. Sparkling water drifted by. It was peaceful, serene. He felt the weight of the world lifted. He felt a cascade of love and caring. He almost cried out from the joy. Yet he saw no one else. Then he did: his mother and father, and good friends who had passed. They were young and strong and beautiful. They stood and watched him. He could not move, though. Why didn't they come to him? Why couldn't he move?

From a far-off place came thunderous explosions.

He was jerked back to awareness.

He reached for his rifle, but something was wrong. He could not raise his arms. He felt no pain, but he could not move. As he slipped down to the floor, he saw the hole on the dormer wall directly in front of him. He looked down and saw the hole in his chest filling up and spilling his life's blood.

Below, a firefight was happening. But the sound faded, and he found himself standing in the field again. This time he could move.

Joan awoke in time to see Stan fall. She went to his side and cried out. Explosions and small arms fire continued. She had the sudden urge to avenge him. She reached for the rifle, but it slipped away. She was suddenly weak. A hole appeared next to the one that had killed her man. This one killed her. She fell next to her husband of over sixty years in the bedroom they shared for decades. But neither she nor her husband felt it. They were far away and moving farther. Together.

The dog did not understand. The pack suddenly laid down. A large black egg came silently. The dangerous, strange things came out. They were invading her pack's territory. She barked furiously. But her pack was unnaturally sleeping. It was up to her. Protect. Protect. She powered toward the nearest thing. Then she jumped sideways as a loud noise passed over her head and a louder noise came from the floating egg. Many more sharp noises came. The pack was fighting with their noise-makers. Some things were falling. She picked a close one and started forward again. Joy in her heart. Rage in her mind.

The other Survivors awoke to the detonations of the first-wave RPGs. The stupor had less of an effect this time. They were becoming immune if they could live long enough. Holes appeared in the trees and brush around them. They struggled to get their guns to bear. Terry was the first to get his bearings. A great rage filled him, and he fired a full clip into the standing aliens from a scant sixty yards. Several went down. A hole appeared in his sidearm. He did not feel it.

Dennis slumped over from the stun effects, the sounds of the battle were muted by the tank. The tank was silent at first. Then, he found the trigger as daylight poked through two more holes in the turret. There was a tremendous blast, and a hole appeared in the upper section on the ship. Inside the unshielded ship, a superheated plasma incinerated the entire upper deck.

Bob and Joe followed the tank's blast a few seconds later, firing triples. Down on the killing field, the aliens who shot the Lakes dropped with multiple hits from Joe's M4. He worked the pattern that was discussed. Stan was to work from the motel bedroom as an enfilade shooter. The aliens theoretically would be in a line away from him. Joe was to work from the left to the center. Terry was to work from the right to the center. And Bob from the center to left. Jan center to right. Dennis in the tank. The rest with rockets.

The plan was corrupted from the start. Terry and Jan were firing at random, and Stan was not firing at all. Dennis was late to the fight but was very effective. After a few rounds, Bob fell. Nevertheless, of the twenty-some-odd aliens who left the ship, most were down, and the others were retreating. They could not match the fire rate or the accuracy of the automatic weapons. Terry spent another clip. He fumbled in a new one. This time, he sighted before shooting. Jan abandoned the plan and shot directly, walking straight at the aliens.

Bill yelled to the RPG shooters, "The door! Fire at the door!"

He, Mary, and Devon responded. Rockets homed in on the lower deck door. The Survivors' practice and experience were telling. Two explosive warheads screamed through the open door and exploded with a dull thud inside. One hit the ship high. The aliens heading for the door were cut down in a withering fire from the remaining riflemen.

"Again!" yelled Bill. This time, Sally fired as well. Wanda was reloading for them. Four rockets flew. Another blew through the door, and others hit the ship and exploded, knocking down aliens that were close.

One rocket hit the ground under the door. Another muffled double boom came from inside. Smoke boiled out the door, then was suddenly sucked back in. The last of the on-hand rockets were expended. There were no standing aliens. The ship seemed to be inert.

Silence. Except for the ringing in everybody's ears. There were no animal sounds. All nature hunkered down. Nothing moved. Then something did. Terry started for the alien.

The engineer collapsed when the shooting began. He felt the others in the vessel leave the slaughter. The dog found him and was savagely mauling him. He did not resist. He had led the Community into a trap. He was doomed.

Then the dog released him. He saw the big, dark savage coming. How had they escaped the sedation? Then it came to him. There were three contributing factors. One, they devised an automated fire ability. Two, they were developing immunity to the sedative. And three, they had deceived him. The Community knew this as soon as he did. A main advantage of the Community was compromised.

At the same time, a message from one of their drones came in. Plans changed within a few seconds, the Community reacting in real time. Leaving these savages was liberating, dealing with their chaotic emotions tiring. There was salvation, after all.

But not for the engineer. He was to be left behind, no longer a member of the Community. It was the cost of thinking alone, of acting alone, and most egregious, of making an avoidable mistake—alone. He stood up. Death was not the end for him. He would move on to the next level. Unsure of his place in the Community at that level. But he had no choice.

The swirling misty air smelled of slowly dissipating gun smoke and a strange cabbage-like smell. Joe was tending Jan, who had sustained a wound to her ear that she had acquired when she went cowgirl. She felt nothing of the actual wounding but knew she was hit when the blood ran down her neck to her T-shirt. This just as she fired the last of the bullets in her clip. Bob was hit through his side. Sally and Mary were tending to him. No major arteries were affected. However, a rib had all but disappeared, and a lot of blood was lost before the holes were plugged. The rib would grow back, but a nasty scar was in his future. Terry noticed the hole in his M17. Shook his head.

Silence.

Alima and the sisters went to find the Lakes. Dennis arrived, driving the ATV, the tank forgotten. Terry moved in to mop up.

Terry found the alien sitting on the ground amid several bodies. The M4 raised and centered on him. The dog watched, joyous and proud of her catch. But the alien put his hand out as if to block the bullets and said, "Wait! I have some information for you. There is nothing left for me now. I go to the next level shortly. If you want to know what I know, then let me speak."

"Sure. You always tell the truth. You were planning on killing us all, and we should believe you now? Hah!"

"The Community is leaving this forsaken world. They are leaving me behind because I betrayed them by making an error with your capabilities. I have no place with them now. And nothing to lose by imparting some knowledge to you. Make a decision, savage."

Sally came over and stepped in. "Wait! Let him speak. We have destroyed his Community here. And can do it again. We are becoming immune to the emotional overload they can project. There is time to see if he speaks true."

"OK. Speak your piece. If I or anyone else feels the least bit like you are trying to influence us, or if we see another ship . . ."

"Agreed. Here is what is going to happen. The Community has discovered another world through use of our scout vessels. It is, by your measurements, over 300 parsecs further out in the galaxy on this spiral arm. Using gravity drives, they will be there in less than a relative year.

"It is pristine. There are no hominid life-forms there. It will be a pleasant world to inhabit while we . . . they progress to the next level. It was determined that this world is too polluted. It would take centuries to remove all the corruption here—the buildings, roads, nuclear power plants, dams, wind farms, photovoltaic farms. The disruptions to the ecosystem, the imbalance in the basic structure of the planet. All would be a bother and an impediment to our . . . their progress."

"That and the fact we are killing you," noted Terry.

"Yes, that, too. Even now, the Ark is approaching. Do not be alarmed. They are coming to retrieve their equipment only. It has no armament, and it would be futile for you to attack it."

Terry leveled his M4 at the alien again.

"Wait!" Sally said again. "I want to say something to this . . . thing. He can relay it to the Community." She steadied herself, walked up to the alien, and said, "You think you are superior, but you are not. You have lost the ability of empathy, of conscience. You are less than we. A sociopathic, hedonistic, narcissistic bunch of children. You have lost God. I pity you."

"I will not argue with you," the alien stated, "except to say we have found no god in our million years of existence. We are content with ourselves. But you should know this: What we were, you are. What we are, you will become . . . that is, if you live."

Jan heard an echo of the cockroach discussion. She looked at Joe, who shrugged. Too far in the future to worry about.

Terry raised the gun.

"I will save you the trouble," the alien said. With that, he slumped and slowly toppled over to the ground.

The dog suddenly jumped up, startled. The strange smelling animal died without cause. She sniffed the corpse absently and walked away, content the pack was now safe again. There were no more things alive. Yet the pack was still agitated. The alpha was barking orders she could not understand, except to know more danger was coming. She again readied herself to fight. She would attack and kill them.

Teressa, Vanessa, and Alima came back with the bad news. Dennis stiffened, then went back into battle mode. Time to process later. If they lived.

All the rest of the RPGs were retrieved from the motel, armed, and aimed. The tank was reloaded. A shot from the aliens had bored a hole through the engine, so it could not be moved, but it could still shoot. Point blank shooting. Dennis rigged it better so if he fell, he would hit the firing button. No delayed dead hand here. Supplies of ammunition were running low; ten more rounds were all that there were left of the RPGs. The tank had more, but after that, it was hopeless. Dead hands were reset for zero. The aiming would have to be done quickly, between the sighting and blackout. They guessed they would have maybe thirty seconds. There was little hope they could prevail, but they would try. They would try with all they had. They were tired and hungry. Nobody had really eaten or slept for two days. They were scared and unsure. Ill prepared.

But resolved. There was no time for long goodbyes or pep talks. There was no real optimism. After a brief meeting, they took their positions and waited. The only change was that the couples stayed together. The sisters wanted to stay with Dennis, but John overrode that. The family would live or die together. Dennis agreed. Hearts breaking, the girls went with their parents.

Devon and Alima waited beside his launcher. He bent in prayer. Alima asked, "Are you asking for help from God?"

"Not exactly. I pray for us. I pray the Survivors may be strong."

"How can this be? Prayer must go to God."

"God will hear, but I ask nothing of Him."

"How can this be?" she asked again.

"I feel compelled to help. But without begging."

"Then I will beg. Please God, save the Survivors."

"I think that is what I was trying to do. I ask not for me but for the others. I pray for Dennis, too."

"As I do."

"We await fate. As Stan said earlier, there is no place I would rather be at this time than with you."

All felt it. A sort of peace settled over them. Live or die. An answer was coming soon. They waited.

It was a short wait.

A ship loomed, coming down the over the Sunset Highway. It was like nothing they had seen before. It was the same basic oblate shape as the downed ships but was perhaps a half-mile long, hundreds of times bigger than the ships that lay dormant below. Around its center line were attached several more ships, each the size of the ones downed by the Survivors.

It moved with precision down the valley. With no hope, the Survivors aimed at the place where the downed ships were. The ship was too big to miss, but all knew there was no way they were going to win this one. Nevertheless, the Survivors prepared for the inevitable.

The dog whined at what she felt from the pack. Then, she growled, deeply and purposefully. Terry looked at her and smiled. "All right!" he called over the com. "Let's give them hell! On my command . . ."

Sally yelled, "No! No shooting!"

"I will not allow us to be killed without a fight. If they're allowed to stun us, we die without even knowing it."

"No! That's not going to happen. Wait and see."

Terry lowered the RPG and nodded. It went against his very essence. But they could spend all day shooting at the monster without effect. And dead is dead, no matter how. He trusted Sally for a reason he did not know. They waited.

The massive ship maneuvered over the wrecked ships. The sky was blotted out. Diffuse shadows covered the land a mile around. The Survivors watched and waited. Was this the last thing they would see in this life?

The behemoth settled down onto the derelicts one by one. As it touched each, there was a thrumming sound and a flash of dark light. It rotated the ships up. Then the massive ship lowered to the ground. There was a rustling in the field. Then it rose, the derelicts attached somehow to the behemoth, carried along with the others. The Survivors watched and waited.

The ship turned in a line pointed almost straight up. A shimmer in the air caused the ship to appear as if it were in sunlit water. Then it was gone. A rush of air filled the space where it was, like a tornado had passed. The Survivors gawked. There was no sign of the aliens left. No ships. No bodies. No weapons. No cabbage smell. There was a sudden emptiness. A void of emotion. Was it over? Everyone sat where they were. Even Terry.

They slowly gathered at the motel, carrying empty weapons. Stunned and numb. Sat and looked at each other in wonder.

"Sally, how did you know that?" asked Terry.

"When I was talking to the alien, I felt it. It was nothing he did, but I knew then he spoke the truth at last."

"I felt it also," said Mary. "He was almost sad."

"Me, too," said Jan. "We are becoming smarter. Almost enlightened." She stopped, thought. "Now we have to ensure we do not become them."

"We won't," asserted Teressa. And some Survivors knew this as a certainty in their hearts as well as minds.

CHAPTER 34

Future

The exhausted Survivors went to the motel deck. The sky was overcast, and the still air held the acrid taint of the battle. The Survivors did not care. The sisters were crying softly for the Lakes. Dennis was turned away, staring at the horizon like he expected to see his grandparents come back. No one knew what to say. Devon felt the need to start a conversation.

"God was with us. I feel the Lakes are in a better place now," he consoled.

The dog felt a sudden chill. She became alarmed. An unseen danger was here. She stood, uncertain, watching, smelling the pack. There were no more strange-smelling things, but one two-paw in the pack was in fight mode.

Dennis turned. His eyes were red, his shoulders tight. "God?" was all he said, bitter and aggressive. His eyes were at first unfocused, then fixed on Devon.

Alima had seen that look on men before Jihad. Without thinking, she stood and walked to Dennis, moved between him and the startled Devon. Joe and Terry also started forward but held up and watched. Alima stood in front of Dennis, who stopped, focused and looked questioningly at her. Seeing a heartfelt concern, he softened.

"Dennis, I see you are vengeful. You lost *lolo* and *lola*, you are hurt, and you want to lash out at something. Please do not become violent. Devon cares for you. You have saved me. Now you must save yourself. I also believe lolo and lola are in heaven. Let me tell you how I know." She had the Survivors' attention now. She took a breath. "I was raised in the Muslim faith." No one said anything. She glanced back and saw only concern, and pride in Devon. She continued, "Here, in this place I see it was not my choice. It was forced upon me. Like Devon, who at first defined himself as a Catholic, I defined myself as a Muslim. I now believe I am a woman who believes. Who can converse with . . . God. I have spent much time with the Lakes. I asked God and believe lolo and lola are in heaven. They are happy and are with those who passed before." She paused, looking up at Dennis as one human to another, not as subservient woman to a man. "Let go of the anger, please."

Dennis stood still for a moment, then slumped down. As before, with Bob and Sally, Teressa and Vanessa went to him and comforted him. Dennis was crying softly, the hurt somehow dissipating through the sisters. Alima waited for the repercussions of her confession.

There were none. "Thank you, Alima," said Devon. "That was beautiful."

With the Lakes gone, there was a void in the elder wisdom area. Jan picked up the mantle of elder woman. "Alima, you are welcome here. I think you know by now that Survivors do not question each other's beliefs. As long as we do no harm to each other. My husband has come to terms with that. As has Terry. We are the Survivors."

"And we will survive," added Terry.

"Just a minute," said Devon. "I think questioning is OK. It's condemnation that is to be avoided."

"Another time, Devon," said Joe. "Now we need to grieve and bury our lolo and lola. Terry, what say you and I prepare the Lakes for burial?" They would spare the others from the gory task.

"I will help," said Dennis.

"No need, Dennis. You will be the one to speak at interment," said Terry, already moving to the stairs.

Dennis nodded, went to the rail, and looked out at the westering sun. He began to think, to remember. The sisters sat and watched him. For a time, he stood there. He could not see them, but he could feel their comfort. And after a while, he thought he saw lolo and lola waving from somewhere far off.

Alima went to help Joe and Terry. The other men started digging.

By dusk, the single grave was ready. The Lakes were cleaned of blood and nestled against each other. "It was how we found them," said Alima. "It is how they should remain."

"Dennis?" said Devon.

"I don't know what to say. I saw so much death during the war. It didn't affect me like this. These people were my rock. I always relied on them to be there. There is a hole in my heart," he continued, "but I will heal. We all will. I need to thank the Survivors for helping. I especially thank Alima for her wisdom. And Teressa and Vanessa for their comfort. I am amazed at the love they have." He took a breath.

"Stan and Joan Lake were the salt of the earth. They taught me humility and strength. They were good Americans and, at the end, good Survivors. Yes, they survived. I believe they are, as our spiritual guides say, at peace in Heaven. Now, let's lay them to rest."

CHAPTER 35

Adam and Eve

Time passed. It was November. The Survivors healed yet again. Life continued. But there was one big question left. How to go forward? If they really were the last of humanity, Jan knew it would need to be addressed. It came up one evening as the Survivors savored another salmon feast in the common room. Blowing rain spattered against the windows, but it was calm inside. The wood stove whispered happily, warming the air.

"What about Adam and Eve?" wondered Teressa. The Survivors looked at the young woman.

"What do you mean?" asked Mary. "Aren't you a little young to be wondering about that?"

"Here it comes," mumbled Joe. "Find a place and shelter."

"Knock it off, Joe. It's here; let's deal with it."

"What's here?" asked Terry.

Joe felt the need to MC this event, if nothing else, to soften the blast. "I think she means, if we, the Survivors, are the last of humanity, we need to think about perpetuating the human race."

"That doesn't mean we are going to commonly decide our mates, so to speak," wondered Devon. Joe breathed out. There would be no blast from Devon.

"Not at all. But we need to look at it. There are fourteen of us. Seven men and seven women," said Jan.

"Don't count my kids as women," warned Mary. Another fuse was lit.

"But we are, Mom," said Teressa. All looked at this young woman and saw she was right. She and her sister were experienced and strong beyond their years, having been through more in their short lives than most in an entire life. And yet they carried so much love. The Survivors saw and were in awe. How could this be? The Survivors were coming to an understanding. But that's still in the future.

"All right. Here is my thought for discussion," Joe said. "We let things go naturally. After all, it is mostly decided now, like my wise wife observed a while back. But it remains a personal choice whether to have a child or not. For our part, Jan and I have agreed to try for a son."

"You wish. It will be a daughter," Jan laughed.

"Well, we know Sally is expecting and Wanda is close," observed Alima. All turned; Sally and Wanda blushed.

"We are ready!" blurted Teressa.

"Oh my God," cried Mary. "No, not yet."

Joe jumped in, worried about the lit fuse. "Let's let it go naturally. There is no need to rush, Teressa. There is time to get it right with whoever. Let your parents help."

Silence as all thought about the future. The fuse went out.

To their surprise, Alima spoke. "I think it is time for me to come forth. For I am ready. Provided I get to parent equally," she said with a knowing smile.

"This is not about simply having babies," cautioned Jan. "It is about love. I think any child should have that assurance. Any who choose to have a child should be in love. Joe and I know that kind of love. John and Mary know it. Terry and Wanda and Bill and Sally know it. The Lakes knew it . . . know it. I think it is necessary, Alima."

"But I do love," asserted Alima. The Survivors looked again and noted the stance of both Devon and Alima. She was straight and sure, glowing; Devon stood next to her, relaxed and proud. Their eyes danced with excitement.

"As do I," said Devon. "The problem is that neither I nor Alima can marry us. That will have to be the new Elder here, Joe . . . or Jan," he quickly added.

"Wow! These vows will be interesting," Mary said. Everybody was stunned for a moment. Then congratulations spread around for the new couple.

"It's a start," Joe said. "It's a start."

Notes from the Author

The "Bugs" and their construction are figments of my imagination. That could never happen, right?

The Drake Equation was used to describe the possibility and type of life on other worlds; the interpretation is mine. None of it came from the History Channel.

The possibility of FTL space travel in a four-dimensional gravitational "sea" is mine.

The possibility of null fields is mine.

Hell, the whole damn shooting match is mine. I can't blame anyone else.

I just hope it makes for a good story.

Ramblings from the author

I am a reader. I am a writer. Over the course of seventy-five plus years, reading thousands of books, it is my observation that, except for the money writers (yeah you, Patterson), I think authors tend to create stories and characters that come from their memories and their fantasies. From Beowulf to Homer, Chaucer, and Shakespeare to Dante, Wilde, Dickens, and Poe, just to name a few. Then, the mass of present writers. Their protagonists and antagonists tend to be their better or worse selves. They populate their stories with characters enhanced by their imagination. Some of the current authors I read—Child, Parker, Cussler, Rollins, Connelly—all unabashedly pattern their protagonists after themselves. Readers will note that there are often very disturbing characters and situations for their alter egos to deal with and navigate.

I also read the local Seaside writers: Myers, Symonds, Perkel, Linkey, and Andrews. These authors also pattern their heroines (I think) after themselves. They tell compelling stories with sometimes disturbingly evil characters in them.

Where do these antagonists come from? How did the writer of Beowulf dream up Grendel? I have made some very bad villains in *A Wandering Man* and *Hit and Run*. And then killed them. I do it again in *Edge of Extinction*. Once I have written a story and killed my villains, I have to start another.

I was once asked whether I identified with any of my characters. Of course I do. As with any author, there is some of me in all my characters, even the evil ones. But more so in Jacob, Whitey, and Brandy, characters in *A Wandering Man*. Yes, even Brandy. Also in William, Sandy, James, Georgia, and Hank in *Hit and Run*. These people are the better parts of me. I know I could never be as smart, capable, and loyal as they are.

And now, when writing *The Edge of Extinction*, I came to admire almost all these characters. (Just for the record, if the aliens came when I was alive, I would be one of the first casualties). A consultant on *The Edge of Extinction* once said that it must be fun playing god. He was right. Writing fiction is a little like that. You make your characters and put them into various scenarios. But then they take on a life of their own.

I find if I try to make them do or say something out of character, they resist. Just like real people. Of course I'm just talking to myself. Right?

My self-stated aim when I started writing (very late in life) was to be entertaining. In the beginning, I was just entertaining myself and my wife, who was my test reader and best critic. I had no hope of actually publishing. But later, some people convinced me to do just that. Thanks, family.

Those who have read my previous books will note the dissimilarities of venue. My first novel, *A Wandering Man*, was historical fiction about a man in late nineteenth-century Oregon. It was a work inspired by my wife, from when we owned a cottage in Seaside, Oregon. The story started about an actual documented gunfight in Seaside in late 1898 and grew into a saga about a boy becoming a man. When Barbara died, with the help of a knowledgeable journalist (and I needed a lot of help), I published it in her memory.

My second novel, *Hit and Run*, is about how ordinary small-town people respond to and persevere under the threat of international terrorism. This was inspired by a chance encounter with a speeding Cadillac limo at a McLaughlin intersection in Gladstone, Oregon, where I lived for a while. One more step into that intersection, and I would have been with my wife that day. After I made out my will, I began to think "what if." The unabashedly self-indulgent novel grew in my mind.

I also started *The Edge of Extinction* while married. This one is science fiction and again is set in the Seaside area, where I now live. I cannot explain how this came to be. I do know that once an idea is formed, the story takes a life of its own. It's like I am simply chronicling, following events like a historian. Except for *Hit and Run* (and even that one seemed to progress on its own), the stories are not really mine; they simply are. I only hope they are entertaining. I had a lot of fun writing them, and I learned a lot, too. Every time I started to describe a setting or character, I had to research it or them.

From the past, to the present, to the future, it's been a continual ride.

CPSIA information can be obtained
at www.ICGtesting.com
Printed in the USA
LVHW022138170720
660993LV00009B/300